Becoming His Master

Books by M.Q. Barber

The Neighborly Affection Series

Playing the Game

Crossing the Lines

Healing the Wounds

Becoming His Master

The Gentleman Series

Her Shirtless Gentleman

Becoming His Master

M.Q. Barber

LYRICAL PRESS
Kensington Publishing Corp.
www.kensingtonbooks.com

LYRICAL PRESS BOOKS are published by
Kensington Publishing Corp.
119 West 40th Street
New York, NY 10018

All Kensington titles, imprints, and distributed lines are available at special quantity discounts for bulk purchases for sales promotion, premiums, fund-raising, and educational or institutional use.

Special book excerpts or customized printings can also be created to fit specific needs. For details, write or phone the office of the Kensington Sales Manager: Kensington Publishing Corp., 119 West 40th Street, New York, NY 10018. Attn. Sales Department. Phone: 1-800-221-2647.

Lyrical Press logo Reg. U.S. Pat. & TM Off.
High Notes is a trademark of Kensington Publishing Corp.

ISBN-13: 978-1-61650-951-4
ISBN-10: 1-61650-951-1

First edition: November 2015

10 9 8 7 6 5 4 3 2 1

Printed in the United States of America

Also available in an electronic edition:

eISBN-13: 978-1-61650-657-5
eISBN-10: 1-61650-657-1

Chapter 1

As a boisterous crowd climbed the winding grand staircase to the adult playrooms above, Henry Webb took a quieter stroll down the narrow hall behind the front desk.

After last week's utter debacle, he'd intended to spend the evening relaxing upstairs. A request from Victor, however, carried the weight of a summons.

A few of his own pieces graced the walls thick with three decades of club history. Victor's office awaited him behind an intricately carved door of well-polished black walnut. His knock skimmed the falling whorls of Persephone's hair.

"Enter."

He stepped inside.

Victor dropped his pen into its holder. "The boy is back."

Clicking the door shut behind him, Henry traced the cool, sinuous antiqued brass handle. If Victor intended to shock him with the announcement, he'd failed. Henry had expected the boy's return. Anyone who'd spent more than five minutes in the novice submissive's company would have predicted it.

"Is that why Emma sent me straight back to your office like an errant schoolboy?" Unbuttoning his suit coat, he claimed a wing chair across the desk from Victor. Firm with a hint of cushioning, the chair, as with every piece in the room, conveyed a power and authority commensurate with Victor's role as president of their little social club.

"My wife hasn't thought of you as an errant schoolboy in a decade." Wolfish amusement lurked in Victor's smile. "Did you tell her how exquisite she looks this evening?"

"Of course." To do otherwise would have offended a beautiful woman and been a lie to boot. The corset shaped Em's body into a feast for the eyes, a centerpiece at a front desk staffed by a handful of beauties of both sexes. "Is the blue a new piece?"

"Mm-hmm." Victor delivered the distant nod of a man chasing fantasies and returned bearing a frown. "She wanted it laced tighter, but it's her first night in it."

Henry favored the cautious approach. Breaking in a new corset demanded time and patience, much like a marathon runner shaping a new set of sneakers.

Pale brown eyes gleaming, creases gathering at the corners, Victor confessed, "She begged so prettily I had to turn her over my knee and deny her satisfaction."

Henry settled back in the cozy leather with a chuckle. Given Emma's masochistic needs, she'd undoubtedly reveled in the attention. "Thus the glowing smile she's wearing while greeting the players tonight."

Victor grunted. "She loves the denial almost more than the completion." He stretched his jaw, sharp and shadowed by his short-trimmed beard. "I have plans to take her this evening, but I've yet to decide whether she'd enjoy it more if I leave her unsatisfied. A bit of time basking in her arousal out front might convince her to climax sweetly for me when the time comes." Flaring his nostrils, he savored a slow breath. "She makes the loveliest sounds."

A truth Henry had witnessed often enough, and one requiring no response. He'd learned from Victor in much the same way, as the older man verbalized his thought process for a scene before directing it. The tutelage had granted Henry deeper insights into the how and why of the choices made—and, perhaps more importantly, the opportunity to see them change on the fly when a sub's needs dictated something different from the anticipated performance.

Victor waved, a dismissal of the subject though likely not of his attention to Emma's upcoming satisfaction. "But that's not why I wanted to speak with you upon your arrival."

The bloodied back. The wrenching cries. The *snap* of the bolt cutters bringing freedom. Henry forced the wash of images aside. "The boy."

Jay Kress, the latest victim of Calvin Gardner's sadistic pleasures.

"He signed the papers. Consensual, inadvertent error." Victor's flat tone struck with all the joy of an untuned piano.

Another missed opportunity to eject a bully from their ranks. A dues-paying dominant couldn't be tossed on his backside without cause, and Cal was clever enough to choose fresh-faced submissives unlikely to make a formal complaint.

Submissives like Jay Kress. "And now he's seeking a new dominant."

"Or the same one."

"Cal is a problem." They'd never be rid of him so long as the subs held their tongues and Cal's father sat on the governing board.

Victor splayed his hands, palms up. "One that time and training might fix."

"He preys on the new faces." He struggled to keep the anger from his tone and didn't quite manage. "He delights in their pain, humiliation, and degradation."

"Some of them want that, Henry." Victor waved off the objection already forming on his lips. "A small percentage, yes, but some do. Most of them young men like our Mr. Kress. Would you tell them their desires are in error?"

"I'd tell them if they're among the vast majority of submissives who want to feel cherished and secure, they'd do well to stay away from Cal." His grip on the chair arms left impressions in the leather. He smoothed them with strict attention for each dark ripple in the surface. "A man or woman who violates a safeword has no honor and deserves no trust."

Preaching to the choir, but Victor hadn't seen the novice after. Hadn't wiped the blood from his back or bundled him into a robe.

"Yes, as Emma told the other board members, to no avail." Victor tapped the desk, his fingers reflecting in the glass atop the mahogany wood. A match for the shade of Emma's hair. "She spoke to the boy in private after his testimony and gently suggested he consider not playing again until he'd listed boundaries for himself and his future partners."

"He couldn't articulate a single one, could he?" An all-too-common problem among new players. Seeking acceptance, they neglected safety. Those with specific fantasies found negotiating easier. Confused submissives lacking self-awareness, however, required careful handling.

"After Cal stalked out in a fit—he left the boy tied, Victor, with no guarantee I'd clean up his scene for him, for God's sake—and I unbound the boy, he was a sobbing, bloodied wreck."

"An outcome that can be the result of a good scene as much as a bad one." Victor wore his lecture face, one eyebrow raised above a chilly gaze. "Would you have me outlaw whipping? My Em loves the sting on her back. Blood and tears can be a component of satisfaction."

"Not for this boy." The cries had pierced him. Not a shred of pleasure in them, and no reason for the young man to have endured the pain. "You didn't hear him calling pitifully for Cal to return. Apologizing for using his safeword, saying he knew he wasn't to do it and it wouldn't happen again."

The blatant betrayal of consensual play strung him tight with rage. "You know as well as I do a dominant can create a vivid mental picture to satisfy a sub's need for pain and swap out the dangerous threat with a safe toy that fulfills the purpose without causing harm."

If Jay Kress wanted to be tortured and violated, the fantasy could have been accomplished without the potential danger of perforating his colon with a whip handle. "The boy didn't want any part of it, Victor. He only wanted to please his master."

"I agree."

Victor's soft tone and expectant stare thrummed awareness of the gap between his spine and the chair. Henry eased back and resettled his shoulders. He ought not allow emotion so much control. Less so in the club and least of all in a situation whose principal players had ceded none to him.

Ever the teacher, Victor nodded. "Which is why my darling Emma is even now putting a bug in the ear of every dominant who enters. She'll encourage them to stay away from the beautiful dark-haired boy in the tight leather shorts with the vivid welts across his back. Unless they want to find themselves in my office explaining their actions."

"He'll beg until he finds someone." Back a week after such an intense, devastating session? The lack of self-control blared alarms. "He's a danger to himself." Denying him access would be a wiser course.

"He is, that's true." Victor frowned, pulling his features into craggy canyons. "If I ban him from the club, he'll find a more dangerous playground."

"The boy needs a teacher." Solution found, he crossed his leg over his knee. Victor would recommend a good one, and all would resolve itself. His own conflicted emotions would subside in time. "A caring dominant to help him find his boundaries and learn to assert himself in negotiation."

"Such was my thought as well." Victor's accompanying stare clarified with nary a waver.

"Me?" No and no again. "He'll associate me with his torture." Better to leave him to someone else. Healthier for all concerned. "Possibly even resent me for stopping the scene and costing him Cal's dubious affection."

"Emma says the boy called you his savior." The return of the wolfish smile didn't bode well. Victor only let the look out to play when he meant to win. "Asked incessant questions. Had she met you, how well did she know you, did you play with boys or girls, didn't you have just the dreamiest green eyes. . . ."

The chair's embrace suffocated. Henry launched himself free. "Hero worship, then." Condensation slipped down the carafe of ice water on the sideboard and joined its fellows in a spreading patch on the robin's egg blue linen beneath. "It'll fade."

"Until it does, why not take advantage of it?"

He tucked his face toward the bookcase. Disgust and fear suffused him. Victor knew where to twist the knife.

"*Positive* advantage, Henry. The boy needs a guide, and you'd be an excellent one. You've a light touch with wounded souls, and he deserves it, doesn't he? If nothing else, the psychological challenge ought to appeal to you."

Shoulders tight, Henry tipped his head back as if he might shake off the suggestion and the problem with it. He whispered his confession to the silent row of unaccusing spines, the pages within full of their own secrets. "I'm attracted to him, Victor."

He'd stood and watched because of the boy's beauty. The lines of his back in sharp relief as Cal had wielded the whip. And then the blood. The shouting. The urgent need to stop Cal without provoking more harm. "He deserves delicate handling, not yet another dominant who might confuse their own desires for his."

"At least talk to him. You enjoy denial almost as well as my darling wife does."

The impropriety of lengthy silence forced him to turn and attend to Victor's words. Their shared gaze acknowledged truth. But the words wouldn't come.

Folding his hands on the desk, Victor leaned forward. "Wouldn't you enjoy the opportunity to sit across from the boy knowing you could have him with a word and forcing yourself to strict control instead?"

Breath flooded his lungs. "You know me too well."

"Age and experience, Henry." Victor relaxed into his seat and straightened his tie. "Talk to the boy. My runners say he's been wandering the third floor as a green-ribbon in search of a partner. Why not give him one?"

Wearing a green ribbon. Attention-seeking behavior. Meat for the lions, tender flesh and a heart more tender still. Henry paced. He'd already lost this battle. The conclusion foregone.

"A talk, then. Tonight only." He'd help Mr. Kress see the need for balance and turn him loose. Perhaps the damage had been superficial, easily remedied with a stern reminder to take care for his own safety.

"Cal's been banned for two months." Victor's blandness only ever disguised spear points beneath. "The boy could explore his desires more freely with your assistance."

"Non-sexual, Victor." Henry bent his back and gripped the top of the wing chair. Smooth, supple leather. The submissive's skin would be even softer. More supple. Twenty-four, twenty-five at the most, youth clinging to smooth cheeks. A crime not to paint him.

"I won't touch him when his need is so raw and untrained." He'd cross any number of ethical lines by becoming involved with the younger man, even if the lines were of his own making and meant nothing to others at the club. No, Victor would understand. William would understand.

"A hands-off approach, certainly, if you like." Victor ran a finger along the edge of his desk. "So long as you don't mind Emma and myself wagering on the outcome."

Henry forced his hands from the chair. "Two months of instruction, and I'll turn him over to an ethical dominant who suits his desires."

Two months ought to be enough. It would have to be, if he meant to keep this innocent from playing with Cal once more. Even an abusive dominant could prove more alluring than loneliness for a submissive desperate for a place to belong.

Victor's casual grunt betrayed his disbelief. "My lovely wife thinks you'll like this boy, and she has a sixth sense about these things. I wouldn't bet against her."

"And her wager is?"

"That you'll put a leash on him and take him home. Not tonight, of course. But eventually."

"I don't collect strays, Victor."

He left his play partners better off than he'd found them and took pride in doing so, but their games stayed at the club. The married straight boys who wanted more punishment than their wives delivered. The sweet-faced girls seeking validation for desires that shamed them.

Short-term or long-term, impact play or sexual possession, it made no difference. None of them had enticed his senses or inspired his passion enough to bring them home. When he found his muse, he would know. He was in his early thirties yet, and the post-college set still found him attractive enough. He had time.

Victor shrugged, an elegant gesture rippling the fabric of his dress shirt. "Then there's no harm in spending the evening with the boy and offering him some friendly advice."

"No harm at all." Henry straightened and buttoned his suit. "If you'll excuse me, I need to track down young Mr. Kress and inform him he may stop searching for a new dominant. For tonight, at least, he has found one."

Advantage.

Victor had sliced deep into the heart of the problem, into the dreams he'd been unable to banish in the last week. The ones where he'd kissed the sweet submissive's wounds closed and fucked him senseless. Where the boy had called out not his safeword but Henry's name, worship etched in his throat.

The narrow hall gave way to the main lobby. He passed the front desk without slowing. Allowing Emma to prod the cut Victor had opened would be unwise.

Only a predator would chase a brutalized, victimized submissive so uncertain of his own wants and needs. Victor's approval mitigated but failed to banish the concern. His wife's approval raised a fearful hope. She'd sat and talked with the young man.

He threaded his way up the staircase, nodding to familiar faces but not engaging in conversation. He kept his amusements within the club's walls, except on those now-rare occasions when he partook in events at Emma and Victor's home or Will's cabin retreat. His home served as his private sanctuary and his studio. He took no one home.

Emma knew those things. In their nearly fifteen-year friendship, she and Victor hadn't set foot inside his apartment. Yet Emma thought he'd take this boy there. Young Mr. Kress must have been quite convincing in more than looks. Or he himself had given away more than he'd realized. In the time he'd spent learning to read Emma's cues, she'd learned to read his as well.

As he reached the third floor, he forced himself to stop. He stood aside from the flowing crowd and locked away the inappropriate attraction. Jay Kress was in pain. He needed a neutral guide and a friend, and he would have one.

No matter how appealing he proved to be. No matter how he attempted to express his hero worship, his little crush. He'd formed an attachment in a moment with emotions running high. He'd come to his senses. Until he did, Henry would tighten the reins on himself and avoid taking advantage of his innocent charm at all costs.

"All right, my dear boy." He pushed off the wall. "Let's see where you wander, how you conduct yourself, and whom you approach." Burying himself in the crowd, he went in search of a shock of black hair atop a wounded boy.

His wounded boy.

For now.

Henry edged as close as he dared in the next hour, catching snatches of conversation from each encounter. The younger man's athletic grace and bowed head, his silent persistence, granted him introduction after introduction with male and female dominants alike, though none approached him first.

Gender lines mattered less than the opportunity to serve, it seemed. All well and good. Finding Mr. Kress a safe long-term play partner would be easier with a wider field of options. Henry ignored the twinges of discomfort the thought caused. This submissive wasn't his to keep.

After introductions, the boy fell apart. Quivering from excitement or perhaps fear, he stumbled over his answers. He wanted to please.

He had no requests, no limits, nothing for a dominant to grab hold of and make real.

The attitude wasn't uncommon in male subs, though in many it covered a challenge. Topping from the bottom, the demand for a dominant to prove himself, or more often herself, by delivering what the sub wanted without knowledge of the desire. A sweetly delivered "whatever pleases you, mistress" meant a "if you're so fucking powerful and better than me, you'll figure it out" lurked beneath. Not likely in this one. A true need burned under his skin.

The too-eager approach and lack of defined desires won him little favor with the fem-doms on the third floor. The mistresses would have turned him away even without Emma's warning. Physically, emotionally, and mentally unprepared for play. Unfit.

Polite, though. He thanked each before moving to the next, despite the growing droop of his neck and the faltering grace in his steps. Twelve in all, a round dozen unaccompanied dominants, and only once did the situation call for dissuasion. One man's eyes gleamed as he beheld the boy's bruises. One hand descended.

Henry coughed before the hand could touch. With a cold stare for the predator, he jerked his head. *My boy. Hands off.*

The man made his excuses, a rejection of the submissive's suitability, and backed away.

A cracked whimper escaped the boy. The sound throbbed its echo in Henry's chest.

More observation would wait for another night. He'd take him around next week and hope a neutral demeanor would serve well enough to prevent Mr. Kress from imprinting on his own desires. Distress demanded immediate action.

He approached with good cheer, a cultivated jocularity, speaking louder than he would otherwise. The submissive's self-worth cried out for bolstering. "Jay, my good boy."

A shudder wracked the slender frame. God in heaven, let it be pleasure and not terror at the sound of his voice.

"The very model of submission I've been seeking." As his quarry turned, a quick check at the sleek black leather in a tight bike short cut confirmed the contents nudged at the tear-open front flap. Pleasure, then. Excellent. "Are you available? I'll require your attentiveness all evening, I'm afraid, and it must be exclusive. Will you be my boy, Jay?"

"Yes." His fervent whisper arrived with an extended sibilant, the sigh of an answered prayer on plump cherry-blossom lips in a tanned face. "Yes, please, sir, Master Henry, anything you want."

Anything intruded on his calm. *Anything* suggested this dark-haired beauty crying his name with delight, naked and bucking to take his master deeper and loving every moment.

He bit his tongue before trusting himself to open his mouth. "And some things you want as well, one hopes. For now, I want you to follow me."

Mr. Kress fell in a half step behind, his excited breaths a repeating wash of awareness across Henry's ear. His responsibility, now. The challenge demanded his best effort. The boy deserved no less.

Behind the front desk, Emma smoothly steered other waiting players to her subordinates. Him, she greeted herself, with knowing eyes and demure posture. "Master Henry." Her smoky blue gaze flicked to his companion and back. "How may I assist you, sir?"

"Step up to the desk, my boy." He kept his voice low. His new submissive's level of comfort with public attention had yet to be determined, and the vivid purple bruising on his back had already drawn glances. "Turn in the green."

He handed over the ribbon without complaint, though his fingers lingered until Emma plucked it from his grasp. An attachment to what the scrap of fabric represented, perhaps. Young Mr. Kress might be dependent upon outward signs of his submission, craving public attention and acknowledgment. Well. That would be easy enough to test.

"Is he to receive a replacement, sir?" Smooth and cool, she betrayed nothing to his companion. Emma was too well trained for that.

He, however, had heard the range of her voice in far too many contexts to be deceived. A note of smug eagerness clung to her lips.

"He's to have red." He leaned forward, splaying his hand on the counter, and raised his voice to cut through the drone of arrivals, requests, and chitchat. "Only red from now on. The boy is mine for the foreseeable future, and I won't have his loveliness sullied by unwanted attentions."

With trembling fingers, Jay accepted his new ribbon and fastened it. His breathing quickened. The motion highlighted his slender abdomen and firm chest, qualities that hadn't gone unnoticed by the submissives behind the desk. Their admiring, envious glances might have been for his attractiveness or his luck in receiving a coveted exclusive arrangement.

Emma, naturally, appeared rather more maternal and appraising. "Privileges, sir?"

Dangerous. Jay couldn't be trusted alone. He lacked judgment and the appropriate level of awareness for his own safety.

"None." If he meant to teach him properly, he couldn't leave anything to chance. "If I'm present when he arrives, he's to be sent to me. If I am not, he's to be detained at the desk and I'm to be called immediately at the number on file."

"Jay." Calling his name in a gentle undertone, Emma tipped her head. Mahogany spirals cascaded from her upswept bun. "Do you agree to Master Henry's terms, Jay?"

Good. Jay ought to understand he had the right to refuse. He wouldn't, of course. His sharp nod came as no surprise.

"Wonderful." Emma moved her fingers over the keyboard. "He's all yours, Master Henry."

All his. A quivering, abused pup who deserved gentleness but required firmness. Strict control.

If all went well, he'd be able to show him he needn't accept humiliation and degradation from any master or mistress who would have him. He would teach him to recognize and respect the gift he offered. To be selective in his choices.

"Thank you, Emma." He turned to his newest acquisition.

Head bowed, Jay revealed exquisite bone structure. His high cheekbones and steep, narrow nose acquired a glow from the lighting. Angelic and sweet to all appearances, a sculpture finished with delicate tools. But inside lay the raw, unformed nature pushing its way out.

"Come along, my dear boy. We've much to do."

The limitations on sexual contact in the second-floor salon served his purpose. Those who wanted to indulge in more than teasing or foreplay—or watch others indulge—would take themselves off to the third floor or above.

He scouted for a suitable seating arrangement. Something private, a bit distant from its neighbors, to encourage his new submissive to give him his full attention and eliminate self-conscious behaviors.

Two seats only, to discourage others from joining them. Out of the main flow of traffic. Perhaps most important, something with an obstruction, a table or statuary or plant, to encourage him to keep his hands off his companion. Tracing the faint tan lines circling his neck and biceps would wait for another night.

A pair of Queen Anne wingbacks upholstered in pale blue with a round cherry side table beckoned, far to the right. Jay fell in behind without prompting as he navigated the room.

Seating himself in the left-hand chair, he gestured toward the other. "Sit, please."

Jay sank to the floor at his feet.

Urgent heat pulsed at the base of his spine. His cock pressed against his slacks. Unintended and too soon. Tonight would be for discussion, not play.

He needed his partner on equal footing. As equal as the misguided man would accept. Questioning and negotiation before submission and play. Curtailing his youthful eagerness in favor of his safety was first on the agenda.

Jay prostrated himself, folding until his head approached his knees. The vivid coloration across the otherwise sleek back spurred an ache in his chest.

"We aren't in a scene, my boy. You needn't abase yourself."

Tentative and slow, his companion lifted his head.

Explicit instructions would be a must, it seemed. Retraining without room for misunderstanding, because Mr. Kress would tend toward greater submission if allowed to run unchecked. "The chair will do, thank you."

"I'm sorry, sir." A mad scramble of flailing limbs and repeated apologies ended with the lithe young man seated in the facing chair, breathing hard and trembling. "I'm sorry."

"Shhh, it's fine, my boy. I neglected to tell you precisely where I wished you to sit. The fault is not yours." He leaned back, attempting to convey calm relaxation. His submissive might learn by example. "Tell me, did your previous masters demand you remain on the floor at all times?"

"Yes, Master Henry."

"Did they ask your preference in the matter?"

Eyebrows dipping, Jay shook his head.

"How long have you been playing as a submissive?"

"Almost four months, sir." Pride colored his tone, but a thin tremor lay underneath. The fear of rejection, most probably.

Henry fought to keep dismay off his face. Four months, and the young man had been participating in the sort of scenes the likes of Calvin Gardner found pleasing. Bound to a St. Andrew's cross and coach-whipped.

"I see." Had no one given this novice even the most cursory, rudimentary safeguards? The guide who'd brought him here ought to have taken more care. "How many masters and mistresses have you served?"

"Eleven, Master Henry." His beautifully dark brown eyes widened. "I mean, twelve, counting you, sir."

Playing dominant-of-the-week. No wonder he'd learned nothing of negotiation and safe play. Likely he'd been picked up by dominants who desired to direct a specific scene. Any submissive who'd play the role would do. The young man's desire to please and need to abase himself would have attracted the edgier players. Ones who wouldn't consider it their duty to educate him. Who wouldn't inquire about his history at all beyond his health status.

"Jay, I'm feeling a bit thirsty." He needed a moment to process this anger. Alone, else the boy would think himself in the wrong. "Are you familiar with the kitchen off the salon here?"

"Yes, sir." Trembling, his companion leaned forward. "Can I get you something, Master Henry?"

"You may. Please bring me a bottle of pineapple-orange juice. You're to choose a bottle for yourself, as well, of whichever flavor juice you find most pleasing. Go directly to the kitchen, make the selections, and return directly to me. Do you understand your instructions?"

"Yes, Master Henry."

He nodded and waved. "Run along, then."

Watching him depart deepened his rage. The slender, athletic submissive trotted away with such eagerness, such pride in serving a master, that any man ought to appreciate having this biddable boy at his beck and call. What need was there to mar innocent perfection?

Believing Jay had requested such intense games was impossible. He hadn't even the self-confidence to instigate pre-play negotiation. He'd agreed to sub tonight without a single question asked.

Henry reached for calm with deep breaths. He had two months to undo four months of misconceptions and instill caution and confidence. If he failed to do so before Cal's suspension ended, he might as well steel himself now for the sight of Jay Kress broken and bleeding again. The boy didn't know how to say no.

He'd have to find a way to begin that training tonight. Before the night was over, he *would* hear his submissive say no and mean it. Introducing the importance of honest communication would make an excellent start.

Jay returned at a fast clip, dodging other players with natural grace and a beaming smile. He placed the drinks on the table and took his seat as directed.

Henry made a show of opening his beverage and sipping. Patience was a virtue he might cultivate in this partner.

"Delicious. The exact thing I needed at this moment. Thank you." He set the drink on the side table, his submissive watching his every movement. "Tell me, are you comfortable this evening?"

"Yes, sir."

Not even a pause to think. With this boy, the instinctive answer would always be yes.

"When you tell me 'yes,' do you know what question you are answering? I note you neglected to ask for clarification. In what way are you comfortable?"

"I don't—" He bowed his head and worried at the chair seat alongside his thighs. "I'm—whatever way you want me to be comfortable, Master Henry. Or uncomfortable. I can be uncomfortable if you want."

"What I want is for you to be honest, my dear boy. If you lie to me, we cannot play together, and that would greatly disappoint me." He kept his tone gentle but firm to avoid flustering his companion when he wished to encourage self-expression. "Would you like to revise your answer?"

Black hair bobbed above a shamefaced nod.

"All right, then. Try again, please."

"I don't understand the question, Master Henry." Speaking in a thin whisper, Jay curled his fingers around the seat.

"Good boy." He ignored the shocked expression. Better the young man learn to accept praise as a routine joy. "A proper submissive will seek assistance when he doesn't understand what's been asked of him. He serves his master's desires more fully in that way. Would you like me to explain the question for you?"

"Yes, please, sir."

"Very well." He settled back in his seat. "First, tell me of your physical comfort this evening. Were the butterfly closures effective in treating your injuries? Did you seek professional medical attention this week? Have you suffered significant bleeding? Are you in any pain from your injuries, and, if so, have you taken medication to ease that pain? Are you clearheaded tonight?"

Young Mr. Kress rattled off answers with no trouble. A quick mind lay behind those deep brown eyes. His tendency toward agreement marked neither lesser intellect or ability but a misunderstanding of the proper role of the submissive. A belief that to be submissive one must be open and accepting of any kink performed on one's body, perhaps, whether a shared desire or not. Training could redirect his energy into discovering his own sources of satisfaction.

The pressure at Henry's groin refused to ebb no matter how he shifted his legs. The more he learned of his partner, the more attractive he became. Not only beautiful and sweet but quick-witted. Temptation burned.

"I'm pleased your injuries haven't caused you overmuch discomfort this week." Either Jay had a high threshold for pain or he bruised easily. The lack of significant rectal bleeding, however, was a relief. No permanent damage done, not from a physical perspective. "Tell me, is bondage your preferred play style? What manner of impact play do you enjoy?"

"I've been tied up a lot, Master Henry. I know how to take pain." Jay flexed and tapped his feet in a pair of thin house sandals, the sort available in the locker rooms for those who would otherwise go barefoot. "Last week was—" His gaze skipped away to the table, the rug. "I'm sorry you saw me like that, sir. It wasn't my best performance, and I promise it won't happen again. I can behave. I can."

Henry gritted his teeth behind a tight smile. He didn't consider himself a violent man. The submissives he'd spanked, flogged, or whipped in the last fifteen years had been thoroughly interrogated about their desires before he'd lifted the first toy. Even as a child, he'd avoided fistfights. At this particular moment, facing this particular young man, had Cal's smirking face appeared, the impulse to break his knuckles on the sadist's teeth would have been too powerful to ignore.

"Your behavior tonight has pleased me thus far, my boy." Fixing his partner's shame, teaching him to see Cal's responsibility in last week's fiasco, would take more than a single night of praise. "I've no doubt you're quite capable of excellent behavior."

Telling Jay he'd yet again avoided answering the question asked would simply upset him. Asking the boy what he enjoyed wouldn't deliver the answers he sought if the boy didn't know them.

"Have all of the masters and mistresses you've served struck you for pleasure?"

Better. His companion cast his gaze toward the ceiling in distant thought rather than spitting out an automatic yes. "All but one, Master Henry."

"Tell me what that one did instead."

"She tied me down and used me for her pleasure. She said she liked my tongue." Jay's eyes gleamed, and his words came faster. "When I got too tired for her, she made me hold a vibrator in my lips. It kinda gave me a headache, but she really liked it. And when she was done, she freed one of my hands and let me jerk off."

Henry nodded encouragement. If Jay could be open about this, so much the better. Power exchanges went hand-in-hand with his submissive attitude. No surprise there.

"Not everybody does." The young man's excitement faded. If he'd meant to attempt a casual tone, he'd fallen far short. "Some of them only wanted someone for the beating and then there wasn't any sex." He sagged, a hunch in his shoulders and a droop in his lips. "Or they had sex with someone else after they beat me, and I just left when they untied me."

Given the boy's unquestioning acceptance, no doubt he hadn't thought to ask or impose limits while negotiating with dominants. He might have assumed all scenes involved sexual contact, when in truth public play more often indulged kinks and fetishes without completion or allowed submissives to finish themselves off afterward.

He'd done it himself often enough, but he'd damn well made certain the submissives understood who'd be doing the finishing before the games started. Some preferred to be worked into a state of fetishistic excitement and left alone to finish or not as they chose. Jay's partners might not have recognized his desire for inclusion or understood how damaging their rejection had been. They'd taught him he was suitable for beating but not tenderness.

Since Jay's introduction to the kink arena, it seemed, his own desires had never come first. "Before these last four months, had you been having intercourse with partners?"

"I wasn't a *virgin*." Eyes scrunched tight, mouth open, his submissive sat tall.

So he did have a backbone. He simply wasn't accustomed to showing it to prospective dominants.

"It's just been tough this last year since I finished my MBA, and I'm working all the time, and—" The slouch returned, a subtle softening as if each word weighed on its owner. "Then this guy I work with said there'd be girls at this hotel party, and then—I saw—I wanted—and then I came here."

A delicate subject, to be sure. He'd no desire to scare his half-formed partner off at this early juncture. The lure of willing women at a hotel party, the sort of event with no rules, would have been a powerful one for a sex-starved college graduate adjusting to the working world.

But an inkling of trouble dripped into his veins. "The encounters you had before visiting this club, were they with men or women?"

"Just women, Master."

Wonderful. He'd developed an attraction for a straight boy who accepted homosexual interaction only in the guise of kink. He might have misread his companion's disappointment earlier. Perhaps Jay desired servitude without sexual experiences from male dominants and preferred to reserve sexual submission for female dominants. If he hadn't known how to convey his desires, he might've been coerced into receiving more than unwanted whippings.

"But I—" Jay swayed sideways. "I like serving men, Master Henry. I didn't know until I saw it, but I," he whispered to the floor, "I wanted it."

More shame. Marvelous. Young Mr. Kress had discovered an unknown predilection for kink and homosexual desires simultaneously, and his initial explorations led to his degradation and abuse for attempting to sate his needs.

The first throb of a burgeoning headache flashed deep behind his eyes. Professional counseling might be necessary if Jay couldn't separate his needs, the right and proper expressions of his sexuality, from the poor introduction he'd been given to fulfilling them. Like a child beaten for masturbating, he might develop an aversion to his own pleasure.

He slowed his questioning, picking through the minefield of emotions and approaching from oblique angles to find a place to begin. He needed more answers before playing with this submissive would be safe, no matter how desirable the prospect.

Hours passed, as throats grew dry and Jay fetched more drinks. A check of his watch—his grandfather's watch, an old-fashioned, classic timepiece—showed they'd gone past two in the morning. He'd done little more than scratch the surface of his conversation partner's psyche.

Well. One night had been an optimistic presumption. Mr. Kress's troubles lay buried far deeper. In truth, he wouldn't begrudge the boy the time spent unraveling them. The younger man made for a beautiful, stimulating companion. One he ought to send home now. Not without a test.

"It's late." He brushed idly at his slacks. "You'll go and get your street clothes on, and I'll take you home."

His submissive bobbed agreeably. "Yes, Master Henry."

"No."

Lifting his head, Jay turned wide eyes on him. "Sir?"

"You won't allow me to drive you home." Though his heart hammered, he contained the pain building in his chest. Nothing but luck, perhaps, that no other dominant had made the same offer. That Jay hadn't fallen afoul of worse than Cal's abuse. Such a sweet boy, and so very, very vulnerable. "You know nothing of me beyond my first name and my penchant for talk over action, hmm?"

Jay's lips twitched. His desire for action had been obvious all night. Being forced to converse undoubtedly tested his patience. Not quite comfortable enough to smile at his dominant's self-deprecating expense yet, but it was only their first night. An encouraging sign. Cal hadn't fully beaten the spirit out of him.

"You've no way of knowing my intentions, dear boy." He hardened his tone, forcing his words into the lower register his play partners always deemed most appealing. "So no, you won't allow me to drive you home, to learn where you live, to potentially take you elsewhere in my car and treat you poorly while you're in my power. You *will not* allow me to drive you home. Say it, please."

"I—" Jay flushed a fetching shade of rose. "I won't allow you to drive me home."

"Because your personal safety is more important than impressing me with your submission," he prompted.

The boy frowned, his lips tight and uncertain, his brow furrowed. He nodded with obvious reluctance. "I'm sorry, Master Henry, but my safety is important to me. I can't allow you to drive me home."

"Excellent. Well done, my boy." Yes, that had perked him up, straightened his shoulders and won back his smile. Verbal reinforcement would be crucial for this student. "I'm going to reward your good behavior with an assignment."

Jay tilted his head, question and confusion in his eyes. A submissive puppy learning a new word.

"Have none of your play partners given you take-home work before?"

"No, Master Henry."

One more thing his pupil had yet to learn. He'd need to tally the lot and set a schedule to be certain he covered the most crucial aspects before Cal's return. "I'd like to give you a task and have you report back to me on the outcome when we meet here next Friday."

There came the response he'd been seeking—the widening eyes, the parted lips, the squirming hips and the fervent nod.

Young Mr. Kress craved attention, good or ill. The opportunity to serve and to be noticed. Degradation was the opposite of what he needed. Telling him he'd been bad likely shamed him without exciting him. He'd accepted such attention from dominants only because he lacked understanding of their games and his own desires.

Well, they'd see next week. Punishment scenes were certain to be under way at any given time, and his submissive's reaction to witnessing them would tell him more than the man himself could.

"Good boy," he murmured. "Tell me, do you shower in the morning or at night?"

"In the morning before work, sir." The note of discomfort in the sweet tenor suggested dissatisfaction with his employment. A sore spot?

"Sometimes at night if I get home early enough to go biking after work." There, that was a happier tone. A favorite hobby, perhaps.

Biking explained his submissive's fine physique and the delightful tan lines. Sloping curves and crisp edges outlined exquisite musculature. A body he ached to pin to the floor and fuck until his partner's sweet face relaxed with post-coital bliss. He'd capture the moment in pencils first, the hazy, half-lidded eyes and the arc of satiation in his smile. Jay cried out for smiles and laughter.

Not mine.

He cleared his throat. "When you touch yourself, which is your preferred hand?"

"I always use my right hand, Master Henry." He half-raised it as he spoke, glanced down, and dropped his arm as if it burned him.

Excess energy gave Jay a natural desire for motion. Previous partners might have tried to beat that out of him as well. Did no one truly look at him and assess his nature and his needs?

"Then you'll use your left for your homework. I want you to masturbate to climax for me twice daily."

Not an onerous task. Giving the young man permission to indulge on a strict regimen would accomplish two things. On one level, it would make his normal behavior an activity with added spice as it was now being performed as an act of submission. On a second level, he hoped, the homework would provide a strong enough outlet for Jay's desires that he wouldn't be inclined to seek out dangerous play elsewhere.

"Your morning session will be in the shower. If that means you need to set your alarm ten minutes early to give yourself time, then you will do so."

Gaze fixed on his face, Jay hung on his every word. A full-body vibration suggested he might perform his first session in his shorts with no stimulation. No harm if he did, though convincing him of that might make for a difficult end to the evening.

"Your evening session will be in the shower if you've gone biking. If not, you're to lie in bed with your eyes closed and think about what you would like to be doing for me." He raised a warning hand, index finger extended.

His submissive snapped to attention.

"Not what you think I wish you to do, you understand, but what *you* wish to do for me. When we meet next week, you'll report to me on your sessions."

Crinkles gathered at the corners of Jay's eyes. Despite the slight pursing of his lips, he held his silence.

"If you've a question, you're to ask it now."

"I don't understand, Master Henry. Report what?"

"Whatever I ask, my boy, so I'll ask you to pay attention to yourself and your desires while you play. That time is my time, and you'll be serving me best by giving it your full attention."

Jay gave a determined nod. "I won't mess up, sir, I promise."

He allowed the smile tugging at his lips to show through. His partner ought to see dominance could be fun, too. "A bit of a mess is to be expected. I won't fault you for that."

The younger man broke into a brilliant smile. One instantly hidden by a bowed head, but a smile nonetheless.

"Don't hide from me, Jay," he murmured. "I want to see your feelings on your face. Will you do that for me, my brave boy?"

The dark head lifted. Earnest brown eyes met his gaze. "I will, Master Henry." His lips moved soundlessly. "Thank you, Master Henry. I want—" He conquered his twitching shoulders and sat still and tall. "I want to make you proud of me."

Thank God for the side table between them. Without it, he'd have pulled the boy to his chest and wrapped his arms too tightly around a still-healing back. As it was, he fought the urge.

Jay had been touched with too much violence and lack of permission to make initiating contact so soon a viable option. He needed to learn such boundaries were desirable and enjoyable. Words would have to do, for tonight.

"You're a good boy, Jay, and your red ribbon tells everyone here that you're my good boy." He leaned forward and held his gaze. "I want you to take good care of my property this week. Treat it well. If you do that, you will have pleased me very much."

Chapter 2

Henry's phone rang at half past six on Friday night. Knife laid aside, he abandoned the mushrooms on the cutting board and wiped his hands on a kitchen towel. "Hello?"

"Good evening, sir," Emma replied, her voice crisp and professional if unexpected. "We're holding a package for you at the front desk."

A package—the boy. At half past six? With the time he'd spent observing last week, he hadn't engaged his new submissive until nine o'clock. They'd agreed to meet at a similar time tonight.

"Describe this package, Em." He'd planned to arrive an hour early in case the younger man's eagerness got the better of him. Clearly he'd misjudged how eager he would be. "No need for formalities on my end."

The front desk's nondescript greetings could be a godsend for married players whose spouses picked up their phones or white-collar professionals taking calls at work, but he had no such concerns.

"A wriggly puppy stuffed into an ill-fitting business suit, sir." She dropped her voice to a teasing drawl on the final word.

"Straight from work?"

"That would be my guess."

"Em, could you spare one of the house girls to show him how to set a proper table in the salon?" The bacon-wrapped filet with sautéed mushrooms would have to wait until tomorrow's dinner. The boy's needs would come first. "One who'll be gentle with him. I don't want his behavior criticized."

"I'll take care of assisting him myself, Henry. A pillow or two chairs?"

"Two chairs for tonight, thank you. I'm confident he'll receive an excellent education in etiquette under your tutelage." He swept the mushrooms into a container and replaced them in the refrigerator. "But if I suspect you're pushing him for the benefit of your wager, be assured I'll have a word with Victor about your behavior."

"If your word with Victor earns me a spanking, I'll have to thank you for it."

He strode down the hall to his bedroom. "I rather think it would lose you a spanking."

Emma topped his chuckle with a laugh. "I might enjoy that, as well."

He grunted to acknowledge the point. "I'm serious now, Em. He's fragile and confused. I won't pull him from the arms of one bully only to push him into the arms of the next."

Suits lined his closet. A basic black would match the boy's coloration. Too formal?

"Only you would put yourself in the same breath as that safeword-violating bastard. The boy's half in love with you already. You ought to have seen the bounce in his step, Henry. He's eager today, but he isn't anxious. He charmed the girls to pieces with his smile and his check-in declaration. 'I belong to Master Henry,' he says, sweet as maple sugar melting on your tongue."

Mmm, confident submission, an elixir stirring heat in—he paused his reach for a suit from the rack. "Please tell me he isn't listening to you right now, Emma."

"Of course not. I ducked into Victor's office to call you. If you want to project a neutral image with him, that's your business, Henry. You know I'd never interfere with your training."

"Directly, no. But a nudge here, a word there? You well know the influence you carry."

"He's a sweet boy, Henry. I just"—her sigh floated, feather-light—"want to see you happy. For you to find what Victor and I share. I realize it isn't my place to play matchmaker. And perhaps this boy isn't the right one. If you want me to send one of the other girls upstairs with him, I will."

"No, he'll be safest in your hands." He tossed the chosen suit to the bed. "Will you transfer the call to the front so I may speak with him? I'll need to issue instructions."

He selected shoes and a tie while he waited on hold. If his submissive had gone straight to the club from work, he'd need to be fed.

They'd be observing rather than playing again tonight in any case, so a full stomach wouldn't be troublesome. Better to teach Jay he expected his submissives to be in good health. Caring for his body with proper food and rest wasn't to be overlooked.

"Master Henry?"

Savoring the sound of his name in the light tenor, he closed his eyes at the tentative hope in his student's voice. "My dear boy. I understand you've arrived early for our playtime."

He counted a short pause, long enough to make the young man reconsider such behavior in the future but not so long as to discourage his enthusiasm. "That's fine. I have a few errands to run before I join you, however. I want you to listen carefully to the instructions I give you, and then I want you to let Emma help you carry them out. Can you do that for me?"

"Yes, Master Henry. I'm sorry I interrupted your evening. I know we weren't supposed to meet until later. I just"—Jay's rapid flow stuttered—"I was so. . . ."

"All's well, my boy. We'll have dinner together when I arrive. You're not to change into your play clothes yet. Emma will show you how to prepare a table for us in the salon. Do you have any food allergies I need to be aware of?"

"No, Master Henry." A thread of excitement wormed its way into Jay's voice. "We're really having dinner together?"

"We are. Be a good boy and wait for me at the table. You're not to leave the second floor. Can you follow these instructions for me?"

"I can, Master Henry. I promise."

With a final reassurance for the boy, he said his goodbyes and ended the call. Now to arrange for carryout from somewhere suitable nearby, shower and dress, and meet his companion for dinner. Training Jay added to his workload. Interrupted his routine.

And yet. The boy's need spoke to him. Having someone to look after fulfilled him in a way short-term liaisons did not.

"Two months." He dialed a satisfactory steakhouse a block from the club. No need to deny himself a filet simply because he wouldn't be handling the cooking. "Two months, and then I'll give him up to someone who'll appreciate him."

Henry's watch showed quarter to eight as he mounted the stairs toting carryout meals for himself and his submissive. The hour found the second floor a modest hive of activity as players donned their preferred personas and headed upstairs to the sandbox. Eventually, he too would join the procession, with Jay in tow. For now, he turned right and stepped through the wide double doors into the salon.

The area set aside for himself and young Mr. Kress showed Emma's unmistakable influence. Tucked into the farthest corner of the room, a three-panel screen of wood and fabric created a private dining nook. Best pray the younger man didn't recognize the scenes depicted, though the intent shouted for all and sundry to pay heed.

A pair of yellow-ribboned women cast admiring glances his way. Muting his growl, he stepped past them with a curt headshake. *Won't interfere, my ass.*

A paean to Greek mythology and literature graced each panel. Achilles and Patroclus circled each other with shields and spears, their sandaled feet the only flesh not on view. Apollo strummed his lyre while a boy—Hyacinth, given the field of flowers—lay at his feet. Beautiful Ganymede proffered a cup beneath the sheltering wings of Zeus-as-eagle.

Stalking across the room, he considered the ready excuses sure to be on Emma's lips. A shield to keep the boy from prying eyes, lest his table manners prove less than impeccable. Hadn't he himself insisted on protecting Jay from possible criticism? No, of course the scenes hadn't been deliberate. Convenience had dictated the choice. In no way had she meant to imply Jay Kress was his *eromenos*.

His beloved boy. His to mentor and protect. His sweet lips to kiss, his beautiful thighs to fuck.

Cock pressing at his fly, he swore in silence. Was there no mercy to be found?

He rounded the screen.

Jay sprang to his feet.

No. No mercy at all.

Despite Emma's claim, his student wore a suit as well as he wore leather shorts. Temptation beat at him, an unrelenting pressure, the image of his submissive on his knees with the same earnest delight on his face.

He forced himself to turn and deposit the bag on the table. Slow and easy.

"You've set a lovely table." He told himself navy wasn't Jay's color, despite the good sense he'd shown to pair his suit with a solid white shirt and a pale blue tie with a diagonal thin-stripe in white. "I trust your wait has been a pleasant one?"

"Yes, Master Henry." Jay stood straight and tall, a slender vision of grace. "Mistress Emma showed me what to do."

"It's just Emma, my boy. No title. She's a submissive here, as you are." He unpacked the tote. Salads first, the light containers atop the others.

"But she's in charge of things." Jay tilted his head. He started to roll his shoulders before stopping himself.

Warm foil container deposited on the table, Henry paused in his work to study his submissive with more care. "Yes, she handles some functions at the club." The neat half-Windsor had to be Emma's doing. "She also submits to her husband." Likewise, the white rose boutonniere pinned with Jay's red ribbon, the symbol of his ownership. The younger man's purity and innocence bound under his protection and control.

Pinned. Of course.

"Tell me, how many pins did it take until Emma was satisfied with the drape of your jacket?"

"I'm not sure, Master Henry." Jay half-smiled, his eyes shining. "She made me stand still for a long time, though. Do you like it?"

With such an enticing invitation, he smoothed the fabric from the lapel to the right shoulder.

Jay caught his breath and rocked his hips.

"Quite handsome," he murmured. Such promising responses his pupil gave, eager physicality impossible to miss. "But you cannot relax, can you? Afraid you'll disrupt her handiwork if you so much as breathe too deeply."

"I don't mind, Master Henry." *If you like it*, he didn't say, though the worship in his gaze made the words unnecessary.

Humming, he traced the edge of the lapel downward and unfastened the button holding the jacket closed. "I mind." Hanging the jacket on the chair back wouldn't do any harm. "Your comfort is my responsibility during our time together."

He pushed the coat from the boy's shoulders. He'd remove his own to ensure his dinner partner felt no awkwardness.

"No, no, please." Jay clutched at the fabric, fighting the motion, his voice rising. "Master Henry, please."

What the devil was he—

"Please don't take my ribbon, I'm your good boy, I'm yours—"

Henry kissed him.

He knew the instant their lips touched he ought not have done it.

Soft and pliant, the younger man opened his mouth with a throaty little whimper.

Irresistible. A possessive haze descended, snarling heat pushing out from his center. He ground his cock against his submissive and claimed his mouth.

Pulling himself away demanded his best effort.

His precocious scholar begged for a reprise with parted lips and an intent stare.

"Hush now." He turned Jay and pulled the jacket free. "I'm not taking your ribbon from you." Hiding the trembling in his hands required deep focus. "Nor your lovely boutonniere." Desire and fear of that desire. Taking this boy would be so easy. "We'll pin them to your shirt."

Jay made no more fuss, though he tracked the ribbon's every move.

"Did Emma find you the flower?"

"She said it suited me." The sweet tenor wavered.

Innocence. Purity. Youth and humility. "It does."

He hung the jacket on the chair and freed the rose and ribbon, re-pinning them to the shirt high and left. "There we are. Still mine, aren't you, Jay?"

Not Jay. The boy. Slip of the tongue. For his own sanity and the boy's, he had to keep his attraction well clear of these lessons. The boy belonged to him temporarily. Jay belonged to no one but himself.

"All yours, Master Henry." Red, kiss-swollen lips enhanced the beauty of his smile.

"Wonderful. Let's plate the meal before it gets cold, then." He ran his fingers through his companion's close-cropped dark hair. "Are you hungry?"

"Starving, Master Henry." Catlike, Jay leaned into his touch. "I got so excited about tonight I forgot about dinner."

All impulse and no supervision. This novice would need a careful minder. One who might tend to his emotional needs as well as the physical ones, and outside the club as well as in. Young Mr. Kress might only attend a few hours a week, but a lighthouse beacon dimmed beside his craving for more. Finding a play partner to meet such a steep commitment would prove difficult.

Issuing instructions, Henry took his seat. He allowed his submissive to fill the salad plates, transfer the filets and sides, and pour water from the elegant carafe from the club's kitchen. A biting almond Madeira Sercial would have enhanced the filet's flavor, but the club's prohibition against alcohol existed as a reasonable precaution. Intoxicated players were careless players, and careless players injured themselves and their partners.

Perhaps he ought to play matchmaker instead. Find Jay a full-time relationship. The young man's preference for women would make that, too, a difficult task. Not many mistresses wanted a man-child to care for. A biddable slave to see to their needs for a few hours a week, certainly. A solid half-dozen colleagues would take the boy off his hands without question for that sort of arrangement.

But to take on a twenty-something like Jay, she'd have to be in the market for a submissive husband or pseudo-son, and the boy had already been wounded by the psychology of the games he'd been playing. He needed clear rules and a better understanding of himself. Perhaps two months wouldn't be enough time. Foisting a half-trained sub on someone else wouldn't be fair to Jay or his new dominant.

Or to yourself. Self-interest. A snide insinuation, difficult to dislodge when it carried a grain of truth. Young Mr. Kress was vulnerable—and burdened with a temporary master rationalizing reasons to keep his own cock happy. *Stop.*

The filled plates awaited his attention, as did the young man standing beside the table.

"Thank you, my boy. Take your seat, please." He'd left the chair with its back to the screen for his submissive. A protected space. The only eyes to gaze upon the boy would be his. The screen's angles provided his own position with sightlines down two walls. Emma's awareness of the dominant need to survey his surroundings, no doubt. "We'll treat dinner a bit casually this evening, shall we?"

Jay knew his own appetites in one area, at least. Starving proved an apt description. Oh, he paced himself as he ate, watching his master's fork and participating in conversation when prompted as an attentive sub ought, but his slender frame bespoke an elevated metabolism.

Henry sliced a quarter of his filet and deposited it on his companion's plate along with a portion of his roasted red potatoes and broccoli with blue cheese.

Jay paused with his fork in mid-air but said nothing.

"You have a question, my boy?"

"That's yours." His student gazed at the plates in turn, his eyebrows drawn together.

"So it is. And what's mine is yours, when I choose to share it, isn't that so?"

Jay fell silent. The pinched lines on his face deepened as if the thought consumed him.

Henry allowed the conversation to lapse and returned to eating his own meal. The more naturally he fostered Jay's thought process, the better the training would be for him.

"Master Henry?" With slow rotations, Jay twisted his fork on the edge of his plate.

"Yes?"

"Can I ask you something?"

He refrained from the obvious answer. Too much teasing might discourage Jay's innate curiosity, and bringing it forth already took effort. "You may."

"Do you do that a lot?"

"Do I do what often?" Clarity worked both ways. Jay would have to learn to articulate his thoughts if he wanted to conduct successful negotiations. He might as well learn in a low-stakes situation.

"Share. With, you know"—the boy dared a quick glance at him—"people like me."

Troubling, that the young man couldn't even name his position.

"People like you, Jay?" If he'd been playing games of degradation and humiliation, perhaps he thought such names would offend. "Do you mean my chosen submissives?" Or perhaps he didn't wish to be called by them at all. "The ones whose service and value are immeasurable to me?"

Jay stared with wide eyes. His sweet mouth cried out for kisses.

Shaking off the urge, Henry cleared his throat. "Are you asking why I would share my meal with you, or are you asking if I routinely do so?"

"Both?"

"I do not routinely dine with my submissives these days, no." In years past, before Victor and Emma had their son, he'd dined at their home weekly, attended by their submissives in training. Happy weekends, long remembered. "I made an exception in your case."

His student dropped his head. "Because I showed up so early."

"In part, yes." In truth, Jay's focus and desire, his sincere submission, reminded him of those days, a welcome gift deserving respect. "But it's a pleasure to have such a thoughtful, well-behaved dinner companion."

"I'm sorry, Master Henry." Jay curled inward with tight, hunched shoulders.

He'd intended to show his new submissive his special place, not deliver a blow to his self-esteem. Jay thought his own value so negligible that a compliment seemed a complaint. Just as he'd thought the crime of being uncomfortable in a dinner jacket made him eligible for dismissal.

"Had I told you to leave the club, find your dinner elsewhere, and return at nine o'clock, you would have obeyed me, wouldn't you?"

"Yes, sir." The boy started to stand.

"Sit." He pointed, rude though it was, to emphasize the command. Jay sat.

"I had the option to brush you aside this evening, and I chose not to. What this decision should tell you is that you occupy an elevated status I do not often grant. You deserve to have your needs met. Do you understand?"

The pink tip of a tongue peeked out between Jay's lips. He stared into the distance. "You're sharing with me because you want to?"

Well. Progress. Jay recognized the enjoyment his master took, even if he didn't yet feel himself worthy of causing it.

"Precisely, my dear boy. Dining with you pleases me, and seeing you well-fed pleases me." He gestured with his fork. "Eat your fill. We've dessert to follow. Did you have lunch today?"

"Working lunch, Master Henry." Jay speared a potato. "Schmoozing with clients, so I didn't really get to enjoy it."

Henry questioned his companion about his job selling financial instruments while they finished their meal. Not a single word about fetishes or sex passed his lips. Hardly the standard negotiation technique. He brushed aside the nagging voice warning him not to become too personally involved in the boy's life. One dinner wouldn't hurt. They'd have time enough to discuss other things when he took Jay upstairs and could gauge his reactions for himself.

If events upstairs elicited as much joy and gushing thanks as the unveiling of a slice of flourless chocolate cake for dessert did, his student would be fine. Swimming in an endorphin coma, perhaps, but healthy and happy.

Henry left the chocolate to his dark-haired devotee and took a judicious bite of his own sliver of key lime pie. A giddy, glowing boy. Yes, he could be content with that.

He accompanied Jay to the auxiliary reception desk on the second floor after dinner. The boy retrieved a battered duffel bag.

After selecting an available changing room, he gestured Jay inside. "Time to change into your play clothes."

To watch or not to watch? Both options offered benefits. The trade-off lay between privacy and desirability.

Jay needed a firmer grasp of boundaries, true. Granting him privacy here, opting not to force his presence upon his submissive in a nude, vulnerable state, could demonstrate the sort of negotiations young Mr. Kress ought to be making for himself.

But abandoning his submissive in a delicate moment might be interpreted as discrediting his desirability. As if his appeal waned. Given Jay's tendency toward self-doubt, the latter might be a more dangerous outcome. Though if he played the mother hen, his student wouldn't learn.

"If you wish me to wait outside, you need only say your safeword." Henry stepped inside and closed the door behind him. "Your body is yours to show or not, as you choose. I will respect your choices."

"You'll stay if I want, though, won't you, Master Henry?" Jay clutched the duffel strap in both hands.

A hint of anxiety, its origins impossible to determine. Self-doubt, or nerves at the thought of using his safeword, or a basic fear of being left alone, or perhaps even a desire for his master's continued company.

"A beautiful boy undressing for my pleasure?" He offered a direct gaze and a slow smile. "I assure you, I'll stay most happily."

Jay smiled in return, white teeth flashing. "Okay. Stay. I mean, please stay, Master Henry."

Claiming a seat on one of the room's two benches, he leaned against the wall and clasped his hands across his stomach. The picture of a patient audience, so long as the arousal thrumming beneath his skin remained undetected.

The duffel unzipped with a singing whirr, and Jay laid his suit coat beside it on the second bench. His fingers lingered on the ribbon wound round the rose on his shirt.

"Shall I hold that for you while you change?" He kept his voice low and gentle, lest his submissive think the question a threat to withhold his attentions. "I'll return it to you directly after, hmm?"

He extended his hand, palm up, and waited. Jay cradled the bundle with the same overzealous care Henry had shown his godson the first time he'd held the child. Their fingers brushed as the boy made his delivery.

Henry hummed with quiet approval. The submissive's shy smile called for praise.

"Good boy," he murmured. "I promise to take special care of you—of your ribbon."

"I like that," Jay whispered. He sped through the top three buttons on his shirt.

Too much to take in at once, beauty arrived faster than his eyes could consume it. As eager as Jay seemed to shed his clothes, Henry ached to extend the experience. "Did you enjoy your homework this past week?"

Abandoning work on the buttons, Jay lifted his head and showcased a brilliant smile. "Yes, Master Henry." He pressed his lips together.

"Go on, my boy. Finish your thought."

The tentative twinkle in Jay's eyes presaged the joke. "It was loads of fun."

He chuckled. "As it ought to be." Heaven knew he'd spilled a few loads of his own this week with thoughts of his new submissive. "Don't let me stop you from undressing while we talk."

Jay hurried back to the buttons and peeled off his shirt. Slim but strong, with narrow shoulders and narrower hips, he offered a delightful feast. Black hair, sparse and swirling, coiled toward his waist. To mark him would be sacrilege.

"Turn, sweet boy, and let me see how you're healing."

Hands at his belt, Jay obeyed as he unbuckled. The faded bruises on his back formed a patchwork of pale greens and yellows.

"Do you have any lingering soreness?"

Thin lines remained where the skin had split, but those, too, would fade in time. Tonight they'd see the extent of the invisible scars.

"Only if I press too hard, Master Henry." Dress pants and boxers dropped to the floor in a bunch. "But I can play."

The cleft between round, tight cheeks stirred his cock.

Turning, Jay revealed his own heightened interest. "I'm all systems go."

Henry took a slow, deep breath. Pacing his own arousal would be the only way to survive the night. "Yes, I see you're firing on all cylinders this evening."

He'd seen the younger man nude two weeks before, after Cal's attention, but this was different. This was Jay's choice, and a safe one. His submissive's pubic hair was as coal black and close-cropped as the hair on his scalp. Trimming must be a regular part of his preparation for play. His cock stood tall and slender as Jay himself. Circumcised and flush with color.

A scant five feet from where he sat. Such a beautiful view. "Did you think on what you'd like to play while you were finishing your homework?"

His student nodded. Play clothes waited in the duffel, but he had yet to reach for them.

"Tell me." A low command.

Left hand straying toward his cock, Jay stepped forward. He stopped short of touching—either his cock or his master.

"I could show you, Master Henry." He sank to his knees. Parting his lips, he took shallow half-breaths, his intention clear as the light in his eyes.

Delicate handling, to be sure. Direct rejection could crush the boy's spirit. Although his cock voted a fervent yes, his head vetoed the idea. This was neither the time nor the place for action.

He cupped Jay's face and tipped his chin up.

"Much as I'd love to allow it, and delighted as I am to know you thought of my pleasure while you sought your own, I must decline." He traced his submissive's lips with a fingertip, seeking to erase the crestfallen expression.

"The prohibition against play on this floor is in place for the safety and comfort of everyone in the club." Could I disregard the rules and have no one know of it? Certainly. The door is closed. The boy is mine.

Minute changes in Jay's face—a slight squint, a tightening of his lips—showed dawning understanding.

"But *I* would know. Better for all concerned that I resist temptation and treat you with the courtesy and respect owed for the gift you offer."

He kissed his forehead, inhaling the faint earthy, woody scent of his scalp. "Put your play clothes on, my dear boy." Cock thudding with his urge to grip Jay's hair and accept his offer, he forced himself to let go. "Your nudity is entirely too enticing."

Jay rose and stepped back. He pulled shorts from his duffel. The same pair he'd worn last week, if Henry wasn't mistaken. A favorite, or perhaps his only set of play clothes.

"Master Henry?" Jay tugged the shorts over his hips and tucked his cock, still at half-mast, into the front pouch.

"Yes?"

Glancing over his shoulder, Jay could've been a male ingénue with his deep brown eyes and trusting face. "I feel safe with you."

He bit down on a groan. The pain in his mouth distracted from the ache in his chest. Jay confessed his comfort, and here he sat, a soon-to-be tormentor. He needed to see Jay's current boundaries, to test his limits, if he meant to demonstrate such things were right and proper things to have. Encouraging his student to enforce his own limits meant showing him scenes to rouse his discomfort. Preferably without further traumatizing him.

"I promise you, Jay, that in the time we spend together, your health and safety will always be uppermost in my mind." He beckoned him closer and pinned the rose blossom and red ribbon over his hip. "I have no wish to hurt or humiliate you, my brave boy."

They gathered up Jay's things together and dropped his bag at the desk. The third floor waited.

Intensity would be the watchword for the night.

Henry scanned the scenes to either side as he navigated the central hallway on the third floor with his submissive at his heels. Escalating intensity would allow him to find the boy's natural comfort level, or what passed for normal after two-week-old trauma. The possibility existed young Mr. Kress wasn't yet aware of the damage done. He'd been seeking out the familiar last week, but experiencing it could trigger a painful reaction.

Ah. There. Two role-play scenarios in adjacent rooms with yellow door tags. Red would have indicated watchers outside only. Green invited guests to participate. Yellow would allow them to step inside if desired but encourage no higher level of interaction. Nothing that might put his submissive on the spot.

He stopped between the pair, pivoted to face the rooms, and drew his partner forward by his elbow. "Tell me what you see."

Jay scanned left to right. "A math lesson, Master Henry."

The scenario on the right. Tutoring role-play. That he'd started there indicated a higher level of comfort than with the medical scene to the left. A female dominant and a male submissive featured in each, so the choice wasn't biased by the players' gender.

"Very good." Three steps carried him to a better vantage point with his sub in tow.

Players passed them at a steady clip, though none paused. Student-teacher role-play didn't often meet the exotic erotic standard for attracting a crowd. Bland as unadorned oatmeal for breakfast to all but the players in a given scene.

Pressing Jay toward the viewing window, he stepped in close behind. The wide hallways accommodated voyeurs with ease, but best to shield him from accidental contact with passersby. A bad reaction to a scene by design would be manageable. A bad reaction to another player could give unintentional offense and cause an entirely different sort of scene.

"Tell me about the scene." He kept his voice low, his mouth a few inches from the younger man's ear. "Where is it happening?"

"At the tutor's house."

"Why there?" The room design featured a family living room, not a classroom, but the setup easily could have been at the student's home.

"He concentrates better there. He's not distracted like he is in class. He can focus on her." Jay swayed toward the glass wall, tipping up on his toes.

Tempting, to deliver a gentle impression of his teeth on the muscled slope of neck and shoulder so near his mouth. But Mr. Kress carried too many unwanted marks. Adding his own would confuse the issue.

"He wants her to smile at him, so he works extra hard." Feet flexing, Jay bobbed. "When he does good, he gets a reward. She tells him stuff or lets him do stuff."

A veritable font of information, this boy. The slightest prod netted a better understanding of his motivations.

"These rewards for good behavior, what are they?" Experience would teach his pupil to speak with more specificity. "What 'stuff' does his tutor allow?"

"She tells him she's proud of him. That he makes her happy, and he's special, and he's not stupid or"—his breath hitched—"or pathetic, or that he can't learn anything right. If he does really good, she takes off her shirt and tells him to touch her how she wants. Or she takes his hand under her skirt and teaches him how to stroke her."

Arms hanging at his sides, Jay rubbed his fingers together. The repetitive motion, thumbs circling, might manifest unconscious desire or a comforting memory.

Jay's constructed scenario didn't match the actions in the room, where the student received an admonishing finger-waggle for trying to touch the tutor's swaying ass as she passed him. And a tongue-lashing, it seemed, though the tutor wasn't loud enough to be heard outside the room.

"If the student does exceptionally well, will he be allowed to climax?" Orgasm control and denial held top slots in many a dominant's toolkit, including his own.

His submissive came close to striking his cheek with a vigorous headshake. "Not in her. Not right away. He's too excited. He doesn't get his pants off, but it's okay. She doesn't laugh at him. She says he can please her other ways."

The fear of premature ejaculation, perhaps, and a desire for acceptance despite it. If Jay had a control problem, a cock ring might help solve it while he learned to slow down. His intense focus on his partner's pleasure could act as a defense to avoid feeling his own too deeply. Or the intense pleasure he felt in serving his partner might bring about his own orgasm. Difficult to say yet which had come first.

He muted his smile and laid his hand at the back of the slender neck. "And if he doesn't do well at his lessons, my boy?" Massaging with gentle strength, he slipped into more treacherous emotional territory. "What sort of punishment does he deserve then?"

"I—he—" Tension gathered in Jay's muscles. "Whatever his tutor says, Master Henry."

Fear and confusion had pushed the younger man from his fantasy in so few words.

"No, not whatever his tutor says." Forcing his sympathetic ache aside, Henry worked his fingers harder to soothe the tightness in his submissive's stance. He pushed the same firmness into his tone. "Tell me what happens when he answers incorrectly."

"They laugh at him," he whispered. "They tell him he's bad. They say he's disgusting and he wants terrible things."

Not she—*they*. The dominants he'd played with, the ones who'd taught him to accept humiliation. Proper negotiation skills could have kept him from engaging in such play.

"Is that what the boy wants to happen?" Interesting, that the verbal unpleasantness remained uppermost in Jay's mind. The physical "punishment" of servile behaviors, restraint, or impact play might be kinks he enjoyed when not accompanied by criticism. "To be told he's a bad boy?"

"No." The word stuck in Jay's throat and emerged as a tiny croak.

Henry cupped the back of his submissive's neck, gauging the pressure to offer security rather than threat. "When he's imagining the scene, and he fantasizes making a mistake, how does his teacher respond?"

"I don't know." A tremble rolled through the slim frame.

"I think you do know, Jay," he whispered. "I think you don't want to tell me. Shall I tell you instead?"

Foot tapping, fingers rubbing at his thigh, the boy jerked with a nod matching the quivering anxiety in his body.

"I think she makes him undress and run laps around her living room while he recites the correct answer. I think she enjoys seeing his beauty in motion and wants him to succeed." He near-tasted the magnificence, the steady flow of energy bleeding off his submissive, light and shadow dancing across the athletic form. "I think she finds ways to harness all of the goodness in this boy so that when he stumbles he will still make her proud with his willingness and determination to learn."

The boy's pleading whimper went straight to his cock. Unexpected, how it plucked a string in his chest along the way. "Is that the response he imagines?"

"Yes, Master Henry." Jay's squirming transmuted from anxiety to eagerness. "He'd like that."

Caressing Jay's back with light strokes, he paid careful attention to the resulting physical cues. His submissive didn't flinch as fingers skated across his bruises. He sighed, relaxing into the touch.

"Wonderful," Henry murmured. "I'm very pleased with you right now. Do you know why?"

Jay shook his head.

No. One so accustomed to hearing criticism couldn't see what called for praise instead.

"You answered my questions in detail, with honesty." Mouth closed, he kissed the pulse point below the younger man's ear. Mr. Kress ought to learn the joys of gentle foreplay and the sensuality of his own skin, even the ninety-five percent of it covering areas other than his cock. "You shared your thoughts with me as I asked you to. Those are the actions of a very good boy, Jay."

He pulled back and gauged Jay's expression, a bit of wide-eyed shock coupled with the beginnings of a smile. Excellent. If he could hold those thoughts as the night progressed, his training would be promising indeed.

"Come along, my boy. We've other things to see tonight." He felt like Dickens's Christmas ghosts, hoping to see a change in Jay's behavior from witnessing three scenes. Ebenezer Scrooge should be so lucky.

Exchanging the occasional nod with familiar faces, he led his partner down the hall in search of something appropriate. A scene with more sting than the first but less identification, one to push Jay's boundaries without making him mentally insert himself quite so much. Not yet, at any rate.

He slowed outside a red-tagged room. Male dominant, female submissive, a mix of sensory deprivation and sensation play. Yes, this would suit.

Three short benches lined the window alcove for voyeurs. A brunette occupied the one at the far right. Alone, mid-thirties perhaps, tastefully outfitted in a floral-patterned corset and flowing skirt. She'd woven her yellow ribbon into her hair like a crown. The sort of partner he might have sought for an evening's entertainment on another night.

He guided the boy to the far left bench. "Turn this sideways, please, and seat yourself at the front, straddling the bench and facing the window."

Sleek and silent, Jay obeyed with a graceful haste. He carried himself with natural talent, his easy acceptance and well-tended appearance fit to be the pride of any dominant.

Nodding to acknowledge the fleeting glance from the unattached submissive, he joined the boy on the bench. He left a thin slice of air between their bodies. The subtle tilt of Jay's head suggested animal awareness of the proximity.

With slow movements, he laid his hands on Jay's shoulders.

A tiny startle reflex greeted him, but his submissive didn't pull away.

Leaning forward, Henry cupped the roundness in his palms and rubbed his thumbs over Jay's back. "Tell me what you see."

The younger man jerked right, aborted in mid-motion, and returned to facing the window.

"It's all right. You're only telling me, my boy. Your words are for my ears alone."

With regal dignity, the yellow-ribboned woman rose and departed in silence. Courteous and insightful. He resolved to speak to Emma after sending the boy home. As the membership coordinator and de facto hostess, she'd be certain to know the woman's name from a description of her style. He'd leave a thank-you note at the desk for her tactful exit.

"I see"—Jay sucked in a breath—"a woman."

The halting words bespoke discomfort, though the cause mystified.

The submissive knelt in a nest of pillows, her body angled toward the viewing area and displaying her nudity. Small clips showcased the rosy tips of her breasts. She arched her back and pushed into the sensation as her dominant tugged the delicate chain connecting them. A fitted blindfold deprived her of sight. Lovely, but tame. Nothing violent or degrading to upset his boy.

"Tell me about the woman." He massaged in slow circles, aiming to ease the tension in his student's neck and shoulders. "What thoughts are passing behind her eyes?"

A sense of danger and anticipation came to mind. The submissive's pain would be little more than a spring shower, and the pleasure following like a summer thunderstorm. Jay might mention the trust showed, or the care the dominant took in placing a clip in his pet's labial folds and the joy she took in it. The way he chose to view the scene and the elements he focused on would say much about his state of mind. A baseline for his future lessons.

"She's in love with him, and she wants to prove it, so she put the blindfold on." Once started, Jay poured forth a flood of words. "But now he's hurting her, and she's not sure she made the right choice, but she doesn't want to disappoint him"—his leg vibrated with a rapid tic—"and she hopes it'll get better but it won't because she's not anything to him."

Chill sweeping through his chest, he focused on evenness. Methodical, constant touch. Steady breathing. Not allowing his shock to show in his hands.

Either the experience with Cal had so colored and tainted Jay's thoughts as to make him incapable of seeing what lay in front of him, or he felt comfortable enough in his new master's embrace to discuss the emotions surrounding the assault, albeit obliquely. Ascribing his own feelings to the nameless woman.

Henry waited until he could be certain his voice wouldn't give him away. "She's not enjoying their game?"

The woman wasn't bound, and the club required the use of safewords for all submissives. The ecstasy on her face as her dominant removed the nipple clamps spoke for itself. The rapid convulsions following refused any other interpretation. Obvious enjoyment, but not obvious to young Jay.

"She thought she would. But he changed it." He carried dull defeat in his tone, rote and drained of energy. "That's not the game she wanted to play, and now she can't say no 'cause she already said yes."

He struggled not to make his questions personal. To demand to know who had taught the boy so badly. To hear every lie this boy had learned from Cal and whatever others had come before him.

Fantasies involving force swam in the minds of any number of power-exchange players. A dime a dozen. A rare sight in the exhibitionist areas of the club, to be sure, but not unknown upstairs, where a submissive might have such fantasies fulfilled in complete privacy with a trusted dom in a space that allowed for comprehensive aftercare for regaining emotional balance.

Despite the surface dynamic, the power lay in the submissive's hands. Unquestioned. A single word to halt the game and take back control. Any dominant worth his creative salt found ways to ask leading questions or back off within the role-play if the sub's response edged close to true trauma.

Yet Jay painted the submissive as a helpless victim, unable to act.

"Does she want to say 'no'?"

"Yes." Rocking, he wrapped firm conviction in an earnest plea.

Wanting to object, but unable to do so. Giving Jay a sense of agency would begin correcting this confusion. "What if she has a responsibility to say no?"

"He won't let her."

"Then that is his failing. Her responsibility, to herself and to her dominant, is to say no when the game has gone too far for her liking. Or if she's gotten a cramp in her leg, or she feels tingling in her extremities, or"—he searched for a lighthearted jest—"or if she's just now realized her DVR will not be recording her favorite show and it starts in five minutes."

Jay jolted and twisted his torso to face him. "But—that's not. . . ."

"Whenever she is uncomfortable with what is happening in the room." Jay's cheek warming under his hand, he tipped his head and aligned their gazes. "*At any time.* A safeword isn't a condom. You aren't limited to using it only once. You needn't walk around with it in your wallet, saving it for the right moment."

Jay's light flush made him look sixteen rather than twenty-five. God help him if no one had given the boy the safe sex talk.

"Pulling out your safeword ought not to occasion mockery. Barebacking leaves you vulnerable to disease and parenthood. Operating without a safeword leaves you vulnerable to much deeper hurts. Promise me from now on you will use your safeword as needed, at will."

"Even"—Jay glanced down and breathed out—"even with you, Master Henry?"

"Especially with me. If I have occasion to test your limits, I want to know we are playing this game together. When I push too hard, you are required to use your safeword. Those are the rules. Do you understand?"

"Yes, Master Henry." Jay confirmed his sincerity with an even gaze and tight lips.

"Good. Tell me your safeword now, please."

Jay moved his mouth, but no sound emerged. After three tries, he uttered a strangled whisper, "Popcorn."

The syllables struck wrong, a hammer and chisel opening a crack deep in the marble. The ruin of the piece, the project entire, if he allowed.

He pressed their heads together, spread his fingers, and cradled the boy's skull. Echoing cries and Cal's caustic scorn played an agonizing accompaniment.

"You'll choose a new word." Hearing the word again would be intolerable. "For tonight, the word 'safeword' itself will do. As part of your homework this week, I want you to think of something you dislike and select a word related to it. You'll tell me your new word when we meet next week."

"More homework?" Sweet hope danced in Jay's tenor. "Next week?"

"Always more homework, my dear boy. It pleases me to think of you applying yourself to your lessons."

With squirming hips, his submissive communicated his pleasure in the thought as well.

Henry edged his own hips back to maintain the distance. The night demanded control, not indulgence. Though he granted himself a slight one, a wisp of a kiss on his companion's cheek before letting him go.

"On your feet, please. We've seen all we needed here." He patted Jay's thigh and stood. "We'll find another source of entertainment."

At his direction, Jay restored the bench to its regular position. He smiled encouragement and delivered praise. But as he entered the general flow of foot traffic with Jay once more at his heels, Henry cursed in silence.

From what he'd seen tonight, testing the boy's boundaries would be painful for them both. Reinforcing the lesson on safeword use, however, would be a kindness. An absolute necessity.

He must be cruel to be kind. Shakespearean phrasing filtered back through uncounted talks with Victor on the joys and frustrations of loving a masochist. Jay wasn't Emma. He would lack the perspective as yet to see the kindness in the cut. Mmm. As if the whole sordid mess had worked out with such loveliness for Hamlet.

A door up ahead swung open, driving a commanding voice into

the hall. "You'll take your punishment, and then you'll begin again the way I showed you."

The sub's answer, if one followed, came too quiet or too slow to be heard before the door closed.

His feet heavy, Henry affected a casual tone as he guided his partner toward the scene. "Tell me your safeword, Jay."

"Safeword, Master Henry."

"Good boy. And when are you to use it?"

"When—" Jay flinched, muscles pulling across his back. "When I'm pushed too hard."

"Or if you're uncomfortable or confused." As Mr. Kress would be soon, a hoped-for and not-hoped-for outcome mixing a muddy brown mess in his veins. The scene came into view on his right. Too late to separate the colors. "You won't be punished for bringing such things to my attention."

A male dominant wielded a leather spanking paddle on a male submissive, which ought to trigger Jay's nerves, but with enough differences to allow for some distance. No whip. The bottom bent at the waist, draped over a spanking bench, rather than tied to a frame.

He eased to a stop and tugged Jay forward, keeping hold of his left wrist to monitor his pulse. The boy's comfort level ought to sprint to intolerable. He would use his safeword, and they would go.

A half-dozen viewers stood inside the room. The *thwack* of the split paddle sounded even with the door closed.

Jay trembled.

Another strike. The submissive's cock bobbed as the force thrust him forward.

The trembling became a full-body quiver.

"Would you like to step inside for a closer look?"

The boy shook his head, so quick as to be instinctive aversion rather than thought. His pulse raced.

Pleading in silence, Henry waited for the sweet sound of a safeword. If Jay didn't speak up for himself, he'd have to pull him away. Better for his self-confidence if he could do it himself.

A green-ribbon reached for the door as a *thwack* reverberated. He pulled it open.

"Please, sir, please." The sub's begging mixed with sobs. "I'll do better."

The green-ribbon stepped inside.

"I'm not convinced you deserve another chance." The dom projected well, with a harsh snarl.

The door began to close.

"I could replace a repulsive cockslut like—"

Jay twisted and flung himself against Henry, arms wrapping like a vise, body shaking, breath whooshing along his shirt collar. "Safeword. Safeword safeword safeword."

"Good boy, Jay." He steadied himself against the onslaught and cradled his tender charge. "My brave boy."

Refusing to permit even the thinnest distance between them, Jay wriggled and burrowed his way inside the flaps of Henry's suit jacket. He clutched at the back of the shirt beneath, his bare chest heaving against the light broadcloth as he held on.

The narrowest threads of propriety. Not all of the shudders rocking them belonged to the boy. The rushed breaths and the woody scent of Jay's skin conspired to raise scandalous thoughts among other, more substantial things.

He sought a bit of privacy, as they'd drawn no shortage of glances. "You've done so well." He sidestepped to an unoccupied alcove.

Jay stumbled along on clumsy feet.

"That's enough for tonight, my brave boy."

"No, please." Jay dug his fingers into his back. "I want to stay with you."

"Shhh, I'm not leaving you." He backed his partner to the wall and shielded his shaking body. "It's all right. You did exactly right. I'm so proud of you."

Jay's heavy, panicked breathing slowed to short, shuddering exhalations at his throat.

He hummed the opening bars of *Für Elise* at half-speed as much to calm his own pulse as the boy's. Nothing like the thought of piano lessons with Mrs. Fogarty to wilt an erect cock.

Plastered to his body, Jay no doubt had already felt his arousal. A reaction to his submissive's achievement and trust, not his fear. The younger man's instinctive turn to him as a protector and the willingness to use his safeword proved a powerful intoxicant.

Muffled whimpers fading, body swaying, Jay brushed his nose along Henry's neck.

A few minutes' comfort wouldn't be enough. The boy needed more aftercare than that.

The hallway traffic would distract. The bright lighting of the salon would inhibit relaxation. The main hall might suit, unless a demonstration was in progress. Somewhere darker, quiet and womblike, would put his submissive back on an even kilter.

Giggles sounded behind him. Jay lifted his head.

"Robin, come back here, pet. Miss Marissa's going to start soon, and we don't want to be late."

"Yes, Daddy." Saccharine-sweet, that one. Over eighteen, or she wouldn't have been allowed access to the club, though she mimicked a child's lilting pout.

The role-playing aspects favored among the age-play set disturbed rather than aroused, but the caretaking and comfort might prove precisely what Jay craved in this moment. Safe, nonthreatening, nonsexual play.

The woman skipped down the hall in footed pajamas, pigtails swinging. She slipped her hand into an older man's outstretched one.

Jay's shaking had stopped, and his gaze followed the pair. Curiosity overcoming fear, perhaps. Well. He'd promised to help his student discover his own desires.

"Shall we see where she goes?" He eased back.

Jay unclenched from his shirt. "Together?"

"You deserve a reward for using your safeword as a good, responsible player should." Best to see where the boy's feelings lay. "I thought we might snuggle a bit."

He nodded. "I don't have to. . . ." He glanced down the hall.

That Jay had started raising an objection at all was a positive sign. Building a sense of boundaries would only benefit him. "Don't have to what, my boy?"

Jay waved at his torso. "You know, with the PJs and the"—he cringed like he'd bitten into a lemon—"the kid voice."

"The trappings aren't necessary." The caretaking mattered. The rest he dismissed. He rubbed the back of Jay's head, ruffling the short hair. "Except the pigtails, of course."

The wide brown eyes in response brought out his chuckle before Jay laughed with him.

"You're teasing, Master Henry."

"I am. There's no reason to make everything serious and painful, is there?" He smoothed his hand around Jay's neck and down the firm muscles and soft hair on his chest. "You deserve to be having fun."

Jay leaned into his hand and bobbed his head in what seemed an unconscious tic.

"Come along, then." He led his submissive through the main hall and beyond, down a hall he rarely traveled. The age-play members had a set of nonsexual role-play rooms for indulging their youthful personas. He passed the cheery classroom setup and stopped outside the next door.

"This is a quiet space, Jay." Precisely what his partner needed, he hoped. "Give it a few minutes, please, and then if you're bored or uncomfortable, tap my knee and we'll go. Understood?"

Despite the wide emptiness of the hall, Jay crowded close. "Yes, Master Henry."

He opened the door on a woman speaking in a calm, friendly tone. Welcoming them with a wave, she kept up her introductory patter.

With Jay trailing, he crossed the back of the room and selected an unoccupied mat with a satisfactory backrest. He kept watch on Jay as he removed his jacket and folded it in a neat bundle. If the childish décor bothered his companion, he had the good sense to hold his tongue out of politeness for the players. Just under a dozen lay scattered about the room, most in pairs, though some had curled up alone.

Settling on the mat, he leaned into the backrest and tugged the boy down. Mouth alongside Jay's ear, he whispered, "Make yourself comfortable."

The reader ended her introduction. Sitting in a waiting rocker, she opened the book and began. *Heidi*. A classic choice, given her audience featured more "girls" with male guardian figures. Slow starting for the boys, perhaps.

He waited.

Jay gazed around the room.

He expected a tap on the knee at any moment, the trappings too much for masculine pride to overcome. As the first chapter ended and the next began, Jay reclined against his chest, curling his body between Henry's outstretched legs. Enthralled either by the story or the closeness, he lay still and radiated heat.

No tapping, even as the second chapter gave way to a third. Cuddling dropped into his mental column of the boy's likes, alongside security, clear directions, attention, and—flourless chocolate cake.

He rubbed slow circles on Jay's chest. Drooping eyelids fluttered. Mr. Kress embodied the unabashed enthusiasm and open acceptance of a youth who ran full-tilt at life until exhaustion dropped him. Developing stronger protective instincts would keep him safe, but he'd lose the sweet innocence wrapped in his submissive nature. He needed the proper balance of wariness and trust.

A black bear cub. Claws to defend himself. Tumbling about, investigating everything, filled with boundless energy and free to explore without the threat of predators. Except for men bent on hunting him.

He'd seen a cub, once, as a child at the family cabin in upstate Maine. Stood transfixed for most of an hour watching. Compositions flipped before his eyes. The cub clambering over a fallen tree. He might paint a series about a shy, playful bear cub. Shaggier hair would suit the boy.

The reader fell silent.

Henry tore his gaze from his sleeping boy's relaxed face. He'd lost track of the time they'd spent here, an inappropriate lapse of focus.

The reader laid the book aside as she stood. "Thank you all for your attentiveness during story time. We'll be continuing at the same time next week."

Players stretched and gained their feet. Some of the pigtails-and-pajamas set approached the reader and received permission for hugs before scampering off. The partnered ones departed with hands clasped, a trusted authority figure and a ward. Not so different from the current mentoring relationship he shared with the boy.

Nestled close, his breathing even and regular, Jay slept. His comfort of primary concern, moving seemed unwise. A reluctance to shift left Henry seated as the reader approached.

"Henry, isn't it?" She whispered in a low alto and extended her hand as she crouched. "Marissa. I haven't seen you in our corner of the club before. Picking up a new kink?"

He raised his hand from Jay's chest and shook Marissa's hand. "Not as such, but my new boy greatly benefited from the calm and quiet here for aftercare. I hope we didn't disturb your regular players."

"Not at all." Her smile blossomed, a field of ivory petals limned in crimson. "He seems very sweet, and you were both model guests.

We'd be happy to see you back." She nodded toward the door. "There's a reservation in fifteen, but the room's yours until then if you want to wake him gently."

"I do, thank you."

She glided off with her kit and closed the door behind her.

He turned his full attention to his submissive. The conversation hadn't roused him. Henry laid his hand on Jay's chest once more, fingers splayed. He nudged his ear with his nose.

"Jay."

His whisper garnered a snuffle in reply.

"You've been such a good boy for me tonight. I'm quite proud of your behavior." He nipped a tempting earlobe. "It's time to wake, my little dreamer."

Jay rolled right, mumbling something that might have been *yes, please.*

He tapped the boy's chest and tugged harder at his earlobe.

Sleepy eyes blinked open. "D'you want me now, Henry?"

"It's time to go, my boy." He kept his voice brisk to avoid thinking about the answer. Or that his sub had neglected an honorific. Or that he wanted Jay asking the same question in the same sleep-slurred voice when he woke hard and aching and ready to fuck in the middle of the night. "You need to wake up."

More blinking before Jay jolted upward. "I'm sor—"

"Hush. You've done nothing requiring apology. You relaxed, as I expected you to." Hoped would have been more accurate than expected, but confidence was half the game. The rest was all sensitivity and skill. "Up on your feet, please."

Rolling forward, Jay briefly gripped his thighs as he gained his feet. He spun in a slow circle. "I didn't know they had this here."

Henry collected his jacket and stood, snapping it smooth. He shrugged into the fabric and buttoned Jay's scent inside, the sweet musk embedded in his dress shirt. "Oh?"

Rubbing sleep from his eyes with a balled fist, Jay almost belonged in the room with its nap mats and crayon artwork. If one excused the well-developed chest and abdominal muscles, and the sleek lines arrowing from his hips and disappearing beneath leather shorts. A potent mix of sexuality and innocence, and all of it trusting enough to fall asleep in his arms.

"You know, with all the kid stuff."

Lack of boundaries, the voice of reason suggested. Jay's trust wasn't hard-won. To believe himself special to the boy would be the height of egotistic, narcissistic folly.

"The fetishes accommodated at the club cross a wide spectrum. You may have heard the ethos expressed as 'your kink is not my kink, but your kink is okay.' Consent is the common bond tying all of us together." Not abusing young Mr. Kress's trust in this delicate time remained a priority. "It's one of the reasons Cal's behavior toward you was so egregious."

"But I"—Jay rolled his shoulders and grimaced—"I agreed. Whatever he wanted."

The sweet submissive's quiet shame and confusion stoked his desire to rectify the situation. To see him safe and well.

"And then you revoked your consent. He was bound to honor your determination that you'd had enough. He did not." Browbeating Jay into belief would be an impossible task. Better to repeat the message as a given as often as possible and let it lie.

"Knowing what you want going into a negotiation will help you set more specific limits up front in the future." He gestured to the childish décor. "Consider what you've learned about yourself tonight. Would you don pajamas and call your partner 'Mommy' or 'Daddy'?"

"Ugh, no." Like a dog coming in from the rain, Jay shook off. "That was weird. I don't want to be somebody's kid. Total boner-killer. I just want. . . ."

To be safe and loved. He held his tongue, prodding only when Jay seemed unable to go on. "Want what, my boy?"

Shifting his weight, Jay twisted his arms behind him. "I dunno."

His gaze flicked upward, the spark of hero worship evident. Unable to separate the action he enjoyed from the person providing it as yet.

"Did you enjoy the story?"

"I didn't mean to fall asleep, Master Henry." He rushed his words in a rising voice. "It wasn't boring or anything."

Again he'd interpreted a neutral question as a criticism. Perhaps praise wasn't merely something Jay enjoyed but something he'd starved for want of.

"Your slumber enchanted me. I would have been saddened to miss it."

Ah, there. Jay lifted his head, and a smile touched the corners of his mouth. "I liked the snuggling, Master Henry. And"—shyness gave way to playfulness—"the way you touch. You could touch me more if you wanted."

Crowding his partner, he lowered his tone. "I know, my boy. Any way I like, hmm? However and wherever I desire."

Laying hands on Jay's waist, he drifted along the edge of the leather shorts. He ignored the whimper in response. He'd calm any fears once he was certain the message had been received.

"Your submission belongs to me. All that holds me in check is my own concern for your welfare and my promise to respect your safeword. We've negotiated no limits. I could do anything I wish to you right now." He leaned in. Brushed Jay's ear with his mouth. "And that is the problem. The one I'm going to help you solve."

Dropping his hands, he stepped back and surveyed his submissive.

Bright eyes greeted him. A rosy flush swept Jay's torso. The tented shorts destroyed all notions but one.

Arousal.

Intense, rapid arousal.

He'd miscalculated. Expected Jay to fear an aggressive approach after witnessing his uncomfortable responses to the scenes tonight. His companion didn't see him as a convincing threat, it seemed. A dominant tone attracted more than it repelled, when it came from the man he viewed as safe.

Flattering and emasculating at once. Arousing beyond measure to have the athletic youth so eager to submit to him. "Tell me, my—"

A knock sounded as the door swung open. "Excuse me—"

He shielded his vulnerable boy from view of the doorway.

"—sorry to interrupt." A woman leaned on the frame. A man dressed as a young girl waited in silence behind her.

"No, the apology is mine. I ought to have kept better track of the time. I'm sorry to have infringed upon your reservation. Please excuse us."

They exited with a modicum of fuss, the woman accepting his apology with grace. Jay kept at his heels all the way to the second floor, dawdling only when Henry stopped at the desk.

"Go on and collect your things, my boy."

A green-ribbon staffer brought out Jay's duffel at his mumbled request.

Henry ushered him into a changing room and joined him. Jay's erection had subsided.

"I owe you an apology as well for letting the time get away from me." He took the bag and unzipped it, drawing out the rumpled work attire.

"Concentration can be difficult when one is with such a delightful companion." His submissive ought to have a proper garment bag.

"Strip, please." He tamped down the urge to purchase one for next week. "I'll play the gentleman's gentleman, shall I?"

"Huh?" Bent at the waist and wriggling out of tight leather, the bare-assed boy presented an intolerable temptation. "What's that?"

Henry flicked his tongue against his teeth and returned to sorting the clothes. "A valet."

"You wanna park cars?"

He held in the chuckle with the thinnest thread of self-control. "I want to dress you, my boy."

"Oh!" Jay shimmied out of the leather. "I'm ready, Master Henry."

Well on his way, at least. Jay's cock pulsed and swelled under his gaze.

"I'd also like to discuss your homework." He shook out the boxers, crouched, and held the shorts at floor level with spread hands. "Step in, please."

Jay slipped his feet in.

Skimming his palms up the outside of the younger man's legs, he raised the boxer shorts. He gave the growing erection a wide berth.

Jay sighed. "I remember, Master Henry. I need to pick a new safeword."

"Indeed you do." He retrieved the shirt and stepped behind his student. "Arms back."

Dragging his fingers along Jay's firm forearms and sloping biceps, he pulled the shirtsleeves up. "I also want you to think of one point you want to negotiate next week. One action or behavior you want from me during our time together. A toy you'd like to try, a roleplay you'd like to experience—something you desire, whatever it is."

He turned him and began fastening the buttons from the top. "Last week I asked you to think of something you wanted to do to me. Did you think on that while you completed your homework?"

Jay's throat worked as he swallowed hard. "Yes, Master Henry."

"I won't ask you for the details now. Keep thinking on it. Perhaps join it to your thinking for this week's assignment. We'll discuss both next week." He finished off the shirt with the buttons at the cuffs, gripping his submissive's hands and stroking his palms as he worked. "Did the masturbation schedule I set for you satisfy your needs?"

Twitching against the boxers accompanied Jay's rapid nodding.

"I kept to the same schedule myself to share your experience." He dropped the words with nonchalance and turned to gather the slacks.

A whimpering moan echoed behind him.

"You'll continue to bring yourself to climax with your left hand during your morning shower."

Jay curled said hand into a fist and squeezed repeatedly.

Kneeling, Henry held out the open slacks. "Step in, please."

His slow strokes covered strong calves and thighs beneath navy slacks as he rose. "In the evenings, you may use either hand this week. However—"

Fastening the belt by touch, he locked their gazes together. "I want you to spend five minutes on light touching only. After that, you may fuck your clenched fist to your heart's content."

He slipped his knuckles up Jay's cheekbone to his ear. Twice. Three times. "Gentle touches," he whispered. "The way I'm stroking your face now, you understand?"

A shudder ran through the submissive, and his breath gusted out. "Yes, Master Henry."

"Good." Leaning in, he claimed his partner's lips for a sweet kiss. "Then you're free to go. I'll see you at eight o'clock next Friday."

Chapter 3

He'd told the boy eight, but the clock hadn't yet chimed seven when Henry entered the club.

Preparations to make. And, it must be said, no shortage of anticipatory excitement contributed to his early arrival.

Emma insisted upon accompanying him to the room. "Sparse, Henry. You're sure you don't want something cozier?"

Yes, he'd like something cozier. A sweet dark-haired lover to cozy up to and command. Where was his much-vaunted control now?

His skin thrummed as if he'd been on the receiving end of electrical stimulation play. If he didn't drain the excess energy, he'd be as fidgety as his submissive. Hardly the image he wished to project.

"You're sure you aren't needling me in the hopes I'll swat your behind for you?" An empty, lighthearted threat. Never mind Victor wouldn't allow such play without his direct supervision—Henry wouldn't be so crass as to presume. Fifteen years of friendship accommodated shifting boundaries.

"I'm sure Jay Kress is a lucky boy." Her smile urged him to check her mouth for the canary. "This is what, your third meeting as his dominant?"

He surveyed the setup. She'd chosen well. The room matched his reservation request for nothing in the way of furniture or frames. Sparse, yes. Perfect for admiring a lovely, graceful body in the form of one Jay Kress. He drew the wood-slat blinds over the viewing windows and locked them in the closed position. The only one admiring his student tonight would be him.

She turned to keep him in profile as he circled her. "I know your tricks, Henry Webb."

"I know yours, you shameless gambling hussy," he teased. "Don't start games you don't mean to finish."

He lunged only to tickle her ribs. A feint in gratitude for her understanding, the playfulness she allowed him to bleed the nerves she had to have seen. Perhaps why she'd insisted upon joining him and started a game both knew would go nowhere beyond a good laugh.

She dashed back, fending him off with her hands. "I could say the same of you. The boy's a sweetheart, isn't he? A proper *eromenos*?" Laughing, she danced away. "I'm going to win the wager, Henry."

Hands falling to his sides, he stopped in mid-stalk. His swirling joy solidified and cracked. "No. You aren't, Em."

"Henry?"

She approached with the gentle steps he himself would use to relax a nervous novice. Did he appear so off-balance to her? The boy didn't know him as well. A blessing, since he seemed to be channeling the uncertainty of his youth. Even the first time he'd wielded a single-tail whip hadn't been so laden with emotion. Young Mr. Kress changed the picture.

"I've upset you."

He squeezed her shoulder. Forgiveness in a clasp. She had no way to know the depth of the river or the speed of the current. How he wanted to let it carry him and the boy downstream, to wash up on some foreign shore where they hadn't met in violence and pain and rescue.

"He isn't a toy to be won, Emma. He's a scared, confused young man who doesn't know half of what he wants and is ashamed of the other half." This was therapy, not a relationship. An odd sort of therapy, but therapy nonetheless. "I won't abuse his trusting nature and throw a leash on him. In two months, he'll have an understanding of himself and his needs, and I—"

A clean break. No playing together once the time was up, not even a play session for old time's sake. Such behavior would complicate the emotional separation.

"I will let him go."

Emma's eyes softened as she pursed her lips. Raising two perfectly manicured hands, she adjusted his pin-straight tie. A blatant excuse to offer comfort in her fingertips, but he said nothing.

"You're an honorable man, Henry. Like my Victor." She patted his chest. A mother's gesture. "He waited a long while for me to come along. But when I did, he snatched me up. I hope you'll seize the moment when it comes for you, too." She shook her head, slow and steady, meeting his gaze. "You rein yourself in so tightly. I don't want to see you alone for the rest of your life."

She let go, dropping her hands from his chest. He captured one.

"Go and play with Victor, Em." He carried her hand to his mouth and pressed a soft kiss to her knuckles. "We both know he's happier with your bottom resting securely in his palm. I've preparations to make for my boy. You've given the desk staff the instructions?"

"Of course I have. They'll send him up to change and then to find you here."

"To knock and wait."

"Would a proper submissive have it any other way?" Her lips gleamed when she smiled. "Excuse me, Henry. I think it's time to knock on Victor's door."

She sauntered out, the sway in her hips elegant and enticing as ever.

He tucked the red card into the holder on the door. No unwanted guests. A closed scene tonight to boost Jay's confidence and allow space for his vulnerability.

Forty-five minutes left, and the boy would be early. Of course he would.

Henry set to work.

When the knock came, he alerted to the sound like a bird dog scenting prey in the bush.

He rose from his half-lotus with a loose calm, confidence descending. He mastered his passions. They did not master him.

Swaying silk teased his skin as he strode to the door. He'd traded his customary formal attire for a shirt and trousers more akin to a martial arts uniform tonight. Black silk concealed and revealed in turns as it flowed to provide a focal point but not a distraction for his student.

He pulled the door open. "Welcome, my boy. I'm delighted to see you."

Jay stood in silence if not stillness, his head bowed and his hands clasped behind him. The picture of perfection in leather shorts and thin sandals but for the trembling in his arms. Waiting was so hard for this submissive. Teaching him to enjoy it—a pleasure, through and through.

"Have you missed me this week?"

"Yes, Master Henry." The answer came tripping on the heels of his question. With a jerk, Jay stifled the beginnings of a nod.

Clasping the back of Jay's neck, he coaxed with a slight tug. "Come here, dear one."

The younger man flung himself forward with the force of Jackson Pollack covering a canvas.

Henry widened his stance to steady himself. Pushing the door closed behind them, he allowed Jay the time to feel whole. He ran his hands over his back with a light touch, reluctant to press until he'd seen the current state of his bruising. Healed, one hoped.

A storm of rapid, hot breaths blew across his ear. Jay's grip compressed his ribs.

The fierce hold stirred a potent mix of protective instincts and desire. Were Jay his lover, an expression of either wouldn't go amiss. Ask how poorly he'd fared this week to require such a desperate embrace. Wrestle him to the floor, pin him on the mat, and take him as he shouted his pleasure.

But Jay was his student, not his lover.

Henry pushed down the growling beast clawing its way out of the basest corners of his brain and demanding to possess its prize. He waited in patient stillness for his partner to relax. Catching the moment between the end of instinctive need and the stirring of embarrassed awareness was crucial. It wouldn't do to make Jay self-conscious about his needs. He struggled with that enough.

"I thought we might forgo viewing other games this evening and instead spend this time together playing one of our own." He slipped his words into the gap with all the painless precision of proper needle play. "Are you prepared to surrender yourself to me?"

Jay's shuddering sigh boded well. "I am, Master Henry. Thank you, Master Henry."

"Wonderful." He put sorely needed distance between their bodies and gestured his student forward. "Leave your sandals here and stand in the center of the sheets."

He'd unrolled one of the club's play mats in the center of the room. A bit larger than his king-size bed, but the fitted and top sheet set he'd brought from home adequately covered the surface. The mat provided a softer embrace than the bare wood floor for a submissive's knees, or back, or other things during a long scene.

"Spread your feet to shoulder-width." Pain had its uses, but it wasn't an element suitable for his boy at this juncture. "An at-ease pose."

Jay jumped to obey. As eager as if he'd been born for it. *For me.*

"Clasp your hands in front, arms relaxed." He sought an unobstructed view of his back. "Excellent. Well done. Stay just like this, please."

The praise produced the expected effect, straightening Jay's shoulders and stiffening his spine. A spine unblemished by last week's motley patchwork of colors.

Concerns about his partner's physical readiness for play laid to rest, he advanced. "Last week we talked about the importance of choosing a safeword and using it as needed. Have you chosen a new safeword as I asked?"

"Yes, Master Henry."

"Tell me your safeword, please."

"Tilt-A-Whirl."

A unique choice. Forcing Jay to disclose his reasoning wasn't a strict necessity, but curiosity pulled at him. "Share with me, my boy. Tell me why you've chosen this word."

Jay shuffled his feet. "'Cause you said I should pick something I didn't like. I don't like carnivals. I ruined it for everybody."

He forced himself to let his foot fall naturally, to avoid revealing the stutter to his partner. Had Jay left his explanation with a distaste for carnivals, he would have judged it a personal quirk, a sweet note of knowledge about his pet, and let it go. But now—not so.

"Everybody?" Best to start simply and ease toward the hurt. "Who went to the carnival with you?"

"Peggy took us, me an' Beth an' Nat. My sisters, I mean, Master Henry. Peggy's the oldest."

"You didn't have fun?" Odd. Jay didn't seem the type to be dismayed by spending time under a woman's thumb, but perhaps he'd been a teenager itching for more freedom. "How old were you?"

"I liked it at first. All the lights and the noise and the food. I'd never seen anything like it."

A hint of wonder edged his tone, sweet and innocent. The desire to hear that tone again, to show Jay such delights in the playground of adulthood, clamped hard in his chest.

"I was five, Master Henry. I hadn't been off the farm much. The carnival came the summer before I started kindergarten. I wanted to try everything. Peggy said I shouldn't be such a piggy. She was right."

Defeat and shame marred the younger man's remembrance. What should have been a happy memory of childhood.

"Tell me what happened, Jay. You rode the Tilt-A-Whirl?"

"I begged like a brat 'til she took me on. An' then it was all spinning an' I"—he whispered, fierce and low—"I threw up. All over me an' her, too. She was so mad."

So the girl had let her baby brother gorge himself, and made the poor decision to allow him to ride the attraction despite his full stomach, and reaped the rewards of her choices. A teenager, undoubtedly. One humiliated in front of classmates or a crush and eager to transfer her failings to a more vulnerable target.

"I see why you dislike the ride. Vomiting is such an unpleasant feeling." He kept his voice light and even. Phrasing his question to give Jay a sense of what ought to have followed, he suspected things had played out much differently. "Did you enjoy the rest of the carnival after she helped you clean up?"

Jay stepped back and turned to face him. "We didn't stay, Master Henry."

"Oh?" He nodded to his student. "Mind your positioning, please. How am I to study every inch of your beauty when it shifts as we talk?"

Quick though he was to reclaim his former pose at the gentle chide, Jay flushed and smiled, too. Good. He hadn't failed to hear his master's praise wrapped in reprimand.

"Tell me what happened when the ride ended." He had no need for harshness to keep this sub in line. The knowledge that he'd given pleasure would do so all on its own.

"Um, I dunno, I cried a lot, I think." The words flowed faster but with a distance, as if he recounted events detached from his own experience. "Nat laughed and Beth kept saying I was gross, an' Peggy yanked my shirt off and threw it in the trash, and Chuck told her no way was he riding home with us when she stank so bad, even if she took off her shirt, too."

The girl's boyfriend, presumably. But the image piercing his mind's eye was of his sweet boy, shirtless and sick, crying in a crowd of strangers at the carnival as his siblings berated him.

"I ruined the whole night. Peggy took us straight home." Jay shrugged, though he kept his head bowed. "I rode in the truck bed so I wouldn't stink up the cab."

Anger twisted into a tempest in his stomach. Callous caretaking had taught Jay to expect no better, perhaps.

"I'm sorry you had such a terrible night at the carnival, my boy." No wonder Jay had cried out for Cal's return that night. He saw love in all but rejection. Blamed himself for the errors of those around him. Excused any behavior but his own. "I hope your sister learned her lesson."

Jay shifted his head. Slight, but signaling his interest.

"She must have been quite upset with herself for not setting a better example and providing clear rules for you to follow. Shirking her responsibilities." He clicked his tongue. "Despite her failings, however, you've made an excellent selection for your safeword."

"I have?" Jay blurted the words and half-twisted before he recovered himself. "I mean, I'm sorry for speaking out of turn, Master Henry."

"It's fine, dear one. Part of your training is learning to ask questions when you need to. You've apologized, as you should. Shall I explain how you've pleased me?"

He would explain regardless of the answer, but he waited to see if Jay would ask for what he wanted. The few short weeks they'd have together, eight nights in all, necessitated reinforcement at every opportunity.

"Yes, please, Master Henry."

"Good boy," he murmured. "I asked you to choose a reminder of something uncomfortable for a reason. During our play sessions, should you begin to feel the discomfort or confusion, the shame or overwhelming helplessness you felt as a child at the carnival, I want you to reach for your safeword and use it. Do you understand?"

"I understand, Master Henry." His student didn't sound happy about it. He'd be reluctant to use his safeword if he thought doing so displeased his dominant, of course, but he seemed disturbed by a deeper fear.

Henry teased the thought forward until it took shape and form, shaded with nuances of Jay's words and behavior over the last three weeks.

"I won't leave you, my brave boy." Stepping in front of his submissive, he cradled Jay's chin and rubbed his thumb across soft, full lips. "If you speak your safeword, we shall stop until I've properly attended to your upset. I won't walk out the door and leave you here alone. I won't exile you to the truck bed."

Jay watched him with trusting brown eyes.

"When we have addressed the trouble spot, we'll begin again." Explaining to Jay that trouble might require more than a single night to address would be sharing too much. As the dominant and trainer, he accepted the responsibility to make such determinations. For now, he emphasized the non-punishment nature of safeword use. "Nothing I do is intended to make you suffer. I wish to bring us both pleasure. Your use of your safeword will help me do that."

Sinking in, the message painted Jay's muscles in pliancy.

Delicious, the mixture of relaxation and anticipation in a submissive as he found safe harbor. The only trigger his dominant instincts required. "Now, tell me your safeword."

Jay puffed out his chest. "Tilt-A-Whirl."

The "w" pushed Jay's lips outward like a kiss against his thumb. A natural motion. Fanciful to believe the younger man intended more. And yet. He breathed out slowly to clear his head.

"Very good." He dropped his hand and stepped back. "I believe we're ready to begin our game."

He surveyed his partner with lingering appreciation. The night's game encompassed two complementary goals. Showing Jay a submissive's fun need not include lasting physical or emotional pain would be the easy part. Demonstrating Jay's desirability without giving in to his own desire to take him? Hard. Well. Not yet, but soon enough. He suppressed a rueful smile as his cock twitched and silk slid.

"Do you know what I do for a living, my boy?" He inspected the musculature of his partner's arm. Sleek and rounded. Not so pronounced as the muscles of his legs.

"No, Master Henry." Jay spoke with gentle, attentive curiosity. He bore a student's hunger. Enticing for one who loved to teach.

"I capture beauty." *In truth, beauty captures me.*

"That's a job?"

"It is for an artist." Pausing his inspection, he met the boy's watchful eyes with a smile. "And you radiate beauty inside and out. Tonight I want to bask in your beauty. Remove your shorts. Nothing about you is to be hidden from me."

His command sent his sub into a flurry of motion. So eager. Nudity suited Jay, and he seemed to enjoy it. More than a few male submissives wore nothing but sandals and a ribbon in the halls.

Yet young Mr. Kress wore shorts, tight and revealing though they were. The choice might reflect the need for a layer of defense or a belief he must dress a certain way to attract a dominant. He couldn't say what his companion had overheard or been told and taken for truth.

Jay handed over the shorts.

He laid them aside. Now nothing obstructed his view. He growled, a low, rolling pleasure.

Jay's muscles tightened, the cheeks of his ass round and firm.

"Delightful." He circled left, admiring the line of shadow gathering under the curving cheeks. "Have you ever been paired with another submissive for play?"

"Oh, yes, Master Henry. Sometimes"—rolling his ankles out and back, Jay bounced taller—"they'd let me watch them with their real sub."

He stopped with an ungraceful jerk. Out of his student's line of sight, thankfully. "A misunderstanding, sweet boy."

Jay saw himself as second-best, a submissive of last resort. On the outside, exiled to watching the real game. No way to tell whether the doms he'd played with had intended to give such an impression or if his lack of experience and propensity for self-blame had played the larger role.

"More precisely, I mean has a dominant ever required you to service another submissive with your hands, your mouth, or your cock while he or she enjoyed the show."

"People do that?" Excitement colored Jay's tone, and a tremor ran through him. "No, Master Henry, I've never."

Wonderful. Perhaps his new pet would enjoy being put to stud. If matters developed satisfactorily, he'd arrange an experience in a few weeks.

"Yes, they do that." He circled back, keeping his distance to take in the angles of Jay's shoulder blades. "I'm surprised you haven't been asked. Your lovely lines and athletic grace make for a powerful visual feast."

Lowering his voice, he let a half-measure of his desire out to play. "When you clench your ass, I cannot help but imagine you in full thrust, muscles flowing and hips writhing to deliver pleasure to an eager partner."

Jay whimpered, a wild and hungry plea. He thrust his hips once and stopped short.

"Yes, just so. Your body an instrument for my enjoyment, moving at my command." He paced far enough to bring himself even with his partner, into his field of vision.

Head bowed, eyelids flickering, Jay sucked air through his teeth.

Black silk shifted over his stiffening cock, the vision he'd intended the younger man to see.

"Quite arousing, your beauty," he murmured. "A shame not to celebrate it, when it does so much for me."

He cupped his groin and stroked upward. A single stroke, to demonstrate Jay's desirability, the counterintuitive power of submission. Teeth clenched, he forced himself to let go afterward.

Jay's low moan nearly upended his plans for the night. Want and need packed into a tight throat, and all of it his to claim. Ordered to the mat, his sub would obey without question. Take a face-fucking with pride if he presented it the right way.

Not yet. Imagination before action. Self-control. His promise to this inexperienced, vulnerable young man.

"Tell me about your homework, my boy. What have you been fantasizing about doing to me?" Knowing the door he'd opened, he anticipated the answer. "How do you want to serve me?"

"With my mouth, Master Henry. I think about blowing you." Jay raced to get the words out. His cock bobbed, mute testimony to the strength of his fantasy. "I've been thinking about it every day this week and last week, too."

Hard did not encapsulate the condition of his own cock. He ached. Every cell in his body ached with desire. A glorious pleasure, the sharp edge of need and the knowledge he might master it.

"When you imagine, do you see the same scene each time, or do the circumstances change?" Details mattered. If the young man had a specific sequence in mind, he would work to create the desired experience in truth. Receiving what he asked for would shore up Jay's self-worth and make him more eager to engage in proper negotiation rather than accepting what was offered.

"Different, I guess, Master Henry." Jay licked his lips.

Henry's cock twitched.

"But you always. . . ." A light flush decorated Jay's face.

"What do I always do?"

"You always say I did good. That you're happy."

Jay rocked on the balls of his feet, his legs stiff. The tension under his skin seemed alive, a ball of energy threatening to burst into motion at any time. Henry held his tongue. Chastising the submissive for the excitement in his very nature only taught him to hide his needs. Correction couched in control and praise would better serve.

"Mmm. Because you do make me happy." He crossed in front of his pupil, noting the way brown eyes followed his steps, keen to keep his cock in sight. "Unlock your knees, please. Your health and comfort will fare better for it. I'd hate to have your knees damaged before I may judge for myself what you're capable of doing on them."

Working against his own instincts to please his masters might make Jay happy on the surface, but the ultimate end would crush him. Working with rather than against created a flowing harmony shared in the bond between dominant and submissive.

Jay's knees unlocked. His stance grew more relaxed. The change heightened the vibrating tension running through him. Without rigid muscle control, his excitement manifested in delightful trembling.

"Thank you, my boy. Looking upon your desire is my prerogative. Controlling and satisfying you is my privilege. Part of the gift you give me."

Jay lifted his head.

"Yes, I said 'gift.'" He passed out of his partner's sight.

Mr. Kress tolerated it well, with minor fidgeting. An improvement.

"As we are on the subject of gifts, I want you to tell me about the other half of your homework. Did you give thought to something you desire for yourself? What do you want your dominant to give you?"

"Yes, Master Henry. I, I like my homework. I know you said a toy or a role-play thing, maybe, but I"—Jay drooped—"I like having you say when and how." He resettled his shoulders with an uneasy shrug. "I just like you saying what happens and me being your good boy. Is that okay? Can I just want that for now?"

The younger man ought to have had a gentle introduction to games. As he'd suspected, degradation and humiliation didn't largely figure in Jay's kinks. He wanted to surrender to a trusted partner who would watch over him. Who would make things easy with clear rules and limits.

"It's a beautiful thought, my boy, and well-expressed." He unleashed his pride in his voice. That Jay's simple desires for security and stability shamed him rankled. Had he been given a proper introduction, a pleasure like bondage could have proven quite appealing rather than feared as a vehicle for pain.

"It—it is?"

Instruction and seduction unified. A potent fuel for his arousal. He'd climaxed in a solo session not fifteen minutes before Jay entered the room, part of his preparation, yet he'd hardened again faster than expected.

"You've given your homework sufficient thought to tell me five things about your desires, my brilliant boy." Orgasm sans ejaculation crept up on him, a beating drum at the edge of his hearing. "I required only two." If the boy continued to . . . *to what, be himself? How could I ask him to be other?* If events continued apace, he might yet reach said peak tonight. "You've exceeded my expectations."

"I did?"

Confusion and wonder. Jay Kress would be the death of him.

"Mm-hmm."

He hummed as he moved in. He'd rouse his partner to a state of raw need and encourage him to give a demonstration. A pop quiz for the work he'd practiced the last two weeks.

"Five things, my boy, you know about yourself and may share in a negotiation to ensure a prospective dominant will provide the experience you seek. I'm going to tell you what they are now."

He stopped three short steps back. The distance allowed for advancement as he increased the pressure. The proximity permitted his words to sound in his submissive's ears.

"I want you listening to my voice, Jay. I know you will, because I've asked it of you, and you want to please me." He aimed to reassure, to affirm with both words and tone that wanting to please was a desired trait.

His submissive nodded, little more than an unconscious tic. He'd internalized the lesson and the acceptance. A promising sign.

"You've told me complex games and elaborate trappings aren't necessary for you to enjoy yourself." He seduced with a lilt of approval. "A simple game of control is appropriate to your fledgling steps here. You seek mentors who will expand your world with patience and care."

Shifting closer, he studied Jay's reaction. The trembling. The in-and-out of his ribcage as his breaths came quick and heavy. Anticipation. He permitted himself a smile.

"You've told me harsh games are not for you. A dominant needn't layer shame or humiliation into a scene to heighten your pleasure. You aren't a naughty boy at heart. Being forced into obedience doesn't excite you, because you take joy in obedience for its own sake."

A half step closer. More would strain his own control as he delivered his next words.

"You're a good boy, Jay. A good boy who wants to show his master how good he can be."

Jay tensed his shoulders. He exhaled in a shuddering sigh.

"You've told me that most of all, you want to give up control not for the helplessness but for the security. The dangerous thrill is not the attraction. Comfort and affection bound in rules to tell you your place, to assure you of your worth—these are the things you seek in your games."

The enticement his submissive represented grew deeper with each revelation. Jay's needs complemented his own. His cock jumped, sending ripples cascading through the silk swirling around his legs. The caress of fabric, sensuous though it was, failed to satisfy. A poor substitute for the image of Jay's willing mouth.

"Three thus far, my boy. Three beautiful things you've told me about yourself tonight. Two left. More specific things you might ask for in a negotiation, hmm?"

No matter that part of him didn't want his student engaging in negotiations with other dominants at all.

"You're willing to take direction. To serve another sweet soul like yourself for the voyeuristic enjoyment of your dominant. You've a bit of an exhibitionist streak."

He imagined the scene, a matched set, trained and responsive, their bodies moving as he guided them to fulfillment. His beautiful boy and a partner. His slow exhale gave his submissive a full-body shudder.

"I expect you'd like very much to please two others and yourself, taking pleasure in following commands, giving pleasure to your playmate, and providing pleasure for your master."

Jay moaned, low and urgent.

He verged on saying too much, of pressing his own desires on his charge. He reached for the calm center he'd found when Jay's knock rattled the door. Waited until he'd reached some semblance of it.

"Fifth and finally, my delightful boy, you've told me you want the fullness of a hard cock in your mouth. An intimate bond." Not always, but it was a safe bet this submissive wanted it to be. He elevated the act to a form of worship in his fantasizing. "You want to serve your master with a personal connection. To show him with your lips and your tongue and the warm pull of your mouth the things you cannot say to him. The things you might be afraid to say to him. But you can show him, can't you?"

"Yes." Jay uttered fierce whispers between harsh breaths. "Yes, Master Henry."

"When you're on your knees and looking up at him, pleading with those wide brown eyes for the opportunity to bring him pleasure? When he slips his cock between your lips, he's sharing himself with you." He picked up his pace, words tumbling. A moment more, a gentle push, and he'd give his pet permission to take himself in hand. "He's powerful and vulnerable all at once, isn't he? Just as you are. How intimate it is for the two of you to be of one mind and one body. Accepting each other for the gifts you bring."

Need burned in his veins. He drifted closer to his shaking submissive.

"I understand you, my boy. I see you for who you are." He whispered into Jay's ear, their bodies a scant inch apart. "And you are *beautiful.*"

As he closed the gap, clasping his hands around strong shoulders, Jay jerked.

Throaty whimpers sounded in the silence, wounded beauty, pain and relief. His submissive's unexpected release spurted across the sheets.

From words alone. Voice and the barest touch, with two pairs of hands and neither anywhere near Jay's cock.

Utter perfection. God himself couldn't have delivered a more exquisite partner into his hands.

Intense satisfaction lasted mere seconds. Curling forward, hiding himself, Jay sank to his knees and babbled apologies.

Rarely did a moment call for indelicate language, but if ever one did. . . . *Fuck.*

Regain control. Distract his sub, divert his attention to interrupt the cycle of shame, and only then return to question his reaction.

Henry followed Jay to the mat and embraced him. He took a slow, confident swipe along the underside of his submissive's cock. Gathered evidence of pleasure on his index finger.

The apologies ceased.

He raised his finger.

The younger man turned his head and watched.

He'd succeeded in capturing his attention, at the least.

Holding his hand over the shaking shoulder, he sucked his finger clean with a satisfied groan. His arousal knocked against Jay's backside, a visitor seeking entry with but a thin layer of silk to preach control.

He'd intended for his companion to come eventually. Jay finishing sooner than expected in no way diminished the success of the game. Besides, the night was still young, and so was the man. Mid-twenties, the prime of youth. He might yet put on another performance.

"An exceptional show," he murmured. "Well done."

"You aren't angry with me, Master Henry?"

The wisp of fear in Jay's voice swept his arousal aside. Reassurance ruled him now. His submissive needed a strong leader.

"Should I be angered by your enthusiastic response?" Clutching him close, he growled in his ear. "Angered you so gratify my ego as to come at the sound of my voice?"

He nuzzled Jay's neck and smoothed his hair. "What is there to anger me in that?"

"But I came. That's against the rules."

A swift and silent review confirmed he'd stated no such rule this evening. "Whose rules, my boy?"

"I don't"—Jay shrugged—"you know, the rules."

Jay had served no long-term masters, but he behaved as if a dominant's rules existed beyond a single night. He craved the continuity and stability of a relationship. Combined with an absolute lack of under-standing of his own power, his need and obedient nature made him vulnerable. Ready to believe every word from another's mouth and carry it over as gospel.

What a jumbled mess this sweet boy had fallen into.

He scraped at the layers of error. He'd peel them back and paint anew. "What happened when you broke that rule?"

Rolling and ducking his head, the younger man shifted his hips. He dared raise a hand and trace his master's finger, the one wet with saliva.

Henry curled Jay's hand into his own. "Tell me."

"She laughed at me." He whispered his confession. "Said I was worthless. Pathetic. And she paddled me." He shook his head, confu-sion plain in his voice. "But she said it was fun, after."

"It likely was, to her. But now you know that isn't a proper game for you. You owe the dominants here courtesy and nothing more. Your submission is yours to grant as you choose." He squeezed Jay's hand. "At present, I am lucky enough to claim it. The only rules you need to concern yourself with in this room are mine. Did I instruct you not to come?"

The boy stilled. "No, Master Henry. But"—his voice hit the higher register of surprise and distress—"but I made a mess and ruined your game."

At last, a problem requiring seconds, not weeks, to set right. "Non-sense." He poured gentle amusement into his tone. "You've christened your sheets."

"Mine?"

Surprising this man was a delight he might never tire of enjoying.

"Part of your homework." Explaining now would do no harm. Would, in fact, encourage Jay to take ownership of his tasks and re-quest what he needed. "Shall I share it with you now?"

"Yes, please, Master Henry." Eager and wriggling, Jay roused his passions. A sweet torment. "I'd like that."

"Where do you believe these sheets came from?"

"The laundry downstairs? I took towels there once."

"Mmm. Not these sheets." He dragged their linked hands across the cotton, soft and smooth as silk. "I took these from my own bed this evening."

Jay clenched, lifting the fabric. "Your sheets, Master Henry?"

"The sheets I lay in this week as I honored our schedule. As I thought of you carrying out your homework."

Whimpering, Jay pushed his hips in his master's groin.

Henry hissed as he inhaled, the pressure on his cock a dangerous enticement. The younger man showed signs of new life already. They sat cradled together on his own sheets. How sweet it would be to slide into his submissive and show him the joys of growing hard thanks to the internal massage from his partner's cock.

Not tonight. He'd done no preparation work with his student. Taking him now would send the wrong message. Jay had granted him rights to his body in ignorance. Held nothing back, negotiated no terms. Impossible to teach safety and control if he couldn't control himself first.

"When you leave here tonight, you'll take these sheets with you. You'll lie on them this week when you take yourself in hand and finish your homework. Next week, you'll bring them back to me."

"Our sheets," Jay whispered.

"Our sheets," he agreed. "You've simply gotten a head start on your homework, my dear boy."

He rubbed a hand down Jay's bare thigh and kissed his jaw. An indulgence. "I think you might manage another for me. Show me how you've been practicing this week, light and slow."

Jay's breath whooshed out in a single gust. "Really?"

"Really." He laid his chin on the younger man's shoulder, their faces side by side. "Show me." Jay's slender waist filled his palms. He stroked trim, solid abs with a feathery touch. "Do you hear my words in your ears when you wrap your fingers around your cock?"

Jay gave a shaky nod, and his hand stuttered as he reached for himself. More than half-hard. Excellent recovery time. Quick to climax lost some of its stigma with a rapid reload and a sustained follow-up.

"Does having my guidance please you?" He stayed close, dismissing the silent voice suggesting he did so to satisfy his own desire.

Cradling Jay offered him comfort and encouragement to diminish his shame. He did so as the young man's dominant to create pleasant associations with the act. The care, the approval and security a dominant ought to provide. That was all.

"Yes, Master Henry." Jay cupped his scrotum, squeezing and releasing with light pressure. "I like knowing I'm doing it for you."

"For us both," he corrected. Jay needed to take ownership. If he tied his pleasure only to his current master, he might backslide when the time came to give him up. "I want to see you take pleasure in it."

Jay gripped his shaft in his other hand. He stroked with delicate slowness, his cock jumping as he hardened fully. Back and forth, avoiding the glans. Worried about his stamina, perhaps. He needn't be. But how sweet of him to want to give his master an extended show.

They were of a size, though the younger man was more slender, in this as in every respect. His tanned fingers paled against the dark flush of his arousal. He worked himself in silence, with only the harsh staccato of his breath to punctuate his heightened excitement.

Henry held his tongue to better observe his habits and responses. He took note of every hitch in his student's breath. The warmth of his skin. The frequency of pauses in his stroke. The changes of pace. The shift from a light clasp to a tighter grip as his climax drew closer. The barest hint of vocalization, strangled in a tight throat. The habit of a boy accustomed to avoiding parental awareness or a roommate's teasing.

"Why so quiet? I hear your want." Flexing his thighs, he squeezed Jay between and hummed at the tremble in response. "Share your need and your joy with me."

The throaty whimpers made his cock throb.

"That's it. I hear you, Jay. I hear your need calling to me. It's all right to finish." He pressed forward, delicious torture, his erection trapped in his silk pants and jammed against his submissive's firm ass. "Do you feel me? How much you please me? Don't hold back."

Jay slicked his hand around his shaft and over the head with the speed of a hummingbird's wings. Rocking, he pushed back. His whimpers gained volume.

"I do," he gasped. "Wanna please you, Master Henry."

Release arrived in a rush. He produced little output, a single jet of white and a few drops spattering over his knees.

Lovely nonetheless. Perhaps more so because of the knowledge he'd drained the boy.

Mine.

He toppled Jay sideways to the sheets and kissed him. A fierce, passionate demonstration of ownership. His weight across his pupil's chest held him down. Jay's eager surrender fed his arousal. Holding his hips back lest the temptation prove too much, he pressed his claim with a thrusting tongue and firm lips.

Satisfaction flooded his chest. The pleasure threatened to spill over. Control at its limits, he pulled back.

"Exquisite." His blood raced in a torrent, pressure humming under his skin. He breathed deep, and Jay's musk filled his nose. "You're a good boy, Jay. My good boy."

Jay's smile rivaled the brush of dawn, bright but slim, a touch shy. A beginning. He wanted to see that smile at noon, sunny and playful in a clear sky, more than beams breaking through heavy clouds.

"Thank you, Master Henry." Jay blinked with dazed eyes. Postcoital stupor catching up with him, perhaps. "Thank you for not laughing. For wanting me. For wanting *me*, I mean."

The fragile hope in the younger man's face urged him to reassure. "No other would serve me so well, brave boy. If there's to be laughter in our sheets, it will be a joyful sound for us both."

His solemn promise to one he held dear.

He patted his pet's chest. "Dry yourself on the sheets, and then we'll fold them together while I explain the rest of your homework."

Jay proved an able helper. As expected, he proffered no objections to an addition to his homework sessions.

"Just lighter, Master Henry?" He wriggled into his shorts.

"Teasing, my boy." Not unlike the enticing display before his eyes. "Draw out your strokes. See how long you can make the enjoyment last before you either lose interest or need to climax. Push yourself."

The more Jay understood of his own limits, the easier his training would be. The better Henry would be able to match him with prospective dominants. That was his goal here, wasn't it? His responsibility. As was explaining the necessity of the remaining item on the homework list.

The sheets had been folded and handed off to his submissive when he raised the subject.

"Jay."

"Yes, Master Henry?" He clutched the sheets to his bare chest, arms crossed in an X.

"I've made an appointment for you with my physician for Mon-

day evening." Jay's blank stare made his lips twitch. "For a physical
and a standard rundown of testing for sexually transmitted infections.
We'll discuss more safety considerations when we meet next week."

"You think I'm dirty?" Wide-eyed, his submissive wailed in a sad,
thin tenor.

Indelicately done, fool. Having no one to care for him, Jay as yet
lacked the understanding of how these things were done.

"Not even a little, my dear boy." He clasped his student's shoulders and kissed his forehead. "I want you to be safe. Are you aware
the desk allows all members to keep their health information on file?
The database permits prospective partners to confirm the date of a
player's last submitted test results and their health status."

Jay shook his head.

Months. Young Mr. Kress had spent months playing games of an
unknown nature without once investigating a potential dominant.

"I want you to stop at the desk and ask to see my record on your
way out tonight." Clean, always, but he maintained a regular testing
schedule. "Submissives, so often the receivers in these games, are
more vulnerable to acquiring an infection." An attention to such details was both a matter of honor, as the responsibility not to harm a
submissive was his, and a courtesy to help submissives make an in-
formed decision to trust him. "From now on, you'll inquire at the
desk about anyone with whom you wish to play."

"I don't want to play with anyone but you, Master Henry." Fingers
tightening, Jay crushed the sheets.

Hero worship, he reminded himself. Not fading yet, but it would.
He stepped away and crouched beside his kit. Emptier now, without
the sheets.

"Then you'll keep your appointment. You needn't give your name."
He pulled the card from the bag's side pocket. "Go here, tell them
you're mine, and they'll handle the rest."

The younger man accepted the card. Good. The bill and the results would come to Henry before their next meeting. Jay had done
well tonight. Coped with challenges, shared a painful memory, and
learned to enjoy himself without pain.

"We'll meet early next Friday, my boy. Have our table in the salon
ready at 7 p.m., please."

Was he mad? He'd issued the invitation without any intention of
doing so.

"We're having dinner?" Jay showed a distinct inability to stand still, and his eyes gleamed.

"Yes." It wouldn't do to go back on his word now. The dinner would serve as a reward for his companion's courage tonight. The invitation owed nothing to the quiet of his table this week. The emptiness of the facing chairs. "We had an enjoyable dinner last week, did we not?"

"I liked it. A lot."

"I'm pleased."

He kissed his partner, thanked him for his submission, and ushered him out. He didn't trust himself to follow Mr. Kress downstairs and keep him company as he changed. Not tonight.

He'd promised himself he'd keep a distance. That this would be no different from the dozens of submissives he'd played with through the years. He'd left them satisfied and parted amicably. Taught the occasional husband how to fulfill his wife's desires when she discovered a submissive kink. Whipped submissive straight boys who feared even asking their wives for such treatment. Indulged his own appetite for voyeurism countless times.

Never had he blurred the line between harmless play and a deeper relationship. Yet he'd handed his sheets off to this boy. Demanded he use them on his bed. He'd overstepped. Made this personal.

For Jay's sake. He needed this level of control and involvement.

Yes, a pretty argument. Jay needed him for the moment. Once trained to defend his own interests, with a few weeks for the hero worship to fade, he would find someone else. Someone who wasn't his rescuer but his lover.

The bare mat in the center of the floor battered at him with its emptiness. Much as he loved to watch, would he be able to watch this boy in another's hands? Without his voice guiding the younger man's behavior?

"A vacation." Once the time was up. "Perhaps it would be best to step away for a few weeks."

Leave the boy alone?

Pain twisted in his chest. No. No. He'd play his role to the end. Introduce Jay around to good-hearted players who would treat him well. For their final week together.

No matter how far off, the date was sooner than desired.

Chapter 4

Stepping into the salon, Henry savored the sight of his obedient student.

Jay had done his work well. Their screen provided privacy in the same far corner, and the fidgeting submissive stood at the edge in a smart black suit.

A forceful kiss and a commanding manner would calm the nerves causing the younger man to shift his weight and rub at the sides of his slacks. His beautiful boy didn't like to be left alone.

The dark head came up. Jay scanned the room. He froze as their eyes met, but a brilliant smile warmed his face in the next instant.

Henry nodded a greeting as he moved forward.

The change in his submissive flowed down through his body. He bowed his head. His shoulders lowered to their proper, relaxed slope. He clasped his hands at his waist.

Perfect stillness.

Jay mimicked the pose he'd been shown last week, an at-ease waiting stance. Delightful. A student who internalized his master's wishes and carried them out to the best of his ability with the tools he'd been given.

Henry's casual stride quickened to a sharp, focused step as he approached. He imagined the beautiful yearning certain to be in his partner's eyes, soulful brown seeking his approval and flooding with contentment and desire when they received it. Jay offered submission without reservation and demonstrated utter joy when commanded with kindness.

Grasping Jay's chin and raising his sweet face, Henry swooped in.

Jay melted into his kiss. Smelling of an evergreen forest and tasting of mint, he whined and sucked at his master's tongue.

Henry allowed no pause, no give-and-take. He slipped his hand around the back of Jay's neck and held him steady even as the force of the kiss threatened to push the younger man back. He released Jay's mouth with a low growl and listened to the harsh breaths that followed.

Called to action, his cock fought to escape confinement, *thump thump thump* against his fly as blood flowed and filled and rose. He let out a single breath and brushed Jay's cheek with his lips.

"I hope you're hungry, my boy. I know I am, with you standing here looking delicious enough to eat."

Jay shuddered and lifted his gaze, soulful and yearning as Henry had longed to see it all week. A shy smile added to his beauty. "I could eat, Master Henry."

He gave his neck a gentle squeeze. "I'm certain you could. Dinner first, and then we'll see what the night holds."

Oral sex wasn't yet on his agenda, but allowing Jay's imagination to run wild with a scenario he'd already admitted to enjoying would do no harm. A bit of wonderment enhanced arousal.

They moved behind the screen to the table set with elegant perfection.

Henry laid their dinner to the side and ran his hand over the back of Jay's suit coat. An exquisite fit. Tailored, if he wasn't mistaken. Perhaps his eager submissive had taken the initiative after playing pincushion for Emma.

He sat and sipped water with lemon between delivering instructions while Jay plated their meals. He'd chosen seafood tonight, a linguine topped with oysters, scallops, and shrimp in a thin white wine sauce. Steamed broccoli added a hint of color.

He ate a few bites before raising the subject.

"You've chosen an excellent outfit for this evening, my boy. The shape flatters your sleek, sensual body with its delightful angles." He smiled at Jay's blush. An innocent pleasure, yet praise seemed so unfamiliar to his student. "Tell me, is it new?"

Shaking his head, Jay laid his fork down. "It's not new, but Mistress Emma helped me fix it when she took me shopping Tuesday."

He concealed his surprise with a long sip of water. Emma had taken the boy shopping. Did Victor know what his devious girl had gotten up to?

"And she helped me pick a tie." The tie popped, a splash of brilliant, deep green with linen pinstripes against Jay's black-on-black shirt and suit coat. "Do you like it, Master Henry?"

"I do, very much so." The tie and the red ribbon stood out, and both cried belonging. "Tell me about your shopping trip. Did you seek out Emma's assistance?"

"She offered while I was looking at your health status at the desk last week, Master Henry. I asked if she'd check my table settings in case I got anything wrong tonight, and we started talking about dinner, and"—Jay shrugged with a sheepish bob of his head—"I wanted to look good for you. Mistress Emma said she'd take me to her tailor if I wanted. Was that"—lines crept across his forehead—"was that okay?"

Jay had done nothing wrong. Emma had overstepped, certainly, but he mustered no more than exasperation for her well-intentioned meddling. Her maternal impulses would have drawn her to the boy after seeing him so wounded, and their own friendship allowed for such emboldened entitlement.

"Of course, my boy." Jay's desire to please his dominant had guided him. Emma's assistance had increased his self-confidence. A positive outcome, despite her trespass. "You wanted to please me, and you have succeeded."

Succeeded too well, in fact. His submissive deserved to be seen, to be flaunted. He envisioned escorting him to a gallery show, the concert hall, a proper dinner in public. Choosing Jay's clothes himself from the skin out.

The only niggling concern was Jay's insistence in granting Emma a title after he'd already explained. The result of misunderstanding, or an instinctive pull toward a female dominant over a male one?

Though it pricked, he made a mental note to consider appropriate fem-doms. A woman who'd treat Jay well. The desire might be temporary, a reaction to his poor treatment at Cal's hands. If so, perhaps a few months spent with a mistress would fulfill those needs.

"The tie, especially." Given that distance, Jay might develop greater perspective on their own relationship. Might come to see him as a potential master in truth rather than the centerpiece of his hero worship fantasies. "Are you making a statement, my boy?"

Jay toyed with his fork and tipped his head sideways. "Not if you don't want me to, Master Henry."

"But you had one in mind by choosing it, didn't you?" Desire warmed his blood. Let the boy go in a few weeks. Be patient and watchful. See if Jay came back to him. Yes. Those things he might reasonably do without abrogating his responsibilities or forcing a relationship upon a confused novice.

"I wanted to match your eyes," Jay whispered. "Mistress Emma said, she said expressing a wish wasn't the same as making a statement. I'll take it off if you want, Master Henry."

"You'll leave it on." He picked up his fork, twirled the linguine, and speared a scallop. "When we go upstairs after dinner and strip off your lovely tailored suit and bare your beautiful body and play our game, you'll wear your tie, my boy. My eyes are always on you."

He met his submissive's gaze with a piercing stare before he returned to his meal, appreciating the surge of confidence across the table. Jay sat taller. He smiled with increasing frequency.

Proffering the boy's clean test results seemed a secondary pleasure, overshadowed by Jay's obvious thrill at having accomplished an appropriate act of submission on his own initiative. Dangerous, to be so enamored with Jay's willing attitude and eager rush to please.

"Get the door, please."

Jay hustled ahead, carrying his own kit and his master's. Rather than having him change downstairs, he'd had him collect their bags and follow him to the third floor, where he'd reserved the same private room. He'd done no preparation on the room this week, the better to have tasks for his submissive. And, of course, the better to enjoy the sight of the lithe young man scurrying about at his direction.

Closing the door behind them, he wasted no time. "Set the bags by the wall and strip to your undershorts and tie."

Jay jumped to obey, unbuttoning his jacket and dropping his pants in an oddly coordinated dance. Shoes, slacks, coat and shirt piled in a heap on the floor.

"Fold them neatly, please. I'll want my property to look as sharp when I allow him to leave as he did when I first saw him this evening."

He removed his own jacket, folding it with a touch more ostentation than necessary, and concealed his gentle amusement at his student's attentiveness. Jay copied his movements, dividing his gaze between his task and his master.

When Jay had a neat stack of clothes, Henry crooked his finger at him. "Come here and show me your tie."

He loosened his own tie and unfastened the top two buttons on his shirt.

Jay's gaze dropped to the revealed skin.

Grazing his submissive's chest with his fingertips, he lifted the end of the tie. Fine weave. Vivid color.

A light tug on the tie prompted a gasp. Tugging again, as if by accident, resulted in a noticeable swallow and a gaze that skittered away as the boy trembled.

Suspicion confirmed, he spoke in an intimate whisper. "Jay."

"Yes, Master Henry?" Nerves thinned his voice.

"Remind me of your safeword."

"Tilt-A-Whirl, Master Henry."

"Mm-hmm." He slipped his fingers up the tie to the knot and scraped the fabric against the younger man. "When did we agree you were to use it?"

"If I'm too uncomfortable." He took a quick breath. "Or gonna throw up."

Stroking the base of the boy's throat, Henry hummed agreement. Jay had well-defined bone structure, soft skin, and a heart beating like a mouse in an owl's talons.

"Or if you feel uncertain, confused, scared, or unsafe." He teased at the knot. "If I told you I intend to bind your wrists with this tie tonight, what would you say to me?"

Heavy, shuddering breaths answered him.

"Speak up," he murmured. "Submission may not be equality, my sweet boy, but it is not silence, either. If I slipped this tie from your neck and began binding your hands, right now, what would you say to me?"

"I—I'd—I'd say Tilt-A-Whirl, Master Henry." Shame laced his submissive's timid delivery.

"Good boy." He wound his arms around Jay and cradled him.

Jay's reflexive clutch dug fingers into his back through his shirt.

"That's precisely what you ought to say to any game you don't wish to play." He tucked Jay's face against his neck and kissed the tip of his ear. "It's hard to admit, isn't it, my brave boy? When you want so badly to be ready for anything?"

Jay nodded, muffled agreement warming his neck.

"A boy with the courage to acknowledge his fears and limitations makes his master proud." He rubbed his partner's back. "Do you know why?"

Shaking his head, the younger man attempted an answer anyway. "'Cause you like to know things, Master Henry?"

He chuckled his appreciation for the earnest effort and squeezed his sub closer. "I do at that, my clever boy. But beyond that, an honest boy may overcome those fears. By telling his master the truth, he enables the master to fulfill his role caring for and guiding his boy."

He allowed Jay another minute to cling to him before disengaging. "Go on and unroll the mat along the wall, please. We've games yet to play this evening."

As Jay trotted across the room, Henry squatted beside the bags and unzipped his own.

Jay tugged the mat into place with ease. "I brought your sheets back like you asked, Master Henry. They're in my bag. Do you want me to spread them out?"

"We'll use these this week." He pulled the new set from his bag and tossed them on the mat. Taken off his bed just this afternoon. "You may lay them out, yes."

Lifting the first sheet, Jay pressed his face to the bundle. "Are they—can I. . . ."

"From my bed, and you'll take them home with you tonight."

Jay's eyes widened over the top of the sheet.

Henry forced himself to hold back his smile, lest he appear patronizing. Delighting his submissive took so little effort. The basic needs for comfort and belonging, for rules and routine, dominated Jay's emotional and psychological map. Yet every step was one in a delicate dance with a new partner.

"We'll try a different sort of bondage tonight." He reached into the bag again as Jay straightened the sheets. "If you become uncomfortable, I want you to find the courage to tell me so."

He'd chosen a quick-release option as both a concession to Jay's inexperience and a practical matter. Beyond providing an instant safety outlet if the younger man panicked, the looser, adjustable fit meant their game wouldn't be rushed.

"Off with your shorts, and stand at ease in the middle of the play space." If Mr. Kress enjoyed the snug support and sense of security, he might wear his new toy all night rather than being forced to remove it after twenty minutes or so. "Hands behind your back, please."

Standing moderately still, Jay squeezed his hands together. The repetitive motion calmed him, perhaps. The word "bondage" had no doubt raised an alarm. Tensed his muscles, if nothing else, and given him a sculpted beauty in his rounded buttocks. A sore temptation.

"I won't tie your hands, because I know what a good boy you can be. But you aren't to touch yourself tonight, do you understand?" His hands would be on his submissive soon enough. After three weeks of nothing but self-gratification, Jay ought to be eager for the touch of another. "Your body belongs to me, and I won't allow trespassing."

"I understand, Master Henry." Jay trembled.

He judged the response excitement rather than fear. Humiliation and degradation didn't factor in Jay's psychosexual makeup, and bondage and pain might be too frightening for now, but possessiveness tied the boy in happy knots all the same.

Circling his property, he assessed arousal. Jay's slight flush and increased respiration attested to his heightened interest, but his erect cock presented a problem. Not an insurmountable one, thanks to the toy he'd chosen, but semi-hard or flaccid would be easier to work with if he didn't want him shooting off before they'd even begun.

"If your fingers go near your cock tonight, I'll be forced to punish you. A disobedient boy doesn't deserve to sleep on his master's sheets. He'll have no homework to busy his hands, because his hands will have offended his master. How sad that would be for the boy, hmm?"

"Very sad, Master Henry." Jay's erection flagged. "I don't want to be that boy."

Perfect. He knelt and took his submissive in hand. Ignoring Jay's excited gasp, he worked fast to secure cock and balls in their proper place and adjust the strap before his student hardened again. Careful work, to ensure he didn't tangle hair or pinch flesh in a painful way rather than a pleasurable one.

Rising to his feet, he studied the overall effect.

Magnificent.

Contradictory desires warred in him to throw open the door and show off his delicious pet for public admiration or hide him away as an object for his lust and his alone. His cock ached with his desire to mark his territory, bathe the younger man in ejaculate and press his claim.

Each urge he locked with care behind a polite veneer of neutral interest. "Have you worn a cock ring before, my boy?"

Black fabric stretched around the base of Jay's cock in a narrow sleeve and split his balls like dangling weights to either side. The snap-closure strap rested against his body. The effect was more akin to compression undergarments than a lovely steel or glass ring set, but testing Jay's enjoyment required slow, patient work.

At the continued silence, he looked up and choked back a laugh. Adorable dishevelment and wonder greeted him, the loose tie swinging from Jay's neck as he tipped his head and gazed at his cock. Each time he moved for a better view, the tie swung forward with him. The novelty held young Mr. Kress spellbound, if perhaps frustrated by the obstruction. Not the reaction of a seasoned wearer.

"I'll take that as a 'no,'" he murmured.

Jay jerked his head. "I'm sorry, Master Henry. I've never worn anything like this. What did you ask me?"

Shaking his head, he smiled his reassurance. "How does it feel? Not too tight, I trust."

"Tight, but nice. It's all *there*, you know?"

"Yes, I can see it's all there." He nodded toward the now-full erection projecting from his submissive's groin. The cock ring held the angle lower, thrust out and away from the slim abdomen like an offering to his master.

Jay laughed, bright and playful.

Henry's heart sang. A bit of bondage the boy hadn't explored yet. From this gentle introduction, Jay might find a lifelong joy.

"I mean it's like, umm, pressure, but. . . ."

He waited. Better to let Jay finish his thought himself and obtain a clearer picture of what he enjoyed about the experience.

"Like squeezing with my fist except not my fist, but I feel it." A happy bewilderment overtook Jay's face. "It makes me think about my homework."

Humming encouragement, he traced the ridge along the underside of Jay's cock. Flesh danced at his touch. Pre-come beaded at the tip.

"Your fist but not your fist. An excellent description, as this sleeve is not an extension of your hand but mine." He splayed his fingers and rubbed his palm lower, cupping Jay's balls. "My property held secure in my grip, safe and protected but accessible to me whenever I wish to play."

An apt description of the young man under his protection even now. He wouldn't allow this boy to be used and hurt again.

"If you're a very good boy tonight"—he stepped in close—"I'll show you how to don and remove the ring yourself and allow you to take it home."

Jay strained toward him.

"You'd like that, wouldn't you?" He massaged Jay's shaft with a slight squeeze. "To feel my hand on you at night as you lie in my sheets and find your pleasure?"

A whimpering moan preceded his affirmation. "Yes, Master Henry."

"On your knees." He stepped back to give his partner room. "Waiting pose."

Jay knelt in a fluid, graceful motion, but once on his knees he waited in awkward silence. Rather than sitting back on his heels, he'd stopped like a penitent soul at a prayer bench. He'd taken to his at-ease posture with no trouble, and he'd dropped like a stone into a waiting pose on their first night in the salon, yet he hesitated now.

"Do you know waiting pose?"

He must, after playing for so many months, with so many dominants. Impossible for him not to have encountered a dominant who expected it of his or her subs.

"No, Master Henry." His student glanced up with wide eyes. "I'm sorry. Am I on my knees wrong? I can do better."

"You cannot do what you have not learned. How convenient for both of us that teaching you is my privilege." Laying a hand on Jay's shoulder, he gave a gentle push. "On your heels, and spread your knees wider, please. Back straight. Present your submission with pride befitting the gift it is."

Jay startled under his hand as he assumed the proper pose. "Oh, yes, I know this pose, Master Henry. I'm sorry I lied. I didn't know it had a name."

"That's not a lie, my boy." He scratched the nape of Jay's neck with steady fingers. "How did you know it before?"

The silence in the room chilled his skin.

Jay ducked his head. "'Get on your knees, slut, and wait for me to want you.'" He dragged the words from his throat with all the enthusiasm of a child sent to bed without dessert. "And the paddle or a flogging, sometimes, when I wasn't fast enough."

Crushing his teeth together, he breathed slow and even through his nose. He'd get Victor to make inquiries. Find out who had played with the boy and make certain none of them touched him again.

Misunderstanding or deliberate sadism, it made no difference. Jay hadn't known to articulate his needs, and the dominants he'd agreed to serve had barreled ahead with their own ideas of entertainment without checking on his emotional readiness.

"What a terribly lengthy and non-descriptive name for a position you imbue with such grace and beauty." He forced lightness into his tone. "That won't suit us at all. When you are in your waiting pose, you're to attend to my voice, to answer my questions and to await the rewards your good behavior will bring."

He crouched behind the younger man. Sleek, rounded shoulders fit his palms to perfection. He breathed across Jay's ear and smiled at the squirming hips in response.

"You needn't wait for me to want you," he murmured. "You may be assured I do so no matter what position I place you in. You are my good boy, and you please me with every sweet smile, every pleading whimper, and every wriggle of desire."

Jay shuddered, his sweet curving bottom bouncing against the up-turned soles of his feet.

Henry nuzzled his partner's neck, nudging at the tie with his nose. Whatever else she had done, Emma had given Jay the courage to wear an outer sign of his inner fantasies. "You wanted to please your dominants, isn't that so?"

"Yes, Master Henry." Jay nodded in a full-body ripple.

"But did you want them to yell at you, sweet boy?" The more often Jay articulated or otherwise expressed his desires and rejected the games he didn't wish to play, the more confidence he would have in negotiation and the safer he would be. "To offer you pain for your lovely service to them?"

"No." Jay stated his dislike in a firm, clear voice without hesitation.

Henry ran his hands down the younger man's arms to his thighs. Relief and pride buoyed his arousal. Stroking Jay's thighs, he peppered his neck with kisses. "No?"

"I want to give pleasure, Master Henry." Jay leaned back, seeking. He pressed forward to lend support and hummed encouragement.

"But I don't want the anger and the yelling." Jay gained strength and volume. Conviction. "I don't want someone telling me I'm a disgusting slut who should be grateful for what they're giving me. I *am* grateful."

"I know you are," he soothed. "You're a polite boy. An eager student." One who responded well to the carrot approach. "The gratefulness should be theirs that such a submissive would offer his service for their pleasure." Only an obtuse, dimwitted dominant would resort to the stick with this one. "It is the heart of the paradox that fuels our games."

Jay tipped his head, rustling their hair together. "Paradox, Master Henry?"

"Indeed. The control is mine." He slipped his hands between his partner's legs and teased the soft skin of his inner thighs, fluttering closer to Jay's weeping cock. "I determine the direction and form of our games."

Closing his hand around the shaft released an explosive exhalation from his submissive, as if every last bit of breath left his body in a single burst.

"You put yourself in my hands," he whispered, "in an immense show of trust and courage."

He squeezed Jay's cock with a slow pull. The heat seared his palm.

Legs trembling, Jay whimpered.

"But you can stop our game at any time." Lips alongside Jay's ear, he spoke low and slow. "You hold the power in a single word, my boy. Paradox."

The emotional response he hoped for wasn't immediate. Silence reigned for a long moment. He raised his arm in an embrace.

A hitching sob erupted. "Not always." Jay mumbled, his voice thick. "Sometimes words don't work."

An exquisite swirl of joy and pain consumed his chest. He'd given Jay an opening to speak, to begin addressing the horrendous wrong done to him, and the young man possessed the courage to take it.

"No, sometimes they don't, my sweet, brave boy." He swayed, cradling his companion close. "Not because of anything the boy has done wrong. Any man or woman who ignores the power in that word is not a proper dominant but an abuser. The failure is theirs."

He traced his fingers along Jay's cock, the compression of the fabric keeping the younger man hard.

"I will always respect your safeword. Without anger and without blame, but with pride at your courage and understanding for your vulnerability in our games."

Tears splashed his hand.

"M'sorry, Master Henry. Thank you, Master Henry."

He stroked the taut skin of Jay's balls to either side of the fabric dividing it.

Jay's stomach jerked as he gasped. He exhaled with a soft moan.

"You've no need to apologize, unless you wish to use your safe-word and have not done so." His teasing fingerplay held his submissive's attention. "Honesty demands no apologies."

Associating pleasant physical sensation with difficult emotional release ought to encourage Jay's openness and honesty. For his effort, the submissive would receive the physical release he'd earned.

"You have endured entirely too many unpleasant experiences in your explorations. Let's imagine a better one together. We'll construct a fantasy scene, and, if all goes well"—he squeezed—"you'll christen these sheets before you take them home."

Jay's eager whine went straight to his cock.

"Close your eyes, please." He'd intended to remove his shirt and slacks, but his partner's need for his embrace trumped any urge to step away or delay the game. "Imagine you're here at the club on a Friday evening but you aren't seeking out a dominant."

He rubbed the boy's chest with his free hand, tracing the hints of sculpted muscle tone.

Jay dipped his head, but his eyes remained closed in perfect obedience.

"Tonight you want only to watch others' scenes, and perhaps join in if invited. What color door cards are you looking for?"

"Green, Master Henry. So I can go in and wait for the chance to join."

"That's exactly right, my good boy."

He slipped along the underside of Jay's cock, massaging with an open palm. The cock ring's embrace added to the submissive's size and deepened his color. A captivating contrast, the pulsing aubergine across his own pale sand.

"You've wandered most of the night, searching. Waiting is difficult, but you want to be certain you find the right scene." He scraped his teeth over Jay's ear and delighted in the shuddering response.

"You won't be satisfied with a scene that fulfills only someone else's desires. You won't settle for a game that makes you uncomfortable. Only the best will do for my boy. Isn't that so?"

"Only, only the best," Jay repeated. His breaths came fast and shallow. "I won't settle."

"Wonderful," he murmured. As a reward, he closed his fingers around Jay's cock and began a slow, teasing stroke. "One door catches your eye, and you squeeze the handle—" He mimicked the action.

Gasping, Jay pushed into his hand.

"—and step inside."

With his other hand, he circled Jay's nipples. Tiny pebbles upthrust from a sea of flat stone, a chest of solid muscle wrapped in soft, inviting skin.

"Two players, a dominant and a submissive. The dominant—a woman? A man, perhaps?" He kept up his stroking, unwilling to clue Jay to his own preference. Let his partner give voice to his own fantasies.

"You." Jay's chest heaved. "I'm watching you, please, Master Henry."

Growling, he tugged Jay's ear between his teeth. "Me, then. I nod to you as you enter our game. Does my submissive notice you?"

Jay shook his head. He swallowed. "She's only paying attention to you, Master Henry. You're her whole world."

She. Interesting. Because Jay enjoyed the beauty of the female form? Because he felt a female submissive wasn't a threat to his own place as his master's best boy?

"Perhaps she can't see you, my boy. Her eyes might be closed or hidden behind the concealing darkness of a blindfold. Might she feel safest there, unseeing, anticipating the thrill of my touch?"

He interrupted his stroke to accommodate a swift brush against the younger man's balls and the fabric pressing on the sensitive perineal raphe between.

Jay's excited leap backward propelled him into his master's groin.

Henry groaned at the all-too-welcome pressure and tightened his hand on Jay's chest.

"She does," Jay enthused. "I know she does. You make her feel so special, Master Henry."

Jay's confidence and trust staggered him. He thrust once against the submissive's backside, slacks rough against the head of his cock as he pushed through the flap in his boxer shorts.

"You'll stand to the side and take yourself in hand as I give her my fingers."

If Jay didn't yet understand he had choices beyond begging for a dominant to serve and accepting whatever offers resulted, he would by the end of their time together. He'd be damned if he'd see this sweet boy go running back to Calvin Gardner in a month's time because he thought it the only way to experience the club—or punish himself for needs and desires that frightened him.

"There is no shame in enjoying her pleasure and your own, hmm?"

"She wants more than your fingers, Master Henry." Jay squirmed, the better to feel him, perhaps.

He thrust again, fingers moving faster over Jay's engorged cock. "Then I will provide what she needs, won't I? While she begs for it with such delightful urgency, shameless in her desire to be fulfilled as she submits to my touch."

Nodding, Jay rocked against his lap. His upturned feet rested beneath Henry's thighs and buttocks, so tight the fit and so narrow the gap between them.

"No shame," Henry repeated. "Only her joy and her arousal and her trust that I will care for her needs. Shall I turn her to face you so you might watch her beauty as I take her?"

"No, please." Jay shook his head, but his hips kept their speed.

He added pressure to his grip as he prodded at his reticent boy's answer. "Cover her on all fours, draping my weight across her back? Is that how I take her?"

"Face-to-face." Jay gasped the words with a low whine, his climax near. "I want, I want you to take her the way I dream you take me."

He fought not to come in his slacks as the image flashed. Jay, naked, writhing on his back, his cock eager and straining as he was penetrated in his master's bed. On the very sheets they knelt upon now. Yes, God, yes.

"On her back, then, with her legs clinging to my hips and my mouth at her breasts until she cries out her satisfaction." He clutched Jay's chest and deepened his voice, every word swathed in possession and command. "But I haven't finished. I crook my finger to my good, patient boy and slide my cock free, hard and wet with my girl's pleasure. Will you taste? Will you drop to your knees and suck me dry?"

Jay babbled as he came, his release soaking the sheets in long arcs as he cried yes and please and master.

Henry drew out his strokes until his submissive could give no more.

Satisfaction flooded him at his success in having Jay take part in describing his own fantasies. A step on the path to self-understanding, self-acceptance, and negotiation.

But his cock throbbed with relentless pressure. His body wouldn't stand for this pace. Either he must find other methods to guide his student's lessons, or he'd have to allow for his own satisfaction at their next encounter. He'd been too close to spilling tonight.

"That was amazing, Master Henry!" Tossing his head like a fractious colt, Jay blew out a breath. "I never stay hard that long or shoot like that. I dunno if it's your hands or your voice, but it feels so good."

The warmth of the younger man's giddy excitement washed over him and overflowed in a mellow laugh. These moments of post-orgasmic bliss seemed the best glimpse of Jay's true nature he'd seen, all uninhibited joy and motion.

He cuddled his partner even as he eased his own hips back. "Impressive work indeed, my boy. I suspect your new toy played a role as well. I'll allow you to take it home, but you must promise me you won't experiment beyond the rules I set."

The supportive constriction, worn loose enough, could snuggle Jay's cock all day, but he wouldn't set a precedent lest the boy think to purchase his own ring in a different style and end up requiring a trip to the emergency room.

"I won't, Master Henry, I promise." Tipping his head back, Jay opened his eyes. Shy delight poured from his face. "I like following your rules, Master Henry. I think about them when you aren't with me, and I remember I'm your good boy."

Resistance impossible, he lowered his mouth and caressed Jay's tongue. Their kiss soothed the urgent need in him, a slow and gentle reminder that this young man worshipped him. To take advantage of that trust to sate his own needs would be a sacrilege of their relationship to one another. "My very good boy."

He spent the rest of the night demonstrating the toy and detailing rules for its use in homework until Jay's ability to put it on and take it off satisfied him. Young Mr. Kress went on his way with his new toy and his master's sheets and the promise of another meeting in a week's time.

Only then did Henry lift the sheets the boy had left behind, the ones they had each used for a week. Raising them to his nose brought Jay's scent to him, the woody musk of his arousal.

Relief refused to wait.

Taking himself in hand, he stroked his cock to a speedy climax in the sheets and growled his ownership to an empty room.

Chapter 5

"I'm concerned about his readiness, Victor." Henry ran a finger along the edge of the bookcase. Spotless. Em would be horrified if guests found her master's office in less than pristine condition.

"Cal will return in a month, and the boy may not be emotionally prepared for that." Some rule, some bylaw must exist to make a delay possible. They'd barely touched upon the issues and misunderstandings that had put Jay in Cal's hands to begin with. "Is there no way to extend his suspension of privileges?"

Victor sighed. "The board has already ruled on the incident—"

"The assault." He stared down his mentor.

The older man shrugged. "The boy refused to label it such."

"He was too intimidated to help himself." Jay would be still. The worry kept him up at night. A moment out of his sight and anything might happen. God forbid he found him in worse condition next time.

"Yes, and you're helping him overcome that. But there's nothing to be done about Calvin." Victor rubbed at his gray-flecked beard. "I cannot bar the doors against him, Henry. He's a dues-paying member. He is guaranteed the same rights you are."

"He doesn't deserve them."

"No." Victor coughed and swatted his desk. "He deserves to have his hands slammed in a car door. A mishap that would sadly leave him unable to wield a whip properly for months until the breaks healed."

Violence surged in his blood, a fleeting desire to see Calvin Gardner broken and begging to apologize to his sweet boy. Swallowing hard, he forced it back. "You know I wouldn't advocate nonconsensual violence against anyone, Victor. Whatever the provocation."

"No, I know, Henry. My wife is more bloodthirsty." Pride warmed Victor's voice. "Motherhood seems to have brought it out in her."

"She's been mothering my boy like he's one of your former pets. Are you aware she—"

Four raps sounded at the door.

"Enter."

Emma stepped inside, her heels clicking as she approached Victor's desk and knelt.

Victor laid his hand on her bowed head. "Speak, beloved."

"Master Henry's boy is here, husband. The standing order is to inform him of the boy's arrival."

"But not, it seems, when one takes his boy shopping."

Mild as Victor's words were, Emma flinched.

Victor winked as he waved toward the door. "Go on, Henry. Enjoy your evening. Emma and I are overdue for a discussion regarding what it means to suggest one has permission from another master to chaperone his submissive for a day out."

"Ah." He nodded to Victor. "An enlightening discussion, I'm certain."

Emma, he expected, was in for a long night. She'd no doubt enjoy every moment.

Jay fidgeted beside the desk, stepping away from each new arrival and keeping his head down. Waiting for Em to return, perhaps. Had she told Mr. Kress he was here or left him to wonder?

"Jay, my good boy."

Jay jerked to attention, the duffel slung over his shoulder banging against his back. "You're here." He breathed the words like a prayer. "Am I late, Master Henry? I'm sorry—"

He shook his head, cutting off the apology. "No, my dear boy, you are quite prompt."

He rounded the desk for a better look at him. Not straight from work, judging by the comfortable jeans and t-shirt. Either Jay felt more relaxed and able to be himself today, or he'd lost interest in looking special for his master. Given the fidgeting, the former wasn't likely. Given the worshipful stare, the latter wasn't, either.

He'd seen this behavior often in female subs. The desire to go unnoticed, to avoid calling attention to oneself as an attractive sexual creature, inevitably accompanied a lack of self-worth. Something had upset and devalued his boy, unless this was extended fallout from his assault.

Pushing the thoughts aside, he projected a smile for his student. "Do you have your ribbon?"

Jay raised his hand, the emblem of his service clutched in his fist. "Yes, Master Henry."

"Wonderful." He tested his submissive's responses with a light brush along his arm.

Jay leaned into his caress.

Whatever afflicted the younger man, he found comfort in his master's touch. Well. Henry had all night to tease the answer out of him and resolve it, should the issue prove problematic.

"Upstairs we go, then, hmm?"

"Yes please, Master Henry."

They'd almost reached the staircase when a man called his name. Hurrying over from the entrance, trailed by a submissive, the man hailed him with a wave.

"Master Robert." He inclined his head, a nod of mutual respect. The dominant was young, no older than Henry's boy, but he'd shown a level of proper attention to his girl's needs.

"Master Henry, I'm so glad we ran into you. I wanted to thank you again for your help." Robert squeezed the lush brunette to his side. "My little trinket is enjoying her whippings so much better since you demonstrated the looser grip and the smooth roll."

Jay's flinch demanded immediate intervention. Henry laid a hand on his back and rubbed slow circles.

Robert remained oblivious to the subtext. "We'll be up on three tonight, and I know my trinket would be honored if you'd attend to see how well she does."

The girl nodded, her head bowed but her excitement obvious in the strength of her nod and the tight nipples beneath her shirt.

"I appreciate the thought, Robert, but I must decline this evening." Ruffling Jay's hair, he pulled him closer and pressed a kiss to his forehead. "My attention belongs to my good boy. I'm certain you understand how important our promises are to those who depend upon us."

"Of course." Robert took the response in stride, though his girl's shoulders sagged.

"Another time, perhaps."

Nodding, Robert squeezed his girl. "Come along, little trinket, and we'll get you your pretty ribbon."

"Up the stairs, my boy. We've games of our own to play." He prodded Jay to precede him so he might watch his posture. Subdued, now.

He watched and waited, biding his time until they'd entered a private changing room. Jay hadn't spoken a word, but that itself wasn't unexpected. The true clue lay in the lack of nervous excitement and the slump in his grace.

As Jay unzipped his duffel, Henry seated himself on the spare bench. "Remind me of your safeword, please."

"Tilt-A-Whirl, Master Henry."

"You understand you may use it at any time?"

"Yes, Master Henry."

Jay laid his play shorts on the bench beside his open duffel. A corner of fabric peeked out of the bag. Pale gray. The soft cotton sheets he'd lain in before sharing them with his submissive.

"Then tell me what weighs on your mind." A flashback to Jay's own whipping, he expected. A straightforward approach might work, if Jay truly trusted him. "What caused your flinch downstairs?"

Still in his street clothes, Jay sank to his knees without being told. "You whipped that girl, Master Henry?"

The pain and confusion in the tenor voice settled under his ribs with a sting not unlike the whip he'd wielded. The first crack cut through the boy's hero worship. Now Mr. Kress would see his dominance, too, in the shadow cast by the whip. The inevitable, necessary end loomed before him. Fallen.

"I did." He willed himself to patience and calm, giving Jay the time he needed to articulate his thoughts.

"You're good enough at it that people want your advice." Not quite a question, but confusion yet clung to the boy. He worried at his jeans with trembling fingers.

"Some of them do, yes."

"You haven't whipped me," Jay whispered. A shudder ran through him.

"No, I haven't." He maintained a neutral tone even as his hopes rose.

Nerves showed in Jay's demeanor, but new territory always carried a current of trepidation. Would he take the next step and vocalize his refusal to play a game? He'd done so with prompting in abstract, hypothetical cases on their previous nights.

To see Jay ready to take such a momentous step on his own would prove his remarks to Victor incorrect. Young Mr. Kress had internalized his lessons in negotiation more than he'd thought. He would let Jay make the initial request to outlaw whipping. Agreement and praise would follow, swift and sure.

"But if you like it, I should do it."

Hope drained in a sick swirl. He closed his eyes, a brief moment to recover himself.

"Am I really your good boy, Master Henry? Am I not good enough? You can tell me, Master Henry." Jay poured forth words in an unstoppable torrent. "I can do it, I promise I can. I won't scream or cry unless you want me to."

So many wrong ideas it seemed impossible to choose one to counteract. His fears made manifest from the boy's own lips. The smallest hint from a dominant, even one not his own, twisted Jay into a submissive mindset focused only on his master's pleasure. Safety discarded.

The lack of self-awareness—or the lack of concern at what submitting to another whipping would do to his wounded psyche—would send Jay back into Cal's dungeon the moment the sadist returned and issued a command.

"Come here, my boy." He whispered the words not on purpose but because his throat ached with the howl he held back. "Come to me and listen."

Jay shuffled forward on his knees.

Yearning to embrace him, he allowed the submissive posture instead. Jay found more security on the floor, and on the floor he would stay.

Henry patted his knee. "Lay your head here and look up at me, please."

Earnest brown eyes gazed at him. Jay rubbed his cheek against the linen-silk blend of his slacks, a repetitive motion that seemed more comfort mechanism than conscious choice.

Resting his hand atop the boy's hair, he found his own comfort in slipping his fingers through the dark strands. He'd planned to expose Jay to more scenes tonight, to test his responses and prompt him through determining which games he might enjoy, which he might tolerate, and which he might declare a hard limit.

No longer. Jay needed more focused emotional support tonight. He had arrived dressed to hide, been relieved to see his master, and pushed a single comment by a stranger into breakdown territory. Something had unsettled him before he'd entered the club.

He would determine the truth before the night was out. For now, he would be his boy's calm, steady rock.

"That's it," he murmured. "Breathe with me, my biddable boy. Slow, deep breaths. How sweet you are, how eager to please."

He slipped his hand across Jay's ear and down to the curve of his jaw. A bit of scruff roughed his palm. He traced Jay's soft lips with his thumb.

The younger man stared as if hypnotized, his gaze fixed on his master's face.

"Before you became my boy, had you ever told a play partner of a desire you had for a scene?"

A slight nod preceded Jay's quiet, "Once, Master Henry."

"Did this partner fulfill that desire for you?" Being a dominant wasn't unlike being a lawyer at times. One asked leading questions whose answers were known lest the witness deliver an unwelcome surprise.

"No, Master Henry. He said"—Jay pressed his lips together—"he said I was 'topping from the bottom' and he'd show me more respect-ful behavior."

"By which he meant discipline?"

Jay nodded, but his face remained smooth and relaxed. Good. Closeness, gentle touching, and focused attention had a calming effect on him. Such small pieces would matter more as the questions grew more difficult.

"And the other times? Tell me your thoughts as you approached these players and agreed to serve them."

"Umm—" Jay drifted, his eyes growing distant. "I guess. . . ."

The silence lasted minutes. He waited, stroking Jay's cheek and hair, pressing his legs to his submissive's sides in a gentle, supportive squeeze. The younger man's easy sigh pleased him.

"They were the dominants, Master Henry. I thought, you know, their desires came first and mine came last. If I was good and did what they wanted, they'd do something I wanted next time, maybe. When I'd earned a reward."

"Did they ask about your fantasies?"

The small headshake wasn't unexpected.

"Do you understand why I ask you about them?"

"No, but I like it." Jay squirmed. Perhaps his jeans had gotten tighter. "I feel good when you ask me, Master Henry."

"I ask you because an honest and obedient submissive does indeed deserve to be rewarded, my sweet boy. But his dominant must know how to best reward him. A good boy who wants to be allowed to suck his master's cock won't enjoy a so-called reward of whipping, will he?"

Jay curled closer and wrapped his arm around his master's leg. "I like that first one, Master Henry."

Ruffling Jay's hair, he smiled. "I know you do, my good boy. Because you've told me so, as an obedient boy should."

His obedient boy's enthusiasm and need for him had given rise to an urgent demand at his groin. The rush of blood to his cock and Jay's sweet face at his knee called for sublime self-control. The carpeted floor of the changing room reminded him of the impropriety. Their room with its mat and new set of sheets waited upstairs.

Dominant urge diverted, he gripped the back of Jay's neck with the firm but protective hold of a bitch carrying her pup. If a fleeting image gripped him in return, an image of Jay's mouth open, willing, and eager as he swallowed on every thrust of his master's cock, the younger man need not know.

"You are never required to accept a whipping or anything else to earn the privilege of giving a blowjob. You needn't *earn* your desires at all, my brave boy." Softening his hold, he smoothed back the dark hair. If he could make Jay understand this much, the rest might follow. "You may state them at the outset and refuse to play with anyone whose desires don't match well with your own."

Strengthen the foundation, build his self-worth, teach him to accept himself and take pride in his submission . . . the work of a lifetime.

He blew out a breath, and Jay echoed him.

"A sadist will always be a sadist, dear boy. You will never earn kindness from one. The kindness is a mask to inflict more varied forms of pain. Nothing you could have done, no perfect service, could have made him love and value you the way you did him."

Whimpering softly, Jay blinked. "But you whip people, too."

"I do, but I am not a sadist." The complications of his own enjoyment, the aesthetic value, the beauty in the snap of the whip and the muscles in the back as the sub responded, the taut strain, the rebounding flesh, the boneless satisfaction afterward, would be too much for his submissive to comprehend.

"Their pain does not amuse me."

Jay would volunteer to show his master those things, the things he wasn't ready for even though he offered them with such guileless innocence. His beautiful Ganymede carried the cup of ambrosia to his lips, and he dare not drink a drop lest he drain the cup and damage the carrier.

"Their enjoyment in the act pleases me."

"I'm sorry, Master Henry. I don't understand."

No, of course he wouldn't. What enjoyment could he find in the act when it had been forced upon him too soon?

"Good boy." He traced a finger down Jay's cheekbone. Such a beautiful face, awash in angled elegance. A noble raven, perhaps. "It's right that you should ask when you don't understand. Thank you for remembering your lesson so well."

Jay's weight rested heavy against him. The physical reminder of the younger man's dependence on him pleased him in ways he refused to examine too closely. These sessions weren't about him. They were for Jay.

No. For *the boy*. Always for the boy. Safer, to keep that distance.

"Imagine for a moment you wait for me at the center of our sheets. As I approach, you see the coils of a whip in my hand. What would you say, my boy? You wish to please me? What would most please me?"

"If I submitted like a good boy, Master Henry." Jay smiled despite the flickering in his eyes and the tightness at the corners. "Positioned myself the way you wanted and listened to your instructions."

Tipping Jay's chin to better capture his gaze, Henry shook his head in a long, slow roll. "'Tilt-A-Whirl.' That is the word from your lips that would most please me, because it would prove to me that you understand you have the right to say no."

"But then you, I mean, no one would want to play with me. No one wants a whiny sub who stops the game all the damn time." Rote cadence flattened his voice.

Had Cal taught him that, or had the sadist's clique of friends passed Jay along from week to week, each dominant reinforcing the shame of the week before? Preparing this gentle boy to accept Cal's advances. Targeting fresh meat for the alpha of their own little pack.

"Some few won't play again with a submissive who safewords, that's true." He wouldn't lie to his student. The truth would better arm and defend him in any case. "That does not mean you've given up your right to safeword nor that you ought to."

Cupping the boy's cheek, he put every drop of confidence and command scraped from the bottom of his soul into the message Jay so needed to learn. "It means you do not play with them. *Ever.*"

Jay widened his eyes at his low growl. Mouth open, he sucked in a breath that shook his body, ribs quivering against his master's calf.

Arousal, if he wasn't mistaken. The gleam in Jay's eyes certainly didn't seem fearful.

"Your affectionate nature, your beautiful grace, your good cheer, and your respectful demeanor will bring you offers from any number of appropriate masters and mistresses once you've had a proper introduction." He'd make those introductions himself in a few short weeks. More a masochist than he'd realized, perhaps. The pleasure of seeing the boy blossom would always be wrapped by a vine choking him with the loss.

"You will never again agree to play without first asking how the prospective dominant feels about safewords, do you understand? You will walk away from any dominant who either refuses to tell you or indicates a safeword will bring less than a complete stop of all activities until he or she has ascertained the nature of your need and corrected the error. This rule extends beyond our time together. You will obey it always."

A demand he had no right to make. A flagrant abuse of his authority.

Jay soaked it up like a cat basking in sunshine. "Always, Master Henry. I will." He squirmed closer, a warm and cuddly body wriggling between his master's legs. Delightful torment. "I'll always obey you."

Residual fear invaded his pores. His student might also always obey Calvin Gardner. Whatever shame conditioning existed in Jay's mind might take years to unravel. Professional help he himself was unqualified to provide.

Four months, Jay had said. Would that he'd seen Jay Kress on his first night. Wide-eyed wonder and mangled manners, no doubt. Had he had the opportunity to take this boy into his care then—

What a magnificent, happy lover he'd have now. All his.

He kissed Jay's smooth brow and his slender nose and his sweet, full mouth.

"Return your things to your bag, please. You needn't dress for play tonight." He raised a warning finger at his submissive's startled reflex. "I am not displeased with you. I am, in fact, so well-pleased with you that I wish to take you directly to our room upstairs tonight rather than observing others at play. The faster you finish your task, the faster I may have you naked on the fresh set of sheets from my bed awaiting us."

Seven seconds. He counted.

He ached to push his submissive against the wall and take him.

Never mind that he had no plans to take Jay at all, let alone tonight. The wall would have to wait in any case. He wouldn't have Jay feeling trapped or pinned with no escape.

He folded his jacket, smoothing out the wrinkles and laying it on the floor alongside his kit. He'd spread the mat and sheets in advance, expecting to be coming in the door with his companion well roused after viewing others' scenes.

Slipping off his shoes, he nodded to Jay. "You may remove your shoes and socks, my boy."

Jay kicked off his sneakers without untying them and yanked at his socks, dropping them beside his bag. He reached for the hem of his shirt. "Clothes, too?"

"No." He slipped his tie free and laid it atop the jacket, careful not to smile at his sub's crestfallen expression. So eager. "Line up your shoes neatly, please, with the socks tucked inside, and then go and stand at ease in the center of our sheets."

He removed his own socks with slow precision as Jay obeyed. A lesson in patience was never wasted, but in truth, he sought more time to calm his libido and consider his revision of the night's goal. Jay appreciated attention and praise. He lacked the ability to assert himself.

So.

"We'll play a new game tonight." He stalked in a broad arc around his submissive. "If you do well at your task, we will both enjoy the satisfaction of release."

Jay jerked his head up and met his gaze. A flush of excitement colored his neck as his breathing deepened. Impossible to say whether the pleasure came from the promise of his own orgasm or his master's.

"Will you try hard at your lesson?"

"I will, Master Henry." Jay bobbed his head. "I promise I'll be perfect for you."

"Yes," he murmured. "Yes, you are."

A belief he ought to have kept to himself. Jay's need for reassurance pulled at him with irresistible force. To deny himself what he wanted was acceptable. To deny Jay—no. To deny *his student* what he needed was not.

Trembling, Jay emitted a quiet whine. Getting his pants off before he came in them would be crucial, lest embarrassment or distress ruin the game. Pants first, then.

"You're going to tell me what you enjoy about sex, my boy." As he stalked closer, he held Jay's gaze until no more than a brushstroke separated their bodies. He leaned in and grazed the younger man's ear. "For every truth you tell me, I will reward you."

"A-anything, Master Henry?"

Humming agreement, he blew a heated breath down his submissive's neck and gloried in the wavering moan he received in reply. "You may share anything with me. The things you have not shared with your play partners. The dreams you harbor. The fantasies you cradle close."

Something to start him off, perhaps. Specific cues helped his pupil better than open-ended ones. "The way the scent and softness of a woman hardens your cock."

"I like when she's on top, when I get to watch how she"—Jay breathed out in a rush—"you know."

A hint of modesty. Embarrassment. Time would cure his sub of that affliction. Time and comfort and growing trust.

He laid hands on Jay's waist and traced the edge of his jeans. "How she slides down on your cock? How her slick and welcoming body takes you in and shelters you in her warmth?"

A gentle tug popped the top button of Jay's button-fly jeans through its snug hole.

"She smiles," Jay whispered. "She says it feels good. I wanna make her feel good."

"Of course you do, my sweet boy." He slipped a second button free. Jay's cock distended the fabric of his boxers beneath. Tension thrummed between them, his fingers close enough to touch. "You're a good boy to think of her pleasure."

"I please her with my tongue, too, Master Henry." Jay's struggle to stand still rippled in his taut forearms. "She's over my face, maybe, maybe after. . . ."

"After you've pleasured her with your cock?" He brushed the third button with a fingertip, adding a slight pressure to the younger man's trapped arousal.

Jay whimpered and jerked his hips before he controlled himself. The tiniest whisper spilled from his throat. "After you have, Master Henry."

Heart tripping, he groaned his delight. His hand stuttered, yanking the third and fourth buttons open at once. A fantasy he could not fulfill for his companion, not without a fluid-bonded female partner, and he had none.

"Lapping at her honeyed center with my taste flowing onto your tongue? Mmm." Giving the jeans a push past slender hips, he licked Jay's neck and sucked at his earlobe. "What a lovely thought."

"You don't"—Jay issued needy whines between his words—"you don't think I'm sick?"

That even such a tame fantasy shamed the boy provoked his ire. A submissive born to serve, the perfect pet for a couple. A master and mistress sharing a sub, or perhaps as the beta sub for a committed dominant and submissive pair. All of that beauty near ruined by Calvin Gardner and his pack of wolves.

"I find you beautiful and giving, my brave boy." He redoubled his focus, squeezing Jay's cock through his undershorts. The younger man would come quick with so much attention. Best to make the release a planned event rather than a spontaneous one that shamed him.

Claiming Jay's mouth with a growl, he nipped at the lips parting for him. He shoved his hands inside Jay's boxers, wrapped his cock in a firm grip, and cupped his balls in the other hand.

He swallowed Jay's moans before pausing his possession to

speak. "You've shared so well, my boy, that I will allow you to come now, in my hands, before we begin again. You're not to hold back. Give me what I demand of you."

He squeezed and stroked with increasing speed. Swarming Jay's face and neck with hard kisses, he had no need to remind his submissive to vocalize. Jay whimpered with each breath, the pitch of his shuddering yips shifting higher as climax neared.

Slim hips thrust Jay's cock farther into the pressure of his hand. The close, commanding hold gave him every intimate moment as Jay's balls tightened and his cockhead swelled.

A growling bite beneath Jay's jaw finished the job. Warmth spurted across his hands.

"My excellent boy, such a beautiful gift." He began his verbal campaign even as his student moaned his completion. No waiting for doubt to set in. "How diligent you are at your studies to come promptly at your master's command. How well you listen and obey."

Jay offered his own reward, a wide smile and relaxed musculature. Calm rather than apologetic panic. A true delight, and one he wished to see more often.

He tugged Jay's boxers down, discreet as he wiped his hands clean on the inside of the fabric. His submissive could go home without his boxers on, but it wouldn't do to make a mess of his jeans and t-shirt. Hmm. Yes, perhaps he'd take Jay's boxers home with him to launder alongside their sheets. The sparking thrill of the thought sent his cock thumping against his own boxers.

He stripped his submissive and tossed the jeans toward one corner of the mat and the boxers toward another. A parting of the ways. Separate journeys lay ahead for the clothing, and for him and his boy as well.

Hands clean, he lifted Jay's shirt in a slow tease. "I believe your behavior deserves another new reward this night."

Jay raised his arms and ducked his head as the shirt came off, compliant and silent in the aftermath of his climax. His eyes, though, radiated love. Worship. Trust.

A master could grow addicted to such things.

"I've a task for you." The shirt landed atop the jeans.

Jay wiggled, an excited shudder his body couldn't contain. "Thank you, Master Henry."

He clasped his partner's hands and lifted them to his collar.

"Undress me," he commanded. "Down to the skin. And then we'll see if we might reawaken your cock to play with mine."

The suggestion made Jay fumble at the button, but he recovered with speed. The gap between shirt halves widened in a steady rush to his waist, where Jay worked to open his belt and loosen his slacks before pulling the shirt free.

"Well done," he murmured. Mr. Kress took the care with his master's clothes that he lacked with his own. An able assistant, easy to train, and one who paid clear attention to his master's preferences.

His slacks dropped to the sheets as Jay peeled his shirt from his back. Only his boxers remained, tented and swaying as his cock nudged the silk.

Jay sank to his knees. His chest rippled. His exhalations grew into shuddering little sighs. He reached for his master's boxers with reverent hands.

The slow, silken tease brushed hyperawareness into his skin as the boxers dropped. Jay flicked his tongue between his lips. Not a hint of disobedience emerged despite his obvious desire to offer his favorite fantasy to his master.

Henry gave his submissive space to gather the clothes and waited to see how he would respond.

Jay's gaze didn't leave his cock.

Erect and aching, fluid beading at the tip and slipping down the glans, beginning to slick his shaft, his cock waited for handling in a trimmed nest of walnut brown hair. The pre-pubescent shaved look had never appealed, but short hair was a courtesy and a necessity for the comfort of one's partners and the ease of use for certain toys.

Jay folded the clothes, darting glances between groin and garments in a sweetly comical show of desire. Unintentional, no doubt, but comical all the same. His uninhibited exuberance resembled nothing so much as a black Lab on a leash desperate to hear the snap of the metal unhooking and the deep warmth of his master's command to fetch.

He took care not to chuckle and sully the boy's enjoyment of the moment.

"Should I—" Jay knelt in a perfect waiting pose, his knees wide and his head bowed. He balanced the clothes across his arms like a gift. "Should I lay the clothes with your jacket, Master Henry?"

"An insightful suggestion. Please do." He continued his praise as his student rose to his feet and carried out his task. "Such a quick mind you have. I'm quite lucky to have you in my service."

"You are?" Clothes deposited, Jay paused at the edge of the mat.

Beauty unparalleled, not only in the perfection of his youthful form but in the shining purity of his soul. Wise men would weep for such a vision. He'd be a fool to give it up.

"I am." He spread his arms and beckoned. "Come here to my embrace and share what else you enjoy. We've rewards yet, don't we?"

Jay flew into his arms in three sweeping strides.

"Such boundless affection," he murmured. His darling pet had never had his need met in return, never received the focused care of a proper master. "Tell me what you most wish. A secret wish. You may be certain I won't tell another soul."

"I wish—" Jay nestled against his body.

Stroking down the younger man's back, tracing the strength of his spine, led his hand to the gentle curve above Jay's buttocks. He held firm and leaned in with his hips. His cock rubbed Jay's stomach.

Jay's answering twitch as he hardened thudded against his master's abdomen.

"I wish I wasn't so—I wish this could be my life, Master Henry." Jay buried his face in his shoulder. "All the time. Doing what you tell me to. I like when you're all hard and growly and you hold me so tight."

"*Yes*." The word escaped without forethought. To have Jay with him always, a constant source of joy flourishing under his dominance. A round-the-clock partner whose needs he'd judge for himself on a daily basis instead of playing catch-up at the end of each week.

Pure fantasy. Unwarranted indulgence.

He was the first master to show the boy kindness. Jay responded to his attitude, his careful demeanor, because he rejoiced in the blush of discovery. Jay's love wasn't for him but for the dominance he offered. In the hands of another, he might find the same satisfaction— or discover something he wanted more.

"Yes," he repeated, more measured. Wedging a hand between them, he stroked Jay's cock with a quick squeeze that earned a whimper. "I see that you do, my good boy."

Jay would enjoy bondage. Not with rope or cuffs at the moment, but once his fears had been expunged. He was clear in his enjoyment of more physical dominance and excited by rough-but-loving handling. Likely that desire had led him to gravitate toward swaggering masculinity in search of a dominant.

Lacking discernment, he'd fallen in with the crude, lesser expressions of dominance. In succeeding at sending Cal scurrying from the room, Henry had become the new alpha in the boy's worldview. Reshaping that view to align with Jay's inner nature provided a heady mix of power and pleasure. A mix he meant to control lest he damage the beauty he sought to protect and cultivate.

"Give me your right hand."

Jay offered his hand willingly, and Henry guided it to his cock.

Jay squirmed, hips shifting back as he bowed his head to look between their bodies.

Henry tugged Jay back by his cock. Hard. Ready to seek pleasure again. The joys of youth.

Realigning their grips, he positioned his submissive's cock alongside his own and created an embrace with their hands. His other hand drifted lower and drove his sub forward.

Jay yelped. Less panic than eager anticipation. Appreciation for how their bodies merged.

The stimulation proved an exquisite enticement. He nipped at Jay's jaw.

"My pleasure is your pleasure tonight." Rocking his hips, he thrust into the tight grip with slow care, cock sliding past Jay's and back again. "I intend to fuck you just like this until your body is soaked in my scent and your chest is painted with proof of my joy."

Jay moaned, a sweet sound, a babbling brook of agreement.

Pre-come slicked down and coated their palms, easing his passage. He quickened his pace. Five weeks he'd waited to come in Jay's presence.

"Do you feel the frenzy of delight humming under my skin?" The desire to mark the younger man as his own, to baptize him in ejaculate, pushed him to the edge. He rode the wild line between expectation and inevitability with the skill of long practice. "I feel it under yours, all of your excitement and concentration fixed between us at the place where my cock takes pleasure in yours."

He squeezed Jay's ass, the taut muscles quivering.

"Such a good boy not to disrupt his master's rhythm. You needn't thrust." Orgasm pulsed nearer. "This will be enough for us both."

Shaking, Jay fixed beautiful brown eyes on him.

"Perhaps you'll think of it during your homework and imagine the shape of your all-the-time submission." He reached for a last push to bring his submissive with him, weaving Jay's wish into a tapestry of fantasies to spark imagination and desire. "Will your master take his pleasure like this? Will he wake you in the morning with a command to suck him dry before work or offer you a bedtime treat?"

Oh how it burned to say *he* and not *I*.

Jay's whimpering ratcheted to its penultimate expression. His release wouldn't be stopped now.

Neither would his master's.

"So many possibilities for pleasure," he growled.

The flash of heat overtook him. His cock jerked alongside Jay's, spurting wet and thick, eclipsing the younger man's emission a half-second later.

He demanded a kiss with near bruising force, more of the roughness Jay had admitted he craved. When Jay had the courage to speak his desires as he had tonight, he would find them fulfilled.

Heart rate slowing, Henry pulled back and peered down at the mess. Satisfying. A burst of ownership, no matter how temporary. He unwound Jay's hand and his own, cocks bobbing without the support.

Staring, Jay lifted his hand.

Pride? Curiosity? His student's intensity defied interpretation. Perhaps he'd never engaged in mutual masturbation this way.

He touched Jay's elbow, question poised on his lips.

Fast as a lightning strike, Jay shoved his fingers in his mouth. He sucked his hand clean in seconds, with a shudder and a moan.

Ah. Lust.

"I'm sorry, Master Henry. I wanted to taste you so bad."

Pure need, followed in rapid succession by satisfaction and panic.

"And next time, you'll ask permission first." Jay hadn't broken a rule per se, and he'd at least seen evidence of his master's clean bill of health, but he'd need a safety reminder regarding bodily fluids at the least. A general discussion might suit.

He proffered his own hand. "I've towels for us in my kit, but you may taste your fill first. You've worked hard tonight, and you request so little of your master. Perhaps this is a reward you ought to add to your list. Something to ask for when you're a good boy?"

Jay nodded, his mouth occupied with cleaning.

Wonderful. He'd slipped in the notion of negotiation with nary a peep. The younger man would take to the skill in time.

Jay's mouth on his fingers mimicked a slow, sweet blowjob. Some week soon, perhaps. He had alternate plans for their next week.

Slipping his mouth off with a *pop*, Jay glanced at him.

"Finished?"

"I am if you want, Master Henry." Jay's gaze darted to his chest.

"Go and fetch the towel from the top of my bag, and then come lie down."

His disappointment obvious but unchallenging, Jay trotted to the bag and retrieved the ivory cotton.

Henry lowered himself to the sheets and lay on his back, a smile twitching at his lips. He patted the space beside him as his submissive approached. "Start with your tongue, my dear boy, and I'll employ the towel."

Unfettered delight shone on Jay's face. The broad midday smile.

Henry cleaned his cock and balls with the towel, unwilling to risk giving rise to the temptation, and left his chest for his student. Tender swipes served to erase his claim on the younger man's skin. Jay's intimate bathing of his chest felt like a blessing.

Kissing his companion afterward to demonstrate his lack of disgust with Jay's desires, he tipped Jay onto his back. A slow roll perched him on his hip beside him. "I want us to discuss safety measures."

"Condoms?" Jay's eyes gleamed.

Eager for penetration, was he?

"An excellent start, as you'll want to protect yourself from potential infection in any scene involving penetration. I'm speaking of more general guidelines in this case." He ruffled Jay's hair. Longer than it had been five weeks ago. He shoved aside the impulse to claim a lock. "Precautions you might take if, for example, a dominant asked you to join him or her for play elsewhere."

"Like a hotel?"

He nodded, though the sort of scene he feared Jay falling afoul of required more discretion than a thin hotel room wall provided. "Or their personal playroom, or a friend's private dungeon."

Anywhere Jay would be vulnerable and alone in a stranger's hands.

"I'd ask—" Jay tipped his head, nudging.

Henry obliged with another stroke through his hair.

"I'd ask for a reference from a previous submissive?"

"Good." He traced the line of Jay's neck to the curve of his shoulder. "What else?"

"Meet somewhere safe first. Downstairs in the salon or at a coffee place or something, just to talk. Say what can and can't happen."

"Lovely. You've been paying attention to your lessons." Pressing his face to Jay's neck, he inhaled the woody musk. "Tell me another."

He dotted Jay's throat with kisses. Tender skin yielded under his lips.

"Umm—I—" Jay squirmed. "I'm sorry, Master Henry. I can't think of one."

"No, the apology is mine." He lifted his head and pecked the younger man's lips. "I've distracted you. Do you remember what I said about a safety call?"

"That I should"—Jay sighed—"have a friend who knows where I'll be and who'll know what to do if I don't call to say I'm safe by a certain time."

"Have you thought about a friend you might trust to ask?"

Jay turned his face away. "No, Master Henry."

Henry rubbed his submissive's chest. No matter the discomfort, allowing Jay to hide on a subject of safety would be unconscionable. "Why haven't you obeyed me in this?"

"I don't—" He shrugged and whispered. "I don't want anyone to know. What I am. What I do."

The pain pierced him. Shame still ruled his submissive. Shame of what they did together. Perhaps young Mr. Kress hated his master as much as he craved his control. "There's no shame in what you are or how you conduct your sex life, Jay."

If the boy had no one else, could he force himself to answer that call? Knowing Jay had spent the time playing under another's command?

Yes. For Jay's sake, and none other. His needs would never be ignored. "Submissive is not synonymous with whore."

Dead silence. A shiver rippled through the boy.

Long minutes he waited, but Jay said nothing. Insight slithered like a snake in the grass. "Someone already knows, don't they? Someone from your life outside the club."

The tight nod in return gripped his heart.

"The guy who brought me here the first time."

"A friend?"

"I thought so."

"Not now?"

"He saw me."

Shame and a hint of despair. Had this friend brought Jay as his submissive or been a submissive himself, Jay would have no reason for upset. "Your dominant friend saw you acting as a submissive ought?"

Another nod, but not even a twitch of hope at the idea that he'd been behaving properly. A deeper problem lay behind Jay's concern.

"How did he treat you afterward? Do you see him often?"

"Almost every day," Jay whispered. "We work out of the same office."

He curved his hand against the younger man's cheek, a gentle but steady pull. "I want you to look at me, my brave boy." He pitched his voice soft and low. Intimate. Private. "And I want you to tell me what he's done."

"How, how do you know he did anything?" Jay's quivering bravado begged for help.

"Because I know *you*, dear boy, and I know others take advantage of your sweet nature."

"It was just—he's been cracking on me, you know?" Jay hadn't yet met his eyes. "Little jokes when nobody could hear. All the time."

"Did his offense end with the harassment?" The pressure of daily bullying might be enough to wear down Jay's defenses, but the shame lay deeper still.

"He—I let him—he said he'd tell everyone. They'd all know. Only once. I only did it once, Master Henry, I promise. I thought he'd stop if I did it once."

"Whatever you've done, it's all right. Tell me what happened."

The younger man rolled onto his side and tucked himself against his master's body. He huddled close, breath hot and fast against Henry's chest. "I sucked him off." Mumbled words, almost inaudible. "In the bathroom at work."

Curling his arm around his submissive's back, Henry forced himself to remain calm. Anger wouldn't help the boy. He threaded his fingers into the hair at the nape of Jay's neck and offered gentle, repetitive scratching. "Was that an act of submission you wanted to perform?"

"No," Jay shouted with a whisper. "I really like giving blowjobs, Master Henry. I do. It's—you're—it's what I think about when I'm doing my homework. But not like that. I didn't want to do it like that. I threw up after, and he said"—Jay shivered—"he said I was such a filthy little cockslut I should be used to the taste."

"Jay, this man,"—this worthless abuser who'd assaulted his sweet, fractured boy—"what is his name?"

"Bryan. Bryan Talbot."

A familiar name. Dennis Talbot's cousin or nephew, perhaps. Something to investigate later at the front desk. "This is the man who introduced you to this club?"

"Yes, Master Henry."

"Then he ought to understand the inappropriateness of his conduct. If he approaches you again, I want you to tell him you are not allowed to engage in sexual activity of any kind without my permission."

"Not allowed." Jay lifted his face and smiled before concern weighed on him. "What if he doesn't believe me?"

"Give him my name, tell him your submission to me is full time, and inform him he's welcome to request a meeting with me at the club to negotiate your services."

"You won't make me serve him." Not a shred of doubt in his submissive's voice, thank God.

"You're learning, my dear boy. No, I won't let him touch you. I will, however, waste his time and teach him a lesson in manners, and do so quite happily."

Perhaps Will would be free of an evening and join him for the meeting. His imposing bulk and steadfast loyalty had their benefits, if he reined in his temper. Brawling over this boy. Not useful, but emotionally satisfying. More useful—ah, yes. Later. When Jay had gone for the night.

He redirected the conversation to a more comfortable topic for his partner, questioning him about his use of the toy he'd been given last week and authorizing continued homework for the week. More games to help his student last longer. A suggestion to spend time fantasizing about women. Preparation for next week.

Sheets handed off, he accompanied Jay as he changed into street clothes and bid good night to him in the main lobby. The moment his submissive climbed into the back of a cab, Henry strode to the desk and inquired after one Bryan Talbot and the sponsor for his membership.

With stationery and a fine fountain pen he'd requested from the desk, Henry settled himself at a small table in the salon with a glass of iced tea.

> *Bryan,*
>
> *It has come to my attention that you style yourself a master and abuse the property of others. How proud your uncle must be. Be assured, I am enclosing a copy of this letter in a note to him, as well, that he might reconsider sponsoring your membership here.*
>
> *The boy Jay is mine. I will not tolerate trespass, whether it happens within these walls or without. You will not approach him again. You will not speak—*

"Henry? May I join you?" Emma stood across from him, a rosy flush in her face.

He stood as well, gesturing with an open hand. "Please, sit."

Her gaze flicked to the tabletop as she sat. A subtle smile flashed across her face.

"Speak, Em." He took his seat. "You'll choke on your self-satisfaction if you don't."

She laughed. "Victor has better things for me to choke on."

The image flashed in his mind against his will. Not of Emma, enjoying her service, but of his sweet boy on his knees, vomiting with shame and disgust in a men's room.

She fingered the edge of the paper. "Writing a love letter to your boy?"

"Wishful thinking, Em. No. A warning letter, in fact."

"Preparing for Cal's return? Much as the bastard deserves it, that's a bit of wishful thinking on your part, don't you agree, Henry? He'd hardly—"

"Not Cal." He crushed the pen against his hand until his knuckle ached. "Another smart-assed little fuck who believes he can stick his cock wherever he likes and is about to learn differently."

The pen ticked on the tabletop as he let go. Flattening his hand revealed the tremor in his fingers. "Pardon my language. I'm not quite myself at the moment."

Emma laid her hand atop his. Warm. Small. Immaculate. A comfort, but not the one he most wanted.

"The boy?"

The boy. As if there were only one in all the world. Unique, and beautiful, and full of need. The perfect outlet for his craving to instruct and care for a partner. But Jay would outgrow his care. Wasn't that always the goal and the fear?

"As well as I can make him for tonight." Not so. He could have taken Jay home. Could be curled around him now. If he threw every standard for his own conduct out the window. If he made the mentoring relationship a personal one.

Personal, ha. He failed to fool even himself. The relationship had already strayed into overly familiar territory. Jay slept on his sheets nightly, for God's sake.

"Let's discuss something else, shall we? The boy's training is private. Tell me what Victor did to put such color in your cheeks."

She allowed the conversational diversion, as he knew she would, with the grace of precise training and the wisdom of longstanding friendship. Even as he listened, his traitorous thoughts remained with the boy.

Chapter 6

He dined with Jay a third time the following week. Tradition, now, to include a shared dinner in his plans every other week. Jay seemed in high spirits, sweet and smiling as he related how he'd spent the previous weekend.

Questioning his submissive about his workday inevitably occasioned bland, almost morose, replies. His leisure habits, however, spawned an endless stream of cheerful chatter, if one oft interrupted by anxious inquiries to be certain his babbling hadn't displeased his master.

Henry took to making active inquiries himself to ease Jay's doubt. Direct questions, quasi-demands for more information, kept Jay relaxed. Loose muscles and giddy eyes.

Outdoor athleticism proved the cause for the toned physique hiding beneath the fine suit. Young Mr. Kress feasted on a steady diet of biking, kayaking, and pick-up basketball all summer. His choices left him radiating health and vitality, intoxicatingly vivid and full of life.

Listening to the younger man, Henry marinated in arousal. While Jay had been riding a fifty-mile loop last Saturday, he had been preparing for tonight with an accommodating brunette.

Periodic glances to his left yielded the results he sought as Jay tucked into his dessert. The brunette—Naomi—approached the table and halted beyond the screen. At his raised eyebrow, she delivered a slow nod he returned. The room would be ready. The woman would be ready.

Would the boy be ready?

The first test came in the changing room as Jay reached for his shorts.

"No play clothes tonight, my boy." He kept his voice calm and steady, firm but undemanding.

If Jay didn't learn to negotiate up front, he'd have to negotiate each item as it arose. His dear one would challenge or submit—and reveal more of himself to his master with every choice.

"You'll wear nothing but the red ribbon of my ownership."

Naked and half-hard, Jay whipped his head up. "Nothing, Master Henry?"

"The required footwear, but nothing else."

The club provided thin play sandals for those who preferred to go barefoot. Jay would be far from the only submissive to be so clad. Appreciating the beauty of the human form was part of the spectacle. For some, the enjoyment surpassed what might be found in a scene.

He himself received pleasure from the pairing. The static beauty of nudity or half-revealed flesh aroused. The dynamic beauty of emotional catharsis fulfilled. A gratifying combination, taken as a whole. And Jay, Jay brimmed to overflowing with the beauty of both.

Drinking such wine for a thousand years would not slake his thirst for it.

Jay hesitated with his hand on his armor. The leather shorts served as a security of sorts. The younger man had been nude when he'd first seen him, bound to the St. Andrew's cross. His response here would serve as a gauge for how deeply he associated his own nudity with that painful vulnerability.

A minute passed. More. Jay's hand didn't budge. His arousal waned, a sign of thought taking precedence over the body's demands, perhaps. Or discomfort. Time to offer his submissive an escape.

"If I demand too much of you, my dear boy, you've only to use your safeword." He affected a casual tone. "Remind me of your word, please."

"Tilt"—Jay cleared his throat—"Tilt-A-Whirl, Master Henry."

Jay stuffed the shorts back into his duffel with his soon-to-be wrinkled suit. "I don't need to use it. I'm not carnival sick. I just"— sandals scuffed at the floor—"just needed a second."

"You're my brave boy, Jay." He stepped forward and clasped the younger man's shoulders in a quick squeeze. "There's no shame in needing a moment to dip into that reservoir of purity and courage within your heart."

Jay stood tall and slung the duffel over his back. "I'm ready, Master Henry."

The green-ribboned girl behind the desk leaned forward, peeking over the counter as Jay slid his bag across. Her breasts bounced on the shelf of a slender blue-and-gold striped corset.

"No shorts for your boy tonight, Master Henry?"

Jay let the duffel go without hesitation.

"No, not tonight, Lindsey." Running his hand down Jay's back, he subtly felt for tension. None so far. "He keeps himself in such fine form, it seems a shame not to show him off a bit."

"He's a nice bit, sir." She flashed a cheeky grin. "But he's adorable with the shorts, too. I hope someday I'll find a master to look at the way he looks at you."

"The most important search of our lives," he murmured.

Sighing, Jay leaned into his hand like a pup begging for another pat.

Henry blinked and wished the girl luck in her search. His hand moved without conscious instruction, stroking his partner's spine. Longing filled him to keep Jay within reach. To roll over in bed at night and count the same vertebrae with his fingers.

They left the younger man's kit at the desk and ventured up the stairs. Jay drew a commendable stream of admiring appraisals from afar.

"You, my beautiful boy, are quite the prize tonight." He strolled with his submissive at his side, a leisurely promenade down the third-floor hall as if they had nowhere to be. Acclimating Jay to nudity in the crowd would ease the shock of being nude for a crowd of one later.

"Half a dozen dominants have inspected you from head to toe with envious eyes." Here, Jay was one among many, a curiosity only for the novelty of a new beauty on display. The weight of expectation and performance was lessened. Once they reached the appointed room, he would become the focal point. Cause for nerves if he failed to accustom Jay to the idea now. "Do you know what thoughts zip to and fro in their minds?"

"No, Master Henry." Jay glanced about, eyes searching beneath a bowed head, his demeanor respectful and unchallenging.

He halted and pressed a kiss to his companion's temple. "That I am an exceptionally lucky man to have such a lovely and well-mannered submissive in my service."

Jay leaned into his kiss. "But how do—"

"Henry! My goodness."

He struggled to place the feminine voice as the woman neared. Poorly dyed blond hair drawn back in a severe bun. An executive's suit, not formal or evening wear but business attire. A role-play kink for disciplining lazy corporate assistants and allowing them to make up for it with sexual favors. M-something. Martha. Miriam. Melody. Yes, that was it. Melody.

"Where have you been hiding this beautiful big boy?" She breezed to a stop close enough for the cloying scent of sweet jasmine to invade his nose. A girl playing at her mother's vanity with no sense of restraint.

Jay ducked his head with a discreet choking sound.

"Melody." He offered a short nod and a thin smile.

"Does he play private parties? I have a pool boy scenario I've been dying to try out with a few friends."

He wouldn't entrust a stable, fully trained submissive to this woman, let alone his delicate boy. If she couldn't judge her perfume choices with restraint, where else did her incompetence extend?

"The boy isn't available." Curling his hand over the join between Jay's shoulder and neck, he found his submissive inching closer as if they'd rehearsed the motion. "He's in training yet. I won't be letting him out of my sight."

"Is that why he's so fresh-faced? I could just pour him into a bowl and eat him with a spoon."

Her covetous gaze hadn't ventured near Jay's face. She'd locked on to a region rather farther south. One experiencing a cold front, if he wasn't mistaken. *For me as well, my boy.* But patience and for-bearance served them all in such a small community.

"Yes, he's an excellent pupil." He tapped his fingers on Jay's collar-bone. "Jay, my good boy, practice saying hello to the mistress and then we'll hurry along to your lesson."

"Hello, Mistress. Thank you for noticing me." Jay gazed at the floor, but he infused his words with a semblance of sincerity. "I'm honored that my appearance pleases you."

Flawless. Jay handled introductions with ease. He'd done so the night Henry had ghosted his steps. The night the boy had agreed to be his.

In the moments after the initial greeting, when the contest for power began, Jay had cowered and stuttered and agreed without negotiating a single point. He'd have to be able to stand straight under questioning or the club would never be a safe place for him. He wouldn't be starting with the likes of Mistress Melody and her intrusive, noisome predation.

"Well done, my boy." He steered Jay forward before the woman took the moment to object. "Please excuse us, Melody. We've an appointment to keep."

"Of course, Henry. Your boy's just as beautiful going as coming." Her laughter grated as her voice followed them. "Be sure and tell me when he's out of school. Or before. Every good boy deserves recess."

They'd gotten five steps before Jay's anxious whisper reached his ears. "Master—"

"Not in your lifetime, my boy," he murmured. "I'd triple-lock a chastity cage around your cock before I let that woman anywhere near you."

Tension flowed out of Jay's shoulders. "Thank you, Master Henry."

"I do, however, have a much more suitable one in mind." He stopped in front of a red-tagged door.

Now he'd see how well Naomi had followed his instructions. Well, he expected. Emma had vouched for her discretion. They'd met on three consecutive Saturdays to assess each other and negotiate the plan for the scene.

"I've a new playmate for you tonight." He pushed open the door. A gentle tug served to bring his submissive across the threshold. "Shall we enjoy her together?"

Jay stared.

Henry closed the door behind them. The room approximated the dining and living area of a small home. Cozy, with a bland, monochromatic design in shades of rose. The slipcovered sofa offered variety in the form of pale gray.

The table, broad enough for six, boasted features unlikely to appear in most homes. Discreet anchor points underneath. Removable padded bumpers to cushion hips, buttocks, and thighs. Floor bolts for safety. The false light fixture above doubled as a restraint bar.

Jay, of course, stared at nothing so much as the naked woman standing at ease in the open space before the sofa. Tucking her arms behind her back had thrust her breasts forward, and the younger man fixated on them, his cock stiffening.

If Jay had a type, he'd at least provided a woman who matched it well enough. He laid a hand against his student's back and rubbed a small circle on his shoulder blade.

Jay jumped, breaking his staring contest with the submissive's chest. "Together, Master Henry? You mean me, too?"

"Of course. You're my best boy, Jay." He delivered the words with authority, leaving no room for doubt.

From Jay's description of his previous encounters, he'd often been used as the warm-up to stoke a dominant's desire for another submissive. An amusement cast aside.

Not tonight.

Henry wouldn't take their temporary playmate at all tonight, though Jay would if all went well. She hadn't so much as lifted her head at their entrance. She excelled at obedience.

"I'd be foolish to put you on the bench when your playing gives me so much pleasure." Given Jay's athleticism, the sports metaphor might do the trick.

Jay tipped his head, adorably uncertain. "It'll please you if I play with her?"

He studied Jay's cues. Judging by the full arousal and straying eyes, lack of desire wouldn't be a concern. Perhaps his submissive sought reassurance that this treat wasn't a trick? He needed more specific details of past experiences to better ascertain where Jay's triggers lay, but shame so ensnared the younger man that digging out the information too quickly threatened to traumatize him.

A faint tan line ringed Jay's bicep. Fingers trailing, Henry crossed the border from white-collar work Jay to playful weekend Jay. "Do you enjoy following my directions?"

"I like it a lot, Master Henry."

He curled his fingers around Jay's, moving their hands as one. "Do you enjoy sexual play with women?"

Jay nodded. His gaze darted between their entwined hands and the silent woman.

Henry parted his lips in a coaxing smile. "Would you like to try both at once?"

Jay's cock bobbed against his stomach, an affirmative response ahead of his, "yes, Master Henry."

"Then yes, it would please me very much to watch my beautiful boy play with our new friend." He brought Jay's hand to his mouth and pressed a kiss to his palm. "Your body belongs to me, my boy. An extension of my own, hmm? If I am the painter, you are the brush and our feminine friend the canvas."

Jay stood taller, thrusting his cock forward. "I promise I'll always bring my 'A' game for you, Master Henry."

"I don't doubt it. I'm certain submissive Naomi will be well-satisfied with your effort, as will I." He released the younger man. "Leave your sandals here, please, and go and stand in front of your playmate."

Jay obeyed without delay, mimicking the woman's at-ease posture. His bowed head would give him an excellent view of her charms, as hers would his in return.

Henry took his time removing his jacket and draping it over a chair at the table. Were Jay engaging in this sort of play with an un-known dominant and submissive pair, he would expect him to question safety and health concerns and run through each participant's hard limits before outlining the type of experience they might create together.

He'd spent two Saturday afternoons with Naomi doing just that. She had a sharp mind and wasn't shy about stating her interests. Most of them wouldn't be indulged tonight. He'd delivered on his half of their bargain last Saturday. Overhead bondage. Nipple clamps. Light flogging. Orgasm denial.

The agreement hadn't included sex. He'd stayed fully clothed the entire time. In return, she'd agreed to more vanilla games with his submissive tonight, including intercourse. Jay would have the oppor-tunity to play with another submissive without being discarded as second best.

He watched the two of them as he slipped off his shoes, socks, and tie. Jay fidgeted. Sweaty hands, perhaps? A mix of anxiety and excitement. Best to get Jay's first orgasm of the night out of the way without shame. He'd be more relaxed after and able to take direction with greater calm.

The woman's satisfaction would be more complex and not some-thing Jay would ever learn the reasons behind. Aside from the ethics of discretion when dealing with others' deepest fantasies, he wouldn't confuse Jay by explaining how Naomi could enjoy intercourse with him precisely because he was his master's boy rather than the master himself.

A degradation kink. She preferred the humiliation she felt in being used to satisfy another submissive's desires, unfit and rejected by the dominant. The more he ignored her, the more she'd enjoy the game. As he intended to focus on Jay's confidence and pleasure, the dynamic suited them both. All information he wouldn't have known if he hadn't sat and negotiated with the woman over tea. Skills Jay had yet to learn.

Tonight, Jay would be safe in trusting his master's judgment. Teaching him not to hand over so much control to any dominant who issued an invitation, however. . . .

"Safety first," he murmured.

Four steps brought him to Jay's back. "Share your safeword with us, my boy."

"Tilt-A-Whirl."

"Excellent. Naomi?"

"Saffron, sir."

"Tilt-A-Whirl. Saffron. These words will stop our game immediately tonight."

His submissive's twitching fingers warranted attention. He raised Jay's arms and left them outstretched to the side, palms up. Holding the position would bleed off nervous energy.

"Jay, if you hear 'saffron' spoken, what are you to do?"

"Stop. Stop whatever I'm doing right away and not touch."

He hummed with pride, tracing the extent of the younger man's scapulae. Beautifully structured, with the perfect thickness of muscle draped overtop.

Squirming hips confirmed the urgency of Jay's arousal.

"Well done, my boy. Naomi, Tilt-A-Whirl?"

"Stop, sir. Leave your boy alone and wait for further instructions, sir."

"Correct." He clipped his tone, downplaying his praise for her benefit. Lowering Jay's arms, he barked a command. "Jay, kneel."

Jay's muscles flexed in smooth motion. Perfection. Naomi's petite frame put Jay's face level with her breasts.

He tousled Jay's hair and walked a slow arc around the pair. Stopping behind the woman excited her. She breathed tense stillness.

He encircled her wrists. Her breath came faster.

Jay watched her expanding chest with greedy eyes. A breast fixation, without a doubt. His own taste ran toward the slope of the buttocks and the deeper curves of the pudendal cleft. Parting that seam displayed a woman's full femininity, brought her blushing flesh into the light and her scent to his nose. Heaven.

As delightful as the bead of pre-come rolling down Jay's stiff cock.

A tighter grip on Naomi's wrists yielded a soft sigh.

Jay opened his mouth, his tongue peeking out.

Empathetic arousal? Jay had a sensitive heart. What brought pleasure to others radiated pleasure to him, as well.

"The air seems dry to me, my boy. We wouldn't want it to chafe Naomi's breasts, would we?" He gave a slow shake of his head that the younger man copied. "No, of course not. Use your mouth to rectify the problem, please. Keep her nice and wet."

Her nipples peaked as Jay worked at them, mouthing the fullness of her breasts. She shaded toward brown rather than pink, her areolae deepening to a sepia tone. Their outline faded into Jay's tanned face, a lovely bit of synchronicity, as if she were no more than a shadow on his skin.

He filed away the thought that a contrast might complement Jay's loveliness equally well. A golden-haired, milky-skinned, rose-tipped girl for his dark boy.

Striking like a snake, he bit down on Naomi's earlobe and crushed her wrists in his hand.

She pressed forward, arching into his enthusiastic boy and moaning. "Yes," she panted. "Yes, sir."

Voice low to avoid rousing Jay from her breasts, he growled in her ear. "No."

His denial made her quake. Dropping her hands as though he'd tired of her charms, he rounded the pair and knelt behind Jay.

The dark head paused. A questioning hum emerged around the flesh in Jay's mouth.

"Keep up your good work, my boy." Hands resting at Jay's hips, he leaned in and inhaled the sharp evergreen of the younger man's preferred beauty products and the earthy musk of arousal mingling at his neck. "I've work of my own to enjoy."

A whimper greeted his sliding fingers as he approached Jay's erection. Controlling his own arousal while playing with Naomi had been a simple matter. She constituted a pleasant, suitable partner for the night, but her desires made her an ill fit for young Mr. Kress in a long-term pairing.

Getting ahead of himself, was he?

The lure of Jay matched with a full-time partner, both his to command, to guide and care for, taunted him. An impossible vision. He was Jay's teacher only. A short-term fixation.

He'd meant this night to be for his student. A demonstration of safe enjoyment with another submissive, a replacement for every night Jay had departed used and discarded. Had he misunderstood his own intention? Pushed Jay into wanting this, steered him toward his own desires as he'd sworn not to do? Selfishness and self-disgust gnawed at him.

If he had, stopping now would accomplish a single, undesirable goal: confusing his submissive. The submissive whose needy cock brushed the backs of his hands.

Playing with Jay emphasized the tight constraint of his own slacks, growing flesh pinched and prodding him for release. He locked down his arousal with a growl.

Jay whimpered in response, a submissive answer to his call that threatened to begin the cycle again. They fed each other in such instinctive harmony.

The woman hadn't felt it—or, if she had, she'd resisted answering the call. Hadn't joined the sphere where he and Jay resided. For two more weeks, at least. A stunning oasis. He intended to provision the boy as best he could for whatever journeys lay ahead.

He curled his left hand around Jay's sack and clenched the base of his cock with the right.

Shaking, Jay rested his head against the woman's breasts. "I'm"—his voice squeaked in a thin, anxious tenor—"I'm real close, Master Henry."

"Of course you are, my sweet boy." He swept Jay's cock in a slow arc, squeezing the base of the shaft. Neither shame nor concern would be permitted here. Not for his partner. "I'm picking up my brush. We cannot place the first streaks of color on our canvas if the paint isn't loaded."

He added a quick stroke up the shaft for emphasis, and Jay squirmed.

"You've your own task to attend to. Tug hard." Swollen and stiff, Naomi's breasts awaited further attention. "See how you've added deeper color already?"

Jay would never cause enough pain to please her. Letting him feast to his heart's content would do no harm.

"I'll handle the brushwork myself."

A slow stroke pulled a shuddering whimper from the younger man. He lowered his mouth to a tight nipple in obedient fascination.

Speedy strokes raised tension in Jay's legs, his thighs curving as climax neared. Delicate, heated skin bowed to the command in the master's fingers. A thready whine presaged Jay's release.

"That's it, my good boy, come for me." Gentle and coaxing, he guided his submissive through orgasm. Panting, shuddering breaths above. Ejaculate spurting below, directed downward to speckle bare feminine calves. A triumph for the man, a degrading joy for the woman.

She trembled and swayed as liquid struck her skin. He'd hit the agreed-upon safe zone. They wouldn't be sharing fluids. Condoms waited in his pocket for Jay.

With a low moan, Naomi pleaded her case for release of her own.

"Our canvas must stay still," he chided.

The greater pressure on her breasts and the humiliation of being used as no more than the boy's bedside tissue would appeal enough to bring her to the edge of the orgasm he denied her now. More enjoyable to her than the permission would be. A trait she shared with Emma, though Em's brand of masochism lacked the compulsive humiliation fetish Naomi favored.

"Enough, my boy." He slid a hand up Jay's chest and nudged. "Let's move our game, shall we?"

Jay stopped sucking. The slight daze in his eyes and his swollen, reddened lips prompted his master's sigh.

"Lovely." He claimed a sweet kiss. Releasing his submissive required focused effort.

He rose to his feet and gestured toward the table. "Jay, go and pull back the chairs, please. Along the wall will be fine. We won't need them."

He could have left the task for Naomi as part of her prep, but giving the job to Jay suited his purposes. Admiring the younger man's lean form and clean lines, he sauntered to a stop behind the woman.

She maintained an attentive poise, silent and still, her head bowed. He'd have a few moments while Jay worked. Enough time to whip her with words, a fast, stinging whisper like the snap of a riding crop in her ear.

"My sleek pup is going to fuck you. Eager. Untrained." He teased her wrists with light touches, the promise of a harsher grip. "His cock is still more than you deserve."

The cock swung flaccid along Jay's thigh for now. Three chairs moved. Three to go. Rousing him again wouldn't require much work. He'd learned that much about his student in the last few weeks.

"He'll take his pleasure in the only value your worthless body provides. And you'll enjoy it, won't you, Naomi?" Her slight nod an encouraging bit of unconscious response, he pushed on. "You'll writhe under his touch, and you'll come for him when I command you."

Her breathing grew louder, a sufficient cover for his guttural whispers.

"Not because you deserve it. You're but an insignificant speck. But the boy—he deserves to own your pleasure."

Gripping her wrists behind her back in his left hand, he marched her forward. Her moans drew Jay's attention as he placed the last of the chairs. If not for Jay's presence, he'd have tripped her and blamed her for the clumsiness herself. A pretext for more punishment play she'd enjoy.

Such behavior would horrify Jay, and his own interest was academic. Cataloguing his partners' preferences had become standard practice over the years. Ensuring their enjoyment enhanced his own.

He ordered her onto the table and raised her legs, placing her feet at the corners and keeping an iron hold on her ankles. The strength in his hands would be all he worked with tonight.

Jay watched at his side with the anticipatory air that often characterized his stillness.

Naomi's eyes flashed. A wish for true restraints, he expected.

"Lie back."

Jay's fantasy included face-to-face encounters. He'd offer a facsimile of it, though he wouldn't claim this woman himself. Not when Jay and his responses were what roused his interest in this room.

Naomi settled on her back, her hips and sex at the table's edge, her legs bent and strained, feet gripping the corners of the short side of the table. The hard surface ought to increase her enjoyment, even if he couldn't provide bondage and impact games tonight.

"Come closer, my boy." Pulling his submissive in front of him, he suppressed a groan at the image assaulting his mind. A pleasant diversion, a slow push between Jay's enticing, rounded buttocks while he in turn took a woman. This one. Another one. Any one he liked. Moving in concert.

He lowered his mouth to Jay's neck with half-savage intensity, pressure and suction sure to leave a mark if he didn't gentle himself. *Easy. Go easy.* A sigh escaped as he gained control, tonguing tanned skin while Jay shivered.

The slender strength of Jay's arms flowed under his caress. He twined their fingers and ran them along the woman's thighs toward her sex. Time to prep her for Jay's entry while he recovered. A glance down showed he hadn't hardened yet, but his periodic whimpers and squirming assured interest and need would win the war over biology soon.

Back and forth, Jay's hands under his, he teased the insides of her thighs to the creases where her sex waited. The threat of rougher handling would have excited her, but young Mr. Kress needed smooth, slick passage. Sure signs of acceptance and desire. Implications of force would distress him.

Guiding Jay's fingers, he traced Naomi's labia. Spread open her sex to their eyes. Stroking revealed more arousal than he'd expected from her at this point. Jay's fingers twitched in his, the end point for a current of excitement.

"See how swollen with need she is?"

He cupped his student's hand around the plump fullness of the vulva and squeezed with gentle pressure.

Naomi tensed. Her chest expanded, her breath a silent pause.

Jay thrust despite the lingering softness in his cock. An adorable wobble at the tip as wrinkles stretched and flattened along his hardening shaft.

More enticement for his own cock, confined by boxers and slacks both.

He'd considered putting a new cock ring on his submissive tonight. A simple silicone band, a step up from the pressure wrap but not yet the more difficult but elegant metal or glass. Its use, however, might lessen Jay's confidence. Imply he wouldn't satisfy otherwise. Far from the truth. Bringing in a new partner was enough of a toy. No sense overwhelming Jay in a single night.

A slide up, a curving angle down, and his index finger and Jay's slipped inside her heat with ease. He pumped twice, slow and steady. Her sex tightened.

"How eager she is to welcome you. Flushed and wet with desire."

He left Jay's other hand on her thigh and brought his own to the younger man's hip. He squeezed with the rhythm of their pumping fingers, a spur to keep Jay's hips in subtle motion. Tiny thrusts made his cock bob until he'd reached full arousal.

"You've something to give her, don't you? A present to make her cry out her satisfaction, unable to help herself."

Naomi moaned, but Jay flinched. His lips pulled in a brief grimace, and his hand stuttered in the rhythm.

Too much. He'd struck a sour note with the helplessness. Something Cal had said to Jay or just the memory of his own inability to escape. A turn-on for bondage fetishists, but the mere hint was understandably beyond Jay just now.

"Do you want that, Naomi?" He went on as though he hadn't intended to stop. "Do you want my boy's cock bringing you pleasure?"

"Yes. Yes, please, sir, if you'll allow it, though I haven't earned it." Her arms stretched above her head, extending to the far end of the table. She imagined cuffs, perhaps. "I'm a bad girl, sir. I don't deserve such a good boy."

Well done. He'd be certain to thank her later for the opening. The verbal opening. He'd always intended to thank her for the physical one on Jay's behalf.

"What say you, my boy?" He kissed the side of Jay's head, inhaling the woodsy scent of his hair. "Will you show Naomi she deserves a good boy like yourself?"

"I, I want to, Master Henry." Clearly. His cock strained as his hips swayed toward the sex laid out before him.

Jay needed to feel both in control and protected in this delicate time. A child building castles in a closely guarded sandbox. Henry would hold his submissive's hands, and they would shape his safe haven together.

"And so you shall."

Pulling a condom from his pocket with his left hand, he eased his right hand free of Naomi's sex.

"Three fingers, my boy, at the same speed. Keep your playmate ready for you while I ready you for her, please."

Combined with Jay's earlier release, the condom might prove adequate to deaden sensation enough for him to last longer once inside. Long enough to wring an orgasm from Naomi, though she'd struggle against it and enjoy it more in the surrender. Jay's gentle and unsophisticated manner ought to be the perfect mix of distasteful and arousing for her. He'd give his submissive a hand if necessary. Jay would be disappointed if he failed to satisfy.

He unfurled the condom over Jay's cock in an easy slide. Lubricated inside and out for a more natural feeling, though in truth nothing matched the intimacy of a slick, bare coupling. Not something this short-term liaison could provide.

Jay's soft whine brought a smile to his face.

"Beautiful work." He tugged the younger man's wrist, freeing wet fingers and placing them around the base of Jay's erection. "Let's switch to a broader brush. Your playmate deserves a thicker tool with more heft."

"If it were me, I'd ask for yours, then, Master Henry."

He growled at Jay's sweet tone. If God granted mercy, his submissive would stop asking. His earnest pleas tempted his master entirely too much.

"Yours *is* mine, my boy. As all of you is mine on our nights together."

A gratifying shudder wracked Jay's body.

Brushing the tip of Jay's cock between darkened lips occasioned a tremor from the woman and a whimper from Mr. Kress.

"Gently, now." He leaned into Jay with caution, prepared to pull back if the weight at his back prompted a negative reaction. Jay allowed himself to be nudged forward, sinking steadily until he'd reached his full depth. "Just so, my lovely boy."

Hands resting at Jay's hips, he guided the pace with fingertips and his own weight. Slow and gentle, listening to Jay's gasps and whines. Encouraging the younger man to let his hands roam along his playmate's tense legs and flat stomach.

"I feel your muscles flexing, my boy. How beautiful you are, the perfect instrument for this application. Made to bring others pleasure, as you do for me each time we play."

Jay whispered his thanks in a shaking voice as his hips jerked. Praise did seem to bring him closer to the edge than anything else.

Naomi's fierce eyes glared at him. She'd want it harder, rougher, faster and with less tenderness. He'd forbidden her to ask. She'd get what she needed from a gentle touch or none at all, and she knew it.

Being forced to accept the opposite of her preference added a perverse excitement to her experience, telling her he found her unworthy of receiving her desires.

All of which operated on a level below Jay's awareness. He had the rhythm down now. Henry lifted his hands.

"Keep going, my dear boy. I want to enjoy watching your exquisite form." Taking a half step back, he rested his hands on the woman's knees as if the location were merely convenient. Jay wouldn't notice the outward pressure he brought to bear, forcing her legs to take his weight as he held her open.

Tight muscles worked in Jay's back and lower, the ever-increasing flex in his ass a delightful vision. Jay's tenor filled the room with a panting song.

"Master, I, I need, I'm gonna—" Jay sucked in a breath. "Do you want me to stop?"

"No," he murmured. "I want you to come."

He darted a hand toward their joining and stopped just above to grip the slippery bundle of nerves peeking out from beneath its hood.

"Come for my boy, Naomi." He pinched and twisted.

Her wail matched Jay's whimper. Her body, unable to budge the table, smacked against the sealed wood as she shook. Jay's thrusts lost coherence and rhythm altogether. Thrice more he drove forward before rocking to a stop, her body shuddering around his.

Henry stroked her thighs with a fluttering touch as he pressed kisses to Jay's back. His cock throbbed with insistent demand. Open his slacks, bend his submissive forward, test that snug fit. He held his hips back, denying himself pressure and relief both.

"A wondrous show, my boy." He nuzzled Jay's neck. "You've pleased me very much."

Jay sagged against his chest, a tentative weight as if he tested his boundaries. Accustomed to stricter, more unfeeling rules, perhaps. Fearing a reprimand.

Henry wrapped an arm around the younger man and clasped him close.

Jay rewarded his gesture with a satisfied sigh and a tiny wiggle.

A tilt of his hips kept Jay from brushing his erection. His submissive had best be still before he forgot himself and fucked him here and now.

Not a perfect night, but not a disaster, either. He'd count it a victory and hope Jay had learned to respect his worth. To see more to the lifestyle than the poor experiences to which he'd been subjected.

He grasped Jay's hand and guided him to the lip of the condom. "Hold tight and pull back."

Jay hadn't softened enough to create a problem yet, but teaching him best practices would help his reputation with other partners later. The thought nagged at him, an irritation he pushed aside. "Courtesy demands we not expose playmates to fluids unless such an exchange is negotiated."

Jay obeyed with a nod. His cock slid free.

Naomi flashed them both a lazy smile.

Sending Jay to discard the used condom in the biobox near the door, he lowered their temporary partner's legs and reached for her hands. "Up you go."

She rose, blinking and stretching.

"Steady?" He held on as she tested her legs.

Dark chocolate hair bobbed as she nodded. "I'll do, sir."

"Go and fetch your things, then. Your behavior was acceptable." More than, though she'd appreciate the lack of praise more than its application, at least until the game had ended.

"Thank you, sir." She scurried to her bag along the wall.

Cock limp and gleaming, Jay wandered back to his side. Studying first the empty table and its missing occupant and then his master, he tipped his head and furrowed his brow. "You're not—" Jay gestured at the woman donning her robe.

"A moment, my boy." Laying a swift kiss on Jay's cheek, he reined in his arousal. His eagerness to paint his partner. His cock rubbing a hole through his slacks.

He crossed to Naomi and gripped her shoulders with a strength she'd appreciate. "Submissive Naomi, I release you from our game and thank you for your service."

She thanked him with solemn dignity in return. Her feet arched with delicate strength as she raised up on her toes.

He bent his head.

"It was more fun than I expected," she whispered. "I hope your boy appreciates how hard you work."

She slipped out the door without another word, leaving him alone with his not-quite-lover and a cock aching for release.

Well. What the woman found degrading, Jay would find empowering. Acceptance. A kind of claiming. He wouldn't deny it tonight, not for himself or Jay either. Next week would be soon enough to begin letting his student go. To usher him out into a wider world. Tonight, Jay was still his.

"Go and sit on the sofa, my boy." He spoke without turning to see his submissive. "Lean back. Spread your arms along the top, please."

Waiting, he listened to Jay's movements. The rustle of fabric as he sat. At the expectant silence, he turned.

"Yes, just like that." Four strides brought him to the sofa. He stood between Jay's spread knees. "Thank you."

A beautiful nude canvas. He slipped his belt free of the buckle. Flicked open the clasp. Paused to appreciate Jay's wide eyes and parted lips.

"Just for me, Master Henry?" Shining adoration and trusting obedience mingled in Jay's eyes. Humble pleasure flowed from his mouth.

"I save my best work for my best boy."

The beaming smile in return made his cock thump. Pressure alone started the slow click of a falling zipper.

He took himself in hand with a quiet grunt. He'd be as fast to finish as his sub tonight, it seemed. A terrible example after he'd focused Jay's homework on slowing his masturbation routine for so many weeks.

The desire to claim his submissive overrode his usual practice. Watching Jay play and guiding his actions embodied the exquisite, excruciating foreplay he craved.

His breath came fast. He locked gazes with Jay, the warm depths of those blackstrap molasses eyes sparking with excitement. The sensation of his hand faded in favor of a more desirable vision, Jay in his arms and his cock working slow and deep.

Jay clenched the slipcover on the sofa. His chest rose and fell, a beautiful target in motion. His gaze dropped. Squirming, he whined an urgent plea.

A low growl escaped Henry's throat as the first streaks of white arced over Jay's lap and landed at his sternum. Ejaculate ran down the firm chest in lazy rivers, a mark of ownership he ought to have resisted indulging.

The sight satisfied to a frightening degree. How much of his vaunted ideals would he willingly set aside to keep this young man under his control? What harm might he do thereby?

Jay lifted his hand and started toward his chest, arresting in mid-motion. "I—Master Henry—can I—"

"It's all right, my boy," he murmured between harsh breaths. "Have your taste."

Jay dragged his fingers through the sticky white glaze coating his skin and brought them to his mouth with all the joy of a gourmand sampling a culinary masterpiece. His sigh as his tongue tip touched his fingers expressed a fulfillment beyond words.

Would that he might satisfy his own desires as easily. They grew stronger each week, and Jay had yet to show him he had the will and the capability to make safe choices for himself. Until he did, claiming him in truth would be the worst sort of trespass.

Next week. Next week he'd test Jay's awareness and capabilities.

Impress me, my dear boy. Please. For both our sakes.

Chapter 7

Henry arrived at Victor and Emma's home early Friday evening to entertain his godson with a round of backgammon. Sharp for a six-year-old, Thomas nearly eked out a victory before his classmate's mother arrived to ferry him to a sleepover.

Emma served a delightful glazed salmon with baby potatoes for dinner, and the conversation sparkled. She carried dessert to the table with customary grace, delivering what looked to be a sublime pecan tart. A whiff of caramel invited investigation.

The end of a fine evening before the painful night ahead.

Fork raised, he set the edge against the point of his pecan wedge. The closer he came to the crust, the closer he would be to introducing his student to other dominants. Ones known to him, of course, whom he'd approached in advance to facilitate negotiation training. None who'd try to take Jay tonight, and yet. . . .

Foolish, superstitious, to believe leaving the tart untouched would be to leave Jay untouched as well.

"Does it distress you also, Henry?"

Dragged from self-absorption, he hummed an inquiry. "The tart, Em? It appears scrumptious. Surely you aren't distressed about the state of your culinary arts."

She shook her head with light laughter.

"The unevenness of our table. Party of three? You ought to bring a friend next time." She cocked her brow and tipped her head in a teasing maternal challenge. "You've had dinner with the boy what, three times now? A record, I'm sure."

The reminder pricked his heart. Fingers tightening on the fork, he managed a flat reply. "Three times, yes."

She returned her attention to her dessert with a graceful shrug.

"What would be the harm in bringing him out of the club? Or isn't he good enough for that?"

Rage hammered at his ribs that anyone should so name Jay. As if he didn't desire a deeper relationship with the sweetest submissive boy he'd ever met. As if he hadn't filled his studio with sketches of Jay in every conceivable pose, with every expression, showing every line and shadow of his musculature. He blinked back the sting in his eyes.

"Emma." Victor cut through the silence. "Go upstairs and wait for me."

Her quiet gasp drew his attention as she rose to her feet. She stared at him with wide eyes and a rapidly paling face etched with regret. "May I apologize to our guest first, husband?"

"You may not. You may reflect upon the value of holding your sharp tongue. Go, and let the prick of conscience keep you company while you await your punishment."

The click of her heels on hardwood echoed as she crossed the dining room and the foyer and climbed the stairs.

Henry gazed at the ceiling and expelled a slow breath until he'd emptied his lungs.

Victor ventured to the sideboard, poured two fingers of brandy, and set the glass in front of him with a thud. "Henry?"

"She's right, you know." He curled his fingers around the glass. "The boy is more than good enough."

"I've never seen you so rattled and indecisive." Victor's trademark mixture of gentle brusqueness, the art of inquiring without inquiring.

"He's perfect for me." The sip of brandy burned going down. "Except in all the ways he's not."

"Namely?"

"He's still a child at twenty-five. No serious relationships, no experience." Jay's gentle naiveté was itself a temptation, but he refused to pluck such tender fruit. Shut off all avenues before young Mr. Kress had explored them. Deny him the pleasures of youth when he himself had been granted time for adventuring.

His own desire to find a serious partner had only manifested in the last few years as he'd watched Victor hover over Emma and their son. A family of his own would be a blessing. Forcing Jay to that maturity at twenty-five would be unkind, no matter how much he desired him.

"So you'll teach him." Victor eased into his chair with his own glass cupped in his palm. "The first time I saw my beloved, she was sixteen. Poised and perfect, even at that age." He raised his glass, studying the color in the light. "The daughter of my newest business partner. Utterly off-limits for years. She had her youthful dalliances, and I kept my distance."

"Precisely. You kept your distance." As he intended to do, once he'd gotten Jay settled. "The boy's past experience is all with women. He hadn't confronted or explored other desires until six months ago, and every bit of it is tied up in his confusion about his submissive desires."

His mentor shook his head. "Don't put words in my mouth, Henry. I kept my distance out of respect for her age, not her inexperience."

Victor drained the glass and set the empty tumbler on the table. "If the boy wants a woman, what of it? I've seen you play with any number of women. Didn't you procure one for him last week? Encourage the boy's flings. Vanilla, if it'll keep him safer. He'll gain experience, and you'll be satisfied you aren't denying, suffocating, or controlling him beyond what he needs. Pick the women yourself if his fragility concerns you."

True, he had, and Naomi had been discreet. She'd done well with Jay, even if playing with another submissive wasn't her usual choice. Perhaps he might search for a woman who suited them both.

"You know all of these things, Henry. So what is your true concern?" Victor leaned forward in his seat. "What is it that so frightens you about this boy?"

"I want to take him home." He closed his eyes and let the words reverberate in his mind. The first time he'd said them aloud. A soaring freedom and a crushing weight both.

"So you'll admit my darling wife was right, and we'll all have a toast to—"

"*Home* home, Victor." Opening his eyes, he pushed his glass past his plate with two fingers. "I've known the boy less than two months. I can count the number of times I've met him on two hands. Yet I want him to meet my mother. I want to take him home and tie him to my bed and fuck him until he can't stand, and then I want to clean him up and buy him a proper suit and introduce him to my mother. I'm at sea. The boy touches something in me."

"Years of searching and not finding," Victor murmured. "But once you have, the rewards are vast and immeasurable."

"If I tell him, he'll agree just to please me. I won't shackle him with that."

Wouldn't he? Hadn't he spent an inordinate amount of time at dinner staring at Emma's neckline? The collar she wore, the pearl choker no one outside their circle would suspect of being more than a favorite piece of jewelry. To her, to Victor, the meaning far surpassed such simplicity.

If Jay held out his arms, wouldn't he lock bracelets around his wrists and claim him for his own? A symbol of submission, of ownership, Jay might wear in all the hours they were apart. The thought tantalized him.

"It can work despite the age difference, Henry." Victor interjected a lighthearted air with his shrug. "He may truly know what he wants. Emma did, and she was far younger than your boy. And if he doesn't, and he leaves, you'll still have taught him how to handle himself in an adult relationship and safe play."

"What if he stays," Henry whispered. "What if he's confused and unhappy but he stays to please me."

"Then you'll break it off gently when you see his unhappiness." Soft lines formed around Victor's encouraging smile. "He won't be able to hide it from you. I've seen him with you in the club. His feelings are plain on his face. He's not the lost boy he was seven weeks ago. You'd know. Trust yourself. You have years of experience to draw upon."

"It's more difficult when the feelings are so strong." Never had they been this tethered to his heart.

"It always is." Victor turned toward the stairs. "If your feelings for this boy are as strong as mine for my Emma, you'll never tire of making the effort—and you'll be amply rewarded for it. To have such dedicated service is a thing of beauty."

"A joy for ever," he murmured. Keats rolled through his mind. *Its loveliness increases; it will never Pass into nothingness; but still will keep A bower quiet for us, and a sleep Full of sweet dreams, and health, and quiet breathing.*

Victor sighed. "You want to offer the boy choices because you wish to be certain he has nothing but the best for himself. You're overlooking a flaw in your design. You want this for him because you love him. Nothing the others offer him could be better for him than your love." His gaze strayed to the stairs once more. "I guarantee you that, Henry."

"He has built me up in his mind, Victor." He could not be all Jay needed. "I am not the paragon of virtue he believes me to be." He'd stumble. He'd fail. Jay deserved perfection. "I'm no more than a man like any other, making uncertain choices. I am not a god."

"Aren't you?" An arrogant unconcern showed itself in Victor's tone. He raised his hand as if to question the importance of such insignificant detail. "He worships you, and you answer his prayers. Is it any wonder the boy believes you a god? Farm him out to others if you must, but don't believe you do it for the boy's sake."

"All I've done for the last two months has been for the boy's sake!" He shoved the chair back as he stood, slapping his hands flat on the table's edge, his breath bellowing like a bull's.

"Yet you'd abandon him now." Victor stood to meet him, rising at a more deliberate pace, his eyes unyielding. "Why do you allow your fear to hold you back? Love demands more of you. Whether master or servant, we are all of us slaves to love."

He swallowed hard and dipped his head in acknowledgment. Victor's wisdom cut as deep as Emma's insight. They'd hunted tonight, flushed him from the undergrowth and given chase. His dread intensified.

A vibration at his hip signaled a call. The club.

"The boy will be waiting," he murmured. "And you've your own matters to attend to. We're still on for next week?"

"Of course, Henry. My wife will consider it a delicious recompense for her misstep tonight."

Henry stepped into the grand salon seventeen minutes after hanging up the phone. Having followed his instructions with precision, Jay waited in his play shorts and his ribbon in a quiet corner. The mere sight of him eased Henry's tumbling thoughts and imposed a kind of order. Attention to Jay took priority. His own turmoil would wait.

Standing at his approach, Jay lacked the eager, wiggling energy he associated with him. The thin smile and slumped shoulders bespoke weariness. A long week?

Impatient to assess his boy, he quickened his steps, threading around the clutches of players chatting. The hastily bowed head deepened the shadows under Jay's eyes.

"You look tired, my sweet boy." Cupping Jay's chin, he nudged upward until their gazes leveled. "Have you been ill this week?"

"No, Master Henry." Listless. Lethargic. "I feel fine." Faded, Jay resembled a painting left hanging in direct sunlight year after year. "I'm ready to play."

He let his hand fall. "I don't believe you are."

"Please, Master Henry, I want to play." Jay leaned forward, a full-body motion matching the quiet desperation in his tone.

"Then you'll tell me why you appear so exhausted."

"I just didn't sleep good. I'll do better next week, I promise." Wide, hopeful eyes watched him.

Jay hadn't appeared so sleepless in previous weeks. Some catalyst had caused his insomnia.

"Have there been more difficulties at work?" If Jay's insufferable co-worker had harassed him again, stronger action would be required.

"Diffi—oh." Jay shook his head. "He hasn't spoken to me in a couple weeks. It's nice, I guess. I mean, I still hate the work, but I don't hafta avoid the bathroom anymore."

Excellent. At least he'd managed to do one good thing for young Mr. Kress. "What has kept you awake so late this week?"

Jay shrugged. "I dunno. Stuff." He scuffed one sandal on the rug. "Are we going to play a new game tonight, Master Henry?"

He'd never need worry about Jay becoming a scheming, demanding submissive. Jay hadn't the skill for guile or deception. Any topic he wished to deflect, however, was one worth pursuing.

"Perhaps we won't play anything at all if you cannot provide straightforward answers to my questions." Pleased with Jay's small gasp, he hardened his tone. "What has kept you from sleeping?"

Silence. He waited. His patience more than matched any stubbornness or embarrassment his submissive could conjure.

"I have nightmares," Jay mumbled. "Since . . . the thing."

Cal's assault. Not unexpected, but Jay had never mentioned nightmares, and he'd arrived well-rested on previous nights. Henry opened his mouth to speak.

Jay hung his head. "I couldn't fall back to sleep. I didn't feel safe."

A tiny whisper followed, so soft he couldn't be certain he'd heard correctly.

"My sheets didn't smell right."

Understanding came close to buckling his knees.

Not wanting to share his sheets with another partner, he hadn't brought a set for their game last week. He knew Jay considered them a reward, perhaps even a tangible reminder of his ownership. He hadn't considered how much emotion his student had invested in the fabric. How soothing his scent would be for Jay. How distressing a change in the routine would be.

Idiot.

His oversight had left Jay frightened and alone in his bed each night. Waking in a sweaty panic without the comfort he'd grown to rely upon.

Opening his arms, he reached for his submissive. "Come here, my boy."

He cradled Jay in a strong embrace, his arms wound tight around Jay's back. Still Jay pressed closer, nuzzling at his throat and trying to sink into him.

"The fault is mine, dear boy. I'm so sorry to have overlooked your need."

God help him if he left Jay now. He'd created the very dependency he'd sworn not to. A breach of ethics. He'd failed to control his own damnable desire to have some claim on Jay outside these walls. What options had he left open to the boy?

A casual, part-time dominant might accept Jay's kink for sleeping on another man's sheets, but Jay needed a more stable, caring relationship than the occasional play date could provide. Explaining the sheet situation to a vanilla partner, if the younger man found one, would be impossible.

"I've sheets for you in my bag tonight. If I neglect to pass them over before the end of the night, you're to remind me, hmm?" He berated himself in silence, a wave of regret washing through him. "We want you well-rested, safe and sound in your bed each night."

He rubbed circles across Jay's back.

"Master Henry?"

"Yes?" He laid his cheek against dark hair. The warmth of Jay's breath on his neck recalled pleasant thoughts.

"Have you ever collared anyone?"

He squeezed his submissive, his fingers moving without input from his brain. Jay meant to give him a coronary. In the months the younger man had spent at the club, it hadn't seemed he'd acquired much knowledge of tradition and protocol.

Henry forced blandness into his voice. "I didn't realize you were familiar with the custom."

"I told Mistress Emma her necklace was nice when she took me shopping for my suit."

Weeks ago. Weeks and weeks ago.

"She explained how it wasn't just a necklace and how proud she was to wear it. To belong."

More of Emma's meddling. If she hadn't been so accurate in her assessment of Jay's suitability for him, he'd ask Victor to let him discipline her himself. As it was, he might yet. Had Jay wondered and worried all this time?

"No, I have never collared a submissive of my own." Though imagination provided an image of one now, Jay with collar and cuffs and cock ring monogrammed with his master's initials, a magnificent sight. "I find the aesthetic often displeases me."

He slipped in a teasing tone and nipped at Jay's ear. "And I prefer free access to my boy's neck."

Squirming in his arms, Jay giggled like a child. Better. Not whole, but on the path to recovery. Just as well his plans for the night didn't involve a lengthy sexual scene. An orgasm might put Jay to sleep on his feet.

He'd made arrangements in advance with four colleagues to ease his submissive into the dynamics of negotiating a scene with a new partner. Two women, two men. A fair sampling of attitudes and styles. The lessons would be useful, even if Jay didn't end up needing the skills immediately.

He pressed a final kiss to Jay's hair. "Are you ready to play?"

"I'm ready, Master Henry." Jay gained warmth and liveliness.

"Wonderful." He slipped his hands down Jay's toned arms and interlaced their fingers. "We'll be starting the night by speaking to other dominants. I want you to practice your negotiation skills."

"You want me to negotiate with you for more things?" Jay cocked his head to the side, eyebrows drawn together. "Is this because of the sheets, Master Henry?"

He squeezed Jay's hands. "Negotiation is a valuable safety skill

for a submissive to cultivate for any situation. You'll be negotiating—
but not concluding—deals with other dominants this evening. I want
to see what you've learned from our time together."

Jay flinched. Disappointment rolled down his face. His gaze
dropped. "Yes, Master Henry."

"Come along, then." He tried to interject a chipper note, but success eluded him.

The mood suffocated him as he led his submissive by the hand to
the third floor. They made a somber, funereal procession amid the
levity, and the more astute players gave them a wide berth.

He owed Jay this, whether the boy wanted it or not. This was the
training he'd promised. The safety skills Jay needed. He would reward Jay at the end of the night, though in truth he'd lost all such appetite since he'd raised his fork over a decadent pecan tart. He'd never
taken that first bite.

Bypassing the themed rooms, he guided Jay straight to the demonstration hall where players mingled. The central platform sat unused,
the spotlights off for the moment. Less extraneous stimuli to distract
his companion, he hoped.

He cast his gaze around the room and spied a familiar face speaking to another player. She looked up, and he nodded. After a brief
touch to the other player's shoulder, she started toward them.

"I'll make the introductions, my boy, but then I want you to conduct the negotiation. I'll stay right here beside you, but the words will
be your own."

"Yes, Master Henry." Jay bore the petulant attitude of a teenager
vacationing with his parents. No time now to correct him.

"Gretchen." He spread his hands in welcome. "It's lovely to see
you. The corset design is quite fetching. One of yours?"

Gretchen ran a hand down the side of the fabric, black lacey pockets between creamy leather straps and antiqued rivets. The full black
skirt beneath no doubt hid a fine pair of boots. She'd always had a
steampunk flair, and the style suited her curvaceous form.

"Lara's, but I'll tell her you said so. She worked weeks on this
one, Henry." Her gaze drifting, she widened her smile. Tight curls in
an unnatural deep vermilion bobbed against her cheeks as she tipped
her head. "What a delicious-looking friend you have today."

"Gretchen, this is my very good boy, Jay." He laid a hand against

Jay's back in a reassuring sweep, but the submissive's posture remained stiff. He'd angered his boy. If the practice protected Jay, he'd accept this sullen distance a thousand times over. "Jay, say hello to Mistress Gretchen, please."

"Hello, Mistress Gretchen." The bare minimum of parroting courtesy escaped his mouth.

Henry offered Gretchen a tight smile. He'd expected this exercise would be difficult for Jay for other reasons, but the younger man had never displayed discourtesy before. Sleep deprivation and anger mixed about as well as a blend of purple and orange. Muddy and unusable.

Gretchen laughed like a champ. "Oh, lift your head, sugar. I want to see those eyes when I talk to you."

Jay graced him with every truculent teen's do-I-have-to expression.

A glare and a nod set him straight.

"Mmm, look at you, like melty chocolate drops. Will you do a little turn for me, Jay?" She twirled her finger in unnecessary example. "Slow, all the way around?"

She'd unquestionably delivered on the marker he'd called in. Bubbly, eager to engage, working hard to draw Jay into the game.

Jay gave a perfunctory turn.

His master held back a sigh.

"You are just a scrumptious little cupcake. I could eat you up. Are you free to play with me, Jay?"

Jay flinched and withdrew a half step.

Henry quelled the urge to reach for him. If Jay meant to play at the club, he'd have to handle such questions with grace unless he expected to wear a red ribbon on every visit for the rest of his life. A pushy dominant, friendly or not, demanded an assertive response from an uninterested sub.

"I, I, I don't know." Jay tossed a glance in his direction. "No. I don't think so. I'm, I'm Master Henry's boy."

Holding a neutral expression in the face of Jay's uncertainty challenged him more than capturing the younger man's sleek lines to perfection in his sketchbook. The rejected attempts littered his studio. He'd held out hope Jay would offer a proper "no" without hesitation.

Gretchen matched Jay's movement to maintain the closer distance. "What you need is a babysitter for the night, sugar."

"I'm too old for a babysitter." Disdain dripped from Jay's mouth. Rude, but acceptable. At least his submissive hadn't agreed.

She advanced with a predatory, sweeping gaze. "Mm-hmm, yes—you—are. That's the point, cupcake. You must've played this game before."

"No I haven't." Jay retreated.

Henry stood with tense muscles. Any more of this, and he'd have to clear a path behind his submissive to allow their dance to continue. Gretchen had obeyed his request that she not touch the boy, but he hadn't issued a moratorium on pursuit.

"Then you're a fast learner, aren't you, Jay?" Sashaying forward, Gretchen flashed a coy smile over her shoulder and mouthed, *relax, Henry*. "Why don't we give your master a night out on his own? You can stay in with your sitter. Maybe he'll come home and find you with her."

Jay gaped at her, eyes and mouth wide. "No, *never*. I'm Master Henry's good boy."

"Even good boys can be naughty sometimes, sugar." She dropped her voice to a low tease. "Maybe you need a little discipline."

He held his breath waiting for Jay's response. Here was the true test. A nice, firm *no* and a *thank you for your time, Mistress* and Gretchen would politely take her leave so he might heap lavish praise on his partner.

Jay studied the floor in lingering silence.

"Would you like that, Jay?" Gretchen gave a gentle push, a direct inquiry a submissive couldn't ignore. "An illicit affair with your sitter after she disciplines you for being such a sassy boy?"

Jay shrugged. "I guess so, Mistress." He directed his words to his shuffling feet. "I must've been bad or Master Henry wouldn't go out and leave me for the night. I should be punished."

Failure thrust into his chest like a railroad spike taking its final drive into the track. He shook his head even before Gretchen looked back for his direction. Pushing further would be cruel and irrelevant if Jay couldn't deliver the answer he needed to. Fear for Jay's safety sparked rising anger that the younger man would use their arrangement as an excuse to accept a game Henry knew damn well he didn't want to play.

"Well, you keep thinking about what you want, cupcake." Gretchen left off the predatory edge in her voice, all sweet understanding and kindness now. "If you decide on something fun, and your master says it's okay, you come look me up and we'll give this another try."

Jay stood still and silent, his head bowed.

Gretchen touched Henry's elbow as she passed, pausing at his side. "Sorry, Henry," she murmured. "Good luck with your boy."

"Thank you, Gretchen." He equaled her quiet tone, though Jay seemed oblivious to his surroundings in any case. "Your patience was much appreciated."

She squeezed his arm, and then she was gone.

"Jay." He called the name with quiet steel. "Come here and explain to me why you aren't treating this exercise seriously."

Jay jerked his neck and slunk over with dragging feet.

"Well?"

"I don't wanna play with her. I wanna play with you. Why don't you wanna play with me, Master Henry?" Childish insecurity thinned his submissive's tenor.

Anger draining away, Henry cupped Jay's cheeks. Petulance borne of fear, not adolescent rebellion, drove his gentle partner. That, at least, he might do something about.

"I very much enjoy playing with you. But I cannot show others how proud I am of you if your behavior makes you unsafe in their company, now can I?" He shook his head in slow motion and mirrored the movement with Jay's head in his hands. "This exercise is about your personal safety. Nothing is more important to me than that, do you understand?"

"If you care so much, why do you want me to play with other people?" Jay's wide, soft, pleading eyes peeked from deep-set shadows. "I don't need them. I just need you, Master Henry."

"I know you feel that way today, my boy. We've bonded quite well in these last few weeks." Stroking his thumbs over Jay's cheeks, he memorized the soft skin above the scruff against his palms, tracing the edge where rough gave way to smooth.

"I will always be here to advise you." He'd abandoned the idea of cutting ties next week. He couldn't do it. The relationship would come to its natural end when Jay was ready, even if the break left Henry bereft. "But surely there are others here you'd enjoy playing with equally well. Women, perhaps? If we're ever to loosen the restrictions on your attendance, you must learn these skills."

"You want me to play with other people." Jay repeated the words with the sting of rejection attached.

"Not necessarily." No, he didn't truly want that in the slightest. But Jay would, eventually, and he'd never ask if he thought the request would displease his master. Better openness now than resentment later.

He'd seen the pattern in countless relationships around him, in infinite variation. One couldn't play in the same club for a dozen years and fail to recognize it. The initial wariness of strangers gave way to trust after the first good scene. The trust grew into dependence and a hint of worship as the submissive entered a honeymoon phase of euphoria in which the dominant could do no wrong.

The cracks emerged. Disaffection and dissatisfaction dominated when a soul-deep connection failed to materialize. An off night and over-high expectations conspired to spill resentment and unhappiness. Three months, perhaps six, and the tide turned. Matches like Victor and Emma's were rare here, where players ever sought something new and different. Fresh faces to manipulate. Unexplored kinks to plumb.

Jay's rush of relief at finding a dominant to guide him enhanced his euphoria, but the need would diminish as it often did. The blinders would come off, and he'd see his master as a man beyond this role. The demands of a full relationship would make certain of it. Authority figures—parents, teachers, the idols of youth—crumbled. He would fare no better.

Striving always to leave his play partners better off than he'd found them, he'd never stayed long enough for those cracks to harm them. He'd never been attached to one the way he'd become attached to Jay.

Could Jay be seeking the same long-term, bone-deep love he himself did? Would their compatibility withstand the test of time and the mundanity of everyday life?

A fanciful, unlikely notion. He owed Jay this training in either case. He cleared his throat, an unnecessary tactic, as Jay's attention hadn't wandered during his overlong silence.

"I want you to assert yourself in negotiations, my boy."

"You want me to ask for what I want?"

"Yes. Respect and courtesy are excellent tools to cultivate for such sensitive topics, but your voice *must* carry equal weight. This holds true for any initial discussion of desires, no matter how submissive you choose to be afterward. Your submission is a choice, and you honor your chosen dominant by making it, but your safety comes first."

Jay fingered the red ribbon on his right bicep. "I understand, Master Henry." His expression slid into a frown and an adorable pinch of concentration between his brows. "I'll try harder to show you what I want."

He beheld Jay's guileless face through narrowed eyes. So little talent for subterfuge, yet something was most certainly afoot. Sighing, he kissed his submissive's forehead. "Thank you for trying. That's all I ask. Let's meet another young woman, shall we?"

A coiled pile of blond braids caught his eye.

"Come along." He held out his hand, and Jay seized it. He gave the younger man a reassuring squeeze. "Remember to assert yourself, please."

He wove through the crowd with his submissive matching his steps.

The statuesque blonde preferred a vinyl look. Striking when captured in a single moment, but a burden for lengthy scenes. The mix of talc and sweat beneath unbreathable fabric didn't appeal. Still, the thigh-high black boots and matching opera gloves made a lovely frame for the pink baby-doll nightie swaying about her hips. He intended to show Jay a variety, and so he would.

"Silke, if you've a moment for us now?"

Turning, the blonde displayed a brilliant smile and no small amount of cleavage. "Henry, as if you need to ask. You know I always have time for you. This is your new boy?"

"Indeed he is. Silke, this is Jay." He squeezed Jay's hand and let go. "Jay, say hello to Mistress Silke, please."

"Is your name really silky?"

He growled out the boy's name in warning. Silke wouldn't take offense during this exercise, but God forbid Jay behave in such a way outside his presence.

"Is yours a name or a letter, little boy?" Silke leaned into his submissive's space.

Jay didn't back away. Progress on one front, though they'd have to review the precise meaning of "assertive" and where it intersected with "courtesy" and "respect."

"I'm not little, I'm Master Henry's." Jay stood tall, squaring his shoulders, and Henry breathed easier.

"Well then, Master-Henry's-Jay." She teased out the syllables in a singsong rhythm. "What interests you? What are you seeking to play with?"

Jay's gaze flicked to his master.

Trepidation stole over him. The urge to pre-empt Jay's answer had him stretching out a hand without conscious thought.

"Do you have a cock, Mistress? Because that's what I really want. One especially."

He gripped Jay's elbow. "You'll apologize to Silke for your manners tonight."

Jay gazed at him with wounded incomprehension. "But I said what I wanted."

The beginnings of a headache pulsed behind his eyes. Jay had followed his instructions. In the rudest way possible, and with a single-minded focus that betrayed just how deeply he'd bound this submissive to him despite every promise he'd made to himself not to.

Light laughter halted his self-recrimination.

"He's fine, Henry. I won't fault your boy for a bit of cheekiness. The feisty ones are more fun."

"Thank you, Silke. Nevertheless, the boy will apologize not for what he said, but for his rudeness. Jay."

"I'm sorry for how I said what I said, Mistress." Jay shifted his weight and dipped his head.

"Apology accepted, Master-Henry's-boy." Silke flashed a raised eyebrow at Henry and tilted her head toward his submissive. *You've got your hands full*, her look said. "To answer your impertinent question, I'm cis, not trans, so no, I don't have a bio cock. But I own more than enough cocks big enough to peg your slender frame."

Jay said nothing, but neither did his body tense. Odd. Given Cal's assault, the suggestion of anal play should have drawn a strong negative reaction.

"Is that what you want, Jay?" Silke cajoled. "A nice strong mistress pegging you all night?"

"If that makes you happy, Mistress," Jay mumbled.

Another failure. Wonderful. Jay had no filters, no concept of the sweet spot. He blundered about like Goldilocks in a stranger's home, first too submissive, then too assertive, then submissive once more. He required a better understanding of *just right*.

"No, he won't be trying it tonight." Henry smiled despite the headache now throbbing. "Please excuse us, Silke."

"Of course, Henry. When he's ready to try it, I'd be happy to give him a lesson, but I suspect you already have plans to fill that position yourself." She winked at him and returned to her prowl. She'd find a partner before the end of the night with no trouble if she chose. Silke always did.

He stepped in front of his submissive. "Define 'pegging' for me."

Jay squirmed under his gaze and refused to meet his eyes. Shrugging, he whispered, "I dunno, Master Henry."

"You agreed to play a game without knowing what it entails." He tried, he truly did, to keep anger and fear from leaking into his voice.

"I, I got nervous. I didn't know what to say. I couldn't help it, Master Henry. I just . . . couldn't."

A "yes" would always be easier for Jay than a "no." The desire to agree, to please, was hard-wired into him. Part of the canvas rather than the paint.

"Do you understand how that behavior terrifies me, my boy? I want you safe." He shoved aside an image of Jay leashed to his bed until he'd learned how to conduct himself. Such an energetic man wouldn't do well denied an outlet for his excitement.

"I know. You said." Jay's flat delivery teetered toward depression. "You want me safe so you can leave me."

Pain. Pain like the dull scrape of a palette knife peeling his skin one layer at a time. He'd never told Jay in so many words, and now he'd hurt him by leaving room for too much confusion and misinterpretation between them.

"I thought I did, that's true." He lowered his voice, mindful of the people milling around them, an uncomfortable oasis in a sea of sensuality. "But not because you are in any way lacking."

He tugged at Jay's wrist and stepped closer. "I stress safety with you, both asserting yourself in negotiation and using your safeword in scenes, precisely because you have such difficulty displeasing others."

Failing to teach Jay these skills, to make him understand the power he held, was unthinkable. Jay's needs would never be met. He'd be prey for any less than ethical dominant. A constant temptation.

"A dominant's role is to make fantasies real. If you describe your fantasies to me, I may choose whether to enact them. If I describe mine to you, you will agree with them simply to agree. I must be so very careful with you, my precious boy."

Jay's hoarse cries yet haunted his dreams. Watching him return to the same treatment because he'd failed to teach him better would be intolerable. Conceding on this point wasn't possible, even if he kept Jay himself. For Jay's safety and his own sanity.

Nightmare scenarios swept through him in a flash flood. If he let Jay out of his sight and found him bloodied in the hands of another. If he forgot himself and Jay feared to safeword.

Jay needed to learn that his own needs mattered. That his master ought to consider them—to put them first, in a sense, because there could be no dominance without submission. Jay's self-worth was so low, but he craved better. Henry refused to fail him in this. He refused to become the man wielding the whip in Jay's nightmares.

Swallowing hard, he shook his head. "Would you have me become your abuser, my boy? Is that the role you envision for me?"

White-faced, the shadows beneath his eyes standing out like bruises, Jay whipped his head in a firm *no*.

"I'm sorry, Master Henry." The thickness in his voice presaged sobs. "I was being selfish. I didn't think about how I'm burdening you. I thought it was just about other people. I'll try harder. I swear I will."

Wrapping his arms around his companion, Henry hummed a few measures of calming nonsense. "You are no burden but a gift. The harder you try, the better you will protect that gift."

Once Jay understood his own strength, he could make a proper choice for himself. Be selective. And, perhaps, choose to stay with him. The choice must be Jay's, even if it was the only one he made for himself from that point forward, else the submission was meaningless. Not a gift but an edict Jay felt compelled to follow.

"Master Henry?"

The whisper at his throat almost made the pain at his temples tolerable. "Yes?"

"What game did I agree to play?"

He sighed. "Pegging is a form of anal penetration, my boy. Silke was offering to don a harness with a dildo and take you."

Jay shuddered in his arms. "I don't, I don't wanna do that, Master Henry."

"No, I know, my sweet boy."

No anal play. No bondage. No impact play. No verbal degradation or humiliation. Nothing overtly childish.

With so many options blocked off for now, Jay would have trouble finding another suitable partner at the club. Or at least finding one who wouldn't require things he shouldn't give but would give anyway at the first hint of a request.

His submissive wasn't ready for negotiations. Continuing would be pointless. He ought to have called a halt to the night from the beginning. Selfish to allow Jay to play at his level of exhaustion. He'd let his own desire to spend time in Jay's company overrule his judgment. The right thing to do now was to take the younger man downstairs, hand over his set of sheets, and send him home to bed.

He rubbed Jay's back, hard and swift, before putting distance between them.

"Finally!" The familiar drawl came from behind him. "I thought you'd never stop hugging that adorable half-naked boy, Henry. However am I to seduce him away when you've unfairly imbalanced the playing field?"

"Not tonight, please, Will." He turned to greet his oldest friend. "We've changed our plan for the evening."

"Ah, stealing the boy away for some private time, are you? Well, I'd hardly blame you." Will's broad smile formed a slash of pink peeking out above his blond beard before he flashed white teeth. "Will you at least make introductions before you spirit him away? I really must meet the boy who has so captivated you for weeks now. We haven't watched a performance together in two months, so single-minded you've been about seeing this boy."

He would have ignored the teasing pokes, apologized to Will for the waste of his time tonight, and walked away were it not for Jay. He hung on Will's every word, casting glances up from his bowed head, standing taller as every sentence registered.

"The boy must have magical properties, Henry. Not to worry, I'll ferret out the spell he's keeping you under if you'll only introduce us." Will rubbed his hands together with undisguised glee.

The crashing in his skull resembled a toddler with a drum kit.

Will's playfulness wouldn't improve on the situation, but the man had been closer to him than a brother since they were eleven years old. And Jay wore a small smile. With the rest of the night having gone so abysmally, anything making his submissive smile was worth suffering through.

"Will, please meet Jay, my very best boy who's having a bit of difficulty with his instructions tonight. Jay, please say hello to my good friend Master William."

Jay squared his shoulders and took a breath. "I'm honored to meet you, Master William. I hope, umm, I hope my behavior brings pride to my master."

Blinking back his shock, Henry halted the tic in his neck attempting to whip his head around to gape. Was Jay finally giving this exercise the seriousness it deserved? God knew Will didn't know the meaning of the word. He'd test Jay's responses with proper care, but seriousness had never settled well on Will's shoulders.

"I'm certain it must, young Jay." Will extended his hand, pulling back as Jay's hand twitched and started to rise. "Terribly sorry, what was I thinking? I know better than to touch a red-ribboned boy without his master's permission. I'm lucky to be speaking to you at all, aren't I? No doubt your master is enormously protective of you. It must be quite boring for an exciting boy like yourself, wouldn't you say?"

Jay shook his head like a dog emerging from a pond. "No, not at all, Master William. Being with Master Henry is the best."

"Is it, now?" Will shot a glance at Henry from beneath raised eyebrows. "He's not a complete Grinch who won't let you play in any reindeer games?"

"Says Santa Claus himself," Henry murmured.

Jay chuckled before he caught himself and regained his composure.

Will winked. "You need more jolliness in your life, Henry. This one's all but gift-wrapped for you, I'd say." Leaning toward the younger man, Will lowered his voice. "A little cricket chirped in my ear that you look simply divine in a suit. Do you enjoy dressing to impress your dominants, young Jay?"

When had Will spoken to Emma? What else might she have mentioned?

Jay held steady, accepting the intrusion into his space without flinching. "I always want to look my best for Master Henry, sir. His opinion is the most important thing to me."

Nodding, Will backed off. "I've always found him a snappy dresser, if a bit fussy. Has Henry's neatness gotten to be too much for you?"

"No, sir, not at all. I'm happy I have Master Henry to teach me and give me tasks. He hands out the best praise after."

Jay's shy smile eased his heart. Perhaps he'd been wrong to present his submissive to women first. Or perhaps his own comfort with Will—nonthreatening, would-never-steal-his-boy Will—transmitted to Jay as well.

"So Henry's a kind master, then? Are you looking for the same treatment or different treatment from a new dominant?"

"The same, sir. The exact same. Master Henry is ideal."

"I can't imagine why you'd be looking for a new one if Henry's so perfect for you. Are you sure you want to leave him, young Jay?"

"Will," he growled, as Jay vigorously shook his head. "If you won't take this seriously, you're no help to the boy."

"Oh, I don't know about that, Henry. I think we've negotiated exactly what the boy wants."

Grinning broadly, Jay glanced at his master and cleared his throat. "Master William, can I ask you something?"

The pounding in Henry's head grew. With Will's teasing encouragement for a guide, Jay might conjure new levels of disobedient rudeness.

"Young Jay, my ears are burning with anticipation. You may."

"How do you feel about safewords, sir? My safety is important, and I won't risk it with just anybody."

He itched to clap, to pull Jay into an embrace, to fuse their lips and growl a challenge to every man and woman in the room. His beautiful student had learned well.

"What an intelligent and thoughtful question to ask. Someone must have been paying attention to his lessons." Will's approving smile would surely boost Jay's confidence. "They are imperative, of course. I control my lovely pets, but only with their consent."

Will extended three fingers and ticked them off one by one. "My submissives must be able to tell me their safeword, their preferred reward, and their hard limits without hesitation before negotiations even begin. Knowledge is power, young Jay, and like your master, I prefer to have as much power in my hands as possible. Has he asked those things of you?"

Henry refrained from snorting. As if he'd asked anything but.

"He keeps asking, Master William." Jay peeked at his master and gave a sheepish shrug. "I'm trying. I don't know all my answers yet."

"Ah, more lessons to come. This must be a thrilling time for you both. The rush of excitement." Will delivered an exaggerated sigh. "How sad for it to come to an end. That's the way of submissives, always moving on to greener pastures. You'll be a confident boy seeking a better master soon enough, won't you, Jay?"

"There aren't any better masters than mine," Jay retorted with heat. He froze in the midst of shifting his weight. "Um, I mean, I'm sure you're good, too, sir."

Will guffawed, his booming laughter drawing glances from the players nearby. "No, no, you're quite right, and your loyalty is a credit to your master's care of you and a testament to your devotion."

Henry breathed easier. Jay had survived. Stood up for himself. Remembered to ask about safewords. A solid beginning.

Will rounded on him. "Well, if it's not the boy's choice, it must be yours. Why are you trying to foist this boy off on me, Henry? Is he secretly disobedient?" He piled on teasing questions with all the subtlety of a punch to the jaw. "Have you grown tired of him? Is his sweetness too overwhelming for you?"

Amusement dissipated. The night had been long enough. He wanted nothing more than to climb into bed with his submissive at his side. Yet another desire destined to go unfulfilled.

"He is the perfect model of submission, Will. I won't play this game with you. I had my fill of it at dinner."

Jay cocked his head.

Wonderful. Now he'd made the younger man wonder how he'd spent his dinner hour and why they hadn't been together. Misstep after misstep tonight.

"You'll make the boy play a game you won't play yourself? Tsk tsk. Bad form, Henry. If you can't stand the heat, why are you shoving the boy into the kitchen?"

Squinting, he pressed two fingers to his forehead in a brief search for relief. "Quite right, Will. The boy's had enough of the kitchen tonight, and so have I. Say good night, Gracie."

He mustered up half a smile for his oldest friend, but Will dropped his joking demeanor in an instant. Once laughing eyes showed concern as he stepped closer.

"Good night, Henry," Will murmured. He clasped Henry's bicep, a quick squeeze. "You look a bit ragged. An early night would do you good. We ought to meet for lunch next week. I'll call you."

Backing away, Will gave Jay a flashy bow, his trademark grin back in place. "Jay, it was a delight to meet such a fine submissive with a level head about what he wants. I hope to have many opportunities to see you with your master in the future."

Jay dragged his feet on the steps.

Henry doubted lingering petulance contributed to the faltering stride. Jay had perked up under Will's questioning. Enjoyed seeing the tables turned and his master needled, perhaps, or needed the light-hearted attention.

No, exhaustion seemed the primary cause of Jay's sluggishness. The lack of sleep overtook youthful energy. Bundling Jay into a cab and calling it a night himself would be the best thing he might do for both of them.

He turned toward the second-floor desk to fetch the bags. Halfway into his third step, he stopped. Body awareness told him his submissive hadn't kept up. A swivel showed his companion standing at a full stop in the midst of traffic flowing to and from the stairs. Tugging Jay's wrist, he guided the stumbling submissive to the wall.

"Not long now." He lowered his voice as much to ease his own headache as for Jay's sake. "Just a change of clothes and home to bed with new sheets, hmm?"

Jay's dull nod failed to hide his longing glance. Not toward the changing rooms but the salon.

"Unless you'd rather something else?" Tipping Jay's chin up exposed raw need and resignation in deep brown eyes. "I'm sorry, my boy. I haven't attended to you properly at all tonight, have I? You deserve better from me. Would you like to sit and talk for a while?"

"Snuggle?" A squirming shrug accompanied Jay's quiet plea.

"Of course, my boy. As you like." For once, he hadn't relished the idea of continued conversation either. Peace and quiet, and the opportunity for comforting contact, would suit them both.

Jay's hand clasped in his, he meandered past the players chatting just inside the salon's open doors. A quick scan of the room showed him what he sought: one oversize chaise with a long back and a single high armrest.

Settling himself and Jay took but a few moments once he'd draped his suit coat over the side. His left leg lay stretched out on the chaise, his back in the corner and his right foot resting on the floor. Jay lay fully on the sofa, body in a fetal curl, his back to the rest of the room and his head tucked under his master's chin.

Jay's chest expanded as he yawned. He wiggled as he settled again. Low-grade arousal pulsed through Henry's veins, unhelpful and ignored. Jay needed stability. Security. And, yes, two or three orgasms a day when he wasn't battling a crippling need for sleep.

Threading his fingers through Jay's hair, he soothed with slow strokes that grew into a light massage. The silence breathed between them, calm and natural, no more worrisome than a gentle rain.

Twenty minutes, and his submissive no longer nudged his chest with his yawns. Despite the ambient noise and the light in the salon, Jay had dropped off to sleep as if they'd been in the womblike age-play reading room. Surrounded by strangers, Jay trusted him to guard his slumber.

As he had then, Henry held his tongue. Let him sleep. What harm would it do? His weight comforting, his steady breaths reassuring, his warmth a soporific of its own. Jay needed the rest. They needed this time together. Ease and relaxation drained the headache from his skull.

More than an hour passed before Jay stirred. A small, urgent whine. A kicking foot. The barest plea, head shaking, eyes closed. "Please don't make me."

Henry huddled close, arms wrapped around him, mouth at his ear. "I have you, Jay. You're safe, my brave boy. No one may touch you without your permission."

No, not without Jay's and not without his own if Jay failed to protect himself.

A hitching sob and another quiet whine had him holding his breath until his partner relaxed. He let the air out in a silent, mindful exhalation, paying attention to the steady current passing through his pursed lips.

The crowd around them thinned and changed. The eager mood of players preparing to go upstairs no longer dominated. Most either lingered in whatever scene they'd found on the upper floors or had returned, sated or dejected, to relax and decompress before heading elsewhere. Scanning the room with lazy disinterest, he paused.

Will raised a glass in a toast.

Well. It wasn't as though he hadn't thoroughly given himself away with his behavior upstairs. Cradling Jay as he slept wouldn't tell Will anything he didn't already realize. And perhaps. . . .

Better to let his boy sleep as long as he could manage. He extricated his hand from their embrace with care and beckoned to Will.

"You rang, Henry?" His voice low and rolling, Will stopped beside the back of the chaise and peered with interest at the slumbering submissive. "Good to see he's finally getting what he needs."

Accepting the chide without comment, he stroked Jay's spine. "A favor, please, Will. For the boy, if not for me. I pushed too hard tonight."

"For you and for the boy. I've had your back since we were eleven years old. Tell me it involves an unpleasant accident for a safeword-violating fuckwit, and you'll make me a happy man." He spread his hands, palms up, and brought them back together in a gesture of prayer.

"You ought to consult with Emma and Victor on the vengeance fantasies, Will." Though the image made him smile more than it ought. If his simmering anger toward Jay's attacker and his constant, nagging fear for Jay's welfare continued, he'd be arranging the counseling sessions he thought the younger man needed for himself instead. "I'd settle for knowing the boy will possess the will to stand up and say 'no' when the suspension ends and he sees his tormentor in these halls."

"You think he'd play with him again?" Concern, but not surprise, colored Will's voice.

"I'm afraid he won't be able to help himself." He twined his fingers in the short hair at the nape of Jay's neck. Coal-black strands, soft and slender. "He's fragile. And my protection is inadequate. I've let him down more than once now, I suspect."

"I don't think your boy sees it that way."

"No, he wouldn't say so, would he?" He shook his head. "But that's not what I intended to ask, Will."

"So ask. Whatever it is, you know I'll say yes, Henry. You're the closest thing to a brother I've got."

"Nothing so onerous. The desk has my bag. Would you bring it here? There's something in it I want."

"If by so doing I'll prevent you from displacing that beautiful boy from your lap, I will accept your charge with the humble servitude of the lowest page in your command, o king." Bowing with a teasing smile, Will backed away several steps before turning and striding from the room.

A boyhood nickname, King Henry, for his mantle of quiet authority. He'd named Will the Conqueror in return, for his prowess in the boxing ring, invading his opponents' space and driving them to the ropes. God, they'd been arrogant boys playing at chivalry and knighthood.

Now he had a vassal who depended on his protection. He listened to Jay breathe until Will returned.

"The central pocket. There's a set of sheets on top. Just one will do, if you would."

Will unzipped the bag and shook out the top sheet. Running it through his fingers, he raised an eyebrow.

"Your own, eh? How long's that been going on?" He draped the sheet over Jay without waiting for an answer.

Henry tucked the fabric around Jay's body, bunching some over the younger man's hand on his chest. Jay snuffled forward, sighed in his sleep, and whispered his master's name.

Will repeated the name with somewhat less love. His sharp smile held the wolfish edge Victor favored. "I'm so goddamn jealous of you right now that I can't even tell you how much," he whispered, low and seething. "You've seen the mess I've made of my own life. If you let this boy go, I'll still be reminding you of it ten years from now."

"I know, Will. I'm a stubborn idiot." He'd deserve the reminder. That and more. "I'll find another way. The one I envisioned—"

Jay's sleeping face, half-hidden in the sheet, roused deeper passions. Possession. Protection.

"It simply isn't possible anymore. I'm not ready to let him go."

Chapter 8

"How have you slept this week, my boy?" Hardly a proper greeting, but he'd wondered all week, and the sight of his smartly dressed submissive standing beside their table had made asking an urgent demand.

"Much better, Master Henry." Jay lifted his head and offered a smile that held all the temptation of a pure, flowing spring in the desert. "Not as good as last Friday, though."

Mmm. No, not as good. His own sleep this week hadn't satisfied him half as well as lying awake and listening to Jay breathe, safe in his arms the whole night through.

"You prefer your scent straight from the source, do you?" He nuzzled the younger man's cheek and brushed his lips.

Jay whimpered and breathed deep. "You bet I do."

Henry gave in to desire and delivered a proper kiss, luxurious and soft. He'd debated taking his almost, wish-it-were-so lover to breakfast last week and settled instead for juice and fresh fruit from the club's kitchen.

Tonight, as he seated himself and Jay plated their dinner, he allowed himself to hope for more. For good or ill, their agreement would change tonight.

Giving his submissive permission to eat, he tucked in as well. Jay ate with quiet enthusiasm and not a few worshipful glances across the table. Henry permitted himself an extension of the fantasy.

He'd made the dinner—chicken in a sauce of bacon and apple cider—himself this evening, disguising the result with plain takeout containers. Jay devoured food he'd made for him with his own hands. How pleasant would it be to spend every weeknight thus?

He envisioned quiet nights at home, sharing meals and assigning

suitable household tasks afterward. Enjoying Jay's homework performance, with a reward for good behavior, perhaps. A bit of aftercare
before bed, snuggling Jay close in his sheets.

A wave of contentment washed over him.

Jay scraped his plate. He stopped, fork half-loaded, and stared at
his master.

"Something the matter?"

"No, Master Henry, nothing." Jay smiled. "I'm just happy. *You*
look happy."

"You make me happy indeed."

Jay danced in his seat. His breathing picked up. "Thank you, Master Henry."

It seemed a shame to steal Jay's happiness, but they had a schedule to keep tonight. Putting off the discussion wouldn't do Jay any favors. "However, we've an unpleasant topic to consider, my dear boy."

Jay's smile slipped.

He reached across the table and clasped Jay's hand. If fear made
his boy bolt, he wanted to know before it happened.

"Calvin Gardner's suspension will end in four days."

Jay shuddered at the name and flinched back against his seat.

He tightened his fingers, an attempt to press reassurance into the
younger man's skin. "By this time next week, he'll have returned to
prowling these halls. You may encounter him here."

Silent terror greeted him. Jay's face grew vacant, his eyes the
grimy panes of an abandoned house. "I don't, I don't wanna—"

He waited, rubbing the back of Jay's hand and holding his gaze.

"I don't wanna be that boy again, Master Henry."

Relief burst in his chest with all the fervor of a fireworks display.

"We'll work together to be certain that doesn't happen." Even if
Jay lacked the strength to enforce such a declaration to his abuser's
face, he'd taken an important step by stating it out loud. "But doing
so may mean confronting some unpleasantness."

With widening eyes and paling skin, Jay shook his head. "I don't
wanna talk about it."

Henry pushed back his chair and stood, keeping hold of Jay's
hand as he rounded the table.

Jay clenched his fingers.

Even had Henry wanted to, he wouldn't have been able to let go.

"Shh, it's all right, my brave boy." Extending his other hand, he tipped Jay's face up. "If you're not ready to talk about what happened, then you're not ready."

He pulled Jay to his chest, feeling the tension in the slender body, and braced for impact.

Jay swung sideways and flung his free arm around Henry's waist with a whimper.

He smoothed the dark hair, holding the silence until Jay's trembling subsided.

"But some things we must know. We must know how you'll react to events around you." Healing would take time, and theirs had almost run out. Jay's behavior tonight would be the deciding factor. "What if he approaches you? What if you see him approaching another vulnerable boy? How will you feel? What response will you have?"

He hugged Jay to him, cradling his back and head. "If I'm to continue as your master, Jay, I must know these things—and so must you."

Jay's slow nod rasped against his shirt. "I trust you, Master Henry. I wanna stay with you. Whatever I hafta do to do that, that's what I wanna do."

The very attitude that most frightened him.

"At the moment, I want you to finish your dessert and clear the table."

After that, they'd see which way Jay would jump.

Tension hummed in him, an unresolved minor chord crawling under his skin.

Unpredictability. Therein lay the problem. Jay had shown flashes of understanding, of assertiveness, in their weeks together, but he retreated to greater submission when pushed. The true limit of his tolerance remained unknown. Would he recognize the point when his discomfort warranted the use of his safeword?

Leading the younger man, now dressed for play, down the familiar third-floor hall, Henry fought the urge to say too much. The club would never change to accommodate individual players' fears or triggers. If Jay wanted to keep their games here—and given the secrecy and shame Jay seemed to attach to the lifestyle, it seemed unlikely he would do otherwise—desensitizing him to certain stimuli would be imperative.

He needed Jay's baseline reaction, to know if they had progressed at all since that second night. Whether Jay could watch without inserting his own emotions in the scene. He doubted it possible. Jay was too sensitive for that. Empathy spilled from his deep brown eyes.

Even if Jay couldn't separate emotionally, he might yet recognize the danger. Protect himself with a word.

Henry stopped before a closed door with a red card. Drawn blinds made the interior impenetrable. "Jay."

"Yes, Master Henry?"

The eager, trusting response bespoke Jay's faith in him. He only hoped he proved worthy of it. "Tell me your safeword."

"Tilt-A-Whirl." Jay stood with level shoulders and spoke in a bold tone.

"And when are you to use your safeword?"

"When I feel sick. When I want the ride to stop."

"Good boy." He took firm hold of his submissive's chin. "Look me in the eyes, Jay."

He waited for Jay to obey and allowed a bit of heat to slip the leash. "Will *not* using your safeword impress me?"

Jay blinked. His mouth moved in silence. "No, Master Henry. I'm not—it's not—"

Biting his lip, Jay grew distant. His smile emerged beautiful to behold.

"I have to tell the truth so my master can care for me properly. Even, even if I don't respect *myself*, I have to respect my master's property. If I try to hide my limits, my master's property might get hurt."

"My brilliant, brilliant boy." Cupping Jay's face in both hands, he pressed hard to keep from revealing his tremor. "You've given me the most exquisite answer to fall from your lips yet. You make me very proud."

Proud and aroused. From concerned and flaccid to lusty and straining at his fly in three sentences. The growling hunger in his chest urged him to bend Jay over the nearest bench and fuck him until he couldn't stand.

He settled for a bruising kiss.

Jay's whimper of surrender exacerbated the thumping rush of testosterone between his legs. Forcing himself to step back, he studied Jay's glazed eyes.

Arousal and obedience shone forth like a beacon.

"Remember your word, my brave boy."

He rapped at the door four times. Paused. Grasping the knob, he opened the door and ushered Jay inside.

Victor had shed his suit coat and rolled his shirtsleeves to the elbow. Ready to work. He ignored their arrival, seemingly standing alone at the far corner of the room. Until one glimpsed the bare, creamy legs not quite hidden by his trousers and the slim fingers flexing above his own as he cuffed thin wrists to a spreader bar attached to the ceiling.

Jay's steps faltered with barely enough space for Henry to close the door behind them. He had no idea of the honor he'd been granted. That Victor had agreed to play on the third floor at all was a concession to Jay's comfort for Henry's sake.

Making him face the fourth floor, to walk the hall that held his own hell, would be unconscionable. Trying to bring him to the sixth floor, to the private suite Victor and Emma maintained for their games, might stoke more fears.

When he'd gone to Victor with the request, he'd expected a flat no. Expected to fall back to a lesser plan. But no example would do so much for Jay as Victor and Emma's. Victor's impeccable control and skill. Emma's love for the sting of the whip, her vocal enjoyment. Their loving communication in a scene.

He'd provide the best for his boy, and they were unquestionably the best for this test. Their public demonstrations were rare these days, an annual event he suspected marked a personal anniversary, though neither had said such in so many words.

Personal invitations to their private games went out perhaps twice or thrice a year, and only to those they considered family. To the doms Victor had personally mentored. Henry. William. To the submissives they'd welcomed into their household for training, and the masters to whom those girls had gifted their service. Scattered across the country, they tried to gather at least once each year to share their happiness.

He suspected Emma had played a large part in Victor's willingness to agree to this. If she'd shown the slightest hesitation, Victor would have denied the request. But she'd seen Jay as Henry's chance for happiness even before he himself had. With Will's happiness impossible to accomplish so long as he remained chained to a woman who despised him, Henry bore the full weight of Emma's maternal need for matchmaking. Woe betide young Thomas when he reached adolescence and began courting romance. His mother's meddling was like to frustrate the boy to no end.

He'd had no one else to ask, not among the committed couples at the club. None he'd trust to witness Jay's vulnerability without comment. None whose style he knew so intimately. None whose judgment he so respected.

If Jay panicked, Victor would let Henry handle the issue without taking offense at the interruption. If Jay was able to stay, Victor and Emma would show him the beauty in the bond Cal had so perverted. The shining example of what could be. Of what *they* could be someday.

Henry swallowed back his thoughts. The hopes and dreams for their future would wait. They'd cross this chasm first.

Bending his head, Victor whispered to his wife and received a sleek, sultry laugh in response. He stepped aside, revealing the nude canvas for his art—and the single-tail whip coiled at his left hip.

Short. A four-footer. Anything longer would be too big for the room. Twelve feet square, fourteen at the most, and Victor would need room for his backswing. A six-foot whip would be dangerous to work with here, an eight-footer impossible. The shorter whip would provide better control in any case, and Jay needed to see safety above all else.

He felt the instant Jay spotted the whip in his bones. The breathless stillness beside him, as if Jay might make himself invisible to the fear stalking him. He brushed Jay's ear with a kiss. "Be truthful."

Jay jerked to life with a short nod and a blown-out breath. Still, his gaze strayed more to Victor's hip than the flowing curves of Emma's bare back.

"Henry." Victor nodded in formal greeting. "My beloved and I are pleased to welcome you and your boy. Emma so enjoys an appreciative audience."

"Victor." He returned the nod, a fraction deeper out of respect for his mentor. "Thank you for the invitation. The boy and I will be honored to witness this expression of your love insomuch as our comfort allows."

He hoped Jay would register the words. The honor. The love. The understanding they might leave at any time if memory and fear proved too much to overcome.

Resting his hand on Jay's back, he offered both reassurance and a check on reactions. Physicality would help him here. Monitoring Jay's comfort level was made easier when his slender body communicated with every twitch, every stiffening muscle, every tremor and indrawn breath.

"Of course, Henry. Pushing beyond one's limits too quickly is a fool's errand. Such behavior only increases the distance to the goal. Done too often, it may place one's desires permanently out of reach." Victor paused, his voice thoughtful, as though he hadn't said the words a thousand times. "Better to know when to say stop and leave the next step for another day."

Victor hadn't once looked at the boy, but the message was unmistakable. Henry could only hope Jay would heed the advice. That his sweet submissive would find his limits—help his master define them and show his understanding of their importance. Then, perhaps, they'd have a lifetime to expand them together.

Victor gestured toward a padded bench to Henry's right. "Please, sit. We'll have a bit of warm-up first."

Brow furrowed, Jay tipped his head.

"Even so experienced a submissive as my beloved Emma wouldn't begin the night with the kiss of a single tail." Turning away, Victor spoke in a casual tone over his shoulder. "We must work up to it, mustn't we, my darling?"

The slight shake of Jay's head stirred a twisting anger in Henry's gut. No warm-up. Of course not. Cal would relish the shock value over his submissives' safety and enjoyment.

"As you say, my husband." Voice low and liquid, Emma captured the hungry restraint evident in the gentle sway of her body as she rocked on the balls of her feet. "Your tenderness makes pain a pleasure I never tire of receiving."

Henry led Jay to the bench and seated him as he had weeks before, straddling the width and cradled in his arms. Emma waited less than ten feet away, her body near perpendicular to their vision. Jay would have a slanted view of the touch of the whip and a window on her reactions to it. If she rolled her head right, he might even watch the enjoyment on her face.

Victor was likely to begin with a light flogging to sensitize his wife's skin and flood her body with endorphins.

Henry doubted Jay would last through the warm-up to the whip at all.

Victor laid his hand on the narrow table across the room and lifted a novice flogger. Deerskin, perhaps, dyed deep black and boasting dozens of falls.

Safe in Henry's arms, Jay trembled.

Victor crossed the floor in silence. Even his footfalls raised no sound. The flogger dangled from his right hand. Rolling his wrist in an absent-minded figure eight created a quiet shirring from the leather, overshadowed a moment later by Emma's answering moan. Pure anticipation of pleasure.

Jay's heart pounded beneath his hand. Less pleasure than fear, he expected, though Jay's shorts showed a suitable physical reaction rising. He rubbed the slim, muscled chest in calming circles with one hand and threaded the fingers of his other through Jay's.

The return squeeze crushed his fingertips to the point of pain. He said nothing.

Across the room, Victor stepped in front of his wife. Arms extended around her neck, he swished the flogger against her back in a caress.

She widened her stance, desire and acceptance in every line of her body.

"Do you remember, beloved, how prettily you begged for more when first I laid the deerskin to your sweet flesh?"

Jay leaned forward. The low, intimate voice seemed to hold him as spellbound as it held its intended target. He hungered for loving praise himself. Not something Calvin Gardner would have delivered.

"I remember, husband. You held me back when I would have charged ahead with blind desire." Her words flowed like music, a song to guide Jay if he let the tune fill his ears. "Protected and sheltered me."

"Did you love me for it?" Victor injected wryness in his tone.

Emma's lilting laugh answered him.

Jay startled, bumping his master.

Henry nuzzled his cheek. This was what he'd wanted Jay to see. That he needn't accept the short-term, transactional nature of play if he desired more. That beautiful, loving relationships existed as part and parcel of dominance and submission, a neatly wrapped gift on both sides.

"I railed against it, husband. I pouted. I stomped. I insisted I knew better. I poured out my anger and my need and my fears."

Victor pressed a kiss to his wife's forehead and slipped around her body to stand at her back. Trailing his fingers down her skin, he nodded. "And now, my love?"

Emma's body rippled with her breath. "I'm grateful, husband. To myself for having the strength to voice my needs. To you for accepting me as I was then and as I am now."

"Always," Victor murmured. His lips brushed his wife's shoulders. "As you were, as you are, and as you will be."

Jay sighed in unison with Emma. His fingers relaxed.

Henry adjusted his grip, massaging Jay's knuckles with his thumb. One hoped he'd absorbed the lesson as well as the comfort.

Victor stepped back. The flogger swung short of Emma's body, though she arched toward it as the air flowed over her skin.

Jay flinched, retreating on the bench.

Henry straightened to offer more contact, a solid wall of safety at Jay's back. *I'm here.* Raising Jay's hand, he leaned over his shoulder and kissed the backs of his fingers.

Jay pressed into his body and dropped his free hand on his master's thigh. He kneaded his fingers like a cat's paw above Henry's knee. The anticipation that woke excitement in Emma fed anxiety in this young man.

The physical nature of Jay's response, combined with the growing musk of desire from multiple bodies, fueled arousal in Henry. Shifting with care, he sought to minimize Jay's awareness of his erection. Arousal was hardly an improper reaction to the love on display before them, but a twinge of guilt settled in his chest nonetheless. The night was to be about finding the depth of Jay's fear and his ability to safeword, not his own joy in witnessing this couple play.

Victor clasped the flogger's handle in one hand, the falls in the other.

Emma swayed in her restraints.

As her body stilled, her master let the deerskin fly.

Thwip.

Emma shuddered, a delighted murmur rising from her lips. The sting at her shoulder would be no more than the barest tease for her, not even the foreplay yet but the kiss of greeting.

For Jay, though, the imagined pain surely begat a psychological assault. Tension gripped his frame.

Henry patted his chest, a gentle tapping over his heart. His submissive required a reminder of his distance. He occupied his own skin, not Emma's. He sat in his master's arms, safe and whole.

The flogger flew again, zipping toward Emma almost faster than the eye could follow. Speed and precision, the hallmarks of control, though Jay would neither recognize nor appreciate the beauty. Not tonight.

A third swing. A fourth. A fifth, and a pink blush spread across unbroken skin.

Each time Emma moaned, each time the flogger landed and the sound registered, Jay jumped. He dug his fingers into his master's thigh with painful intensity. He shook his head, the motions tiny and frantic. Squirmed back as if he meant to crawl away by any means.

Jay's breath crashed like waves on a rocky shore, filling Henry's ears. He squeezed Jay's hand to offer comfort.

His sweet submissive yanked free.

What is he—

Jay cupped his hands over his groin and drew his knees together. He rocked forward, hunching in a fetal curl.

"Tilt-A-Whirl," he gasped. "Tilt—"

Gripping Jay's biceps, Henry muscled him to his feet.

"Good boy, it's all right my beautiful boy, we're going now." He guided Jay to the door with no more than a glancing nod for Victor. Expecting the emotional response and Jay's need to escape, they'd prepared the adjacent room for recovery and aftercare. "All's well, brave boy. You've done so well."

The door clicked closed behind them.

Jay pressed his back to the wall and breathed with heaving gulps. Tears cascaded down his cheeks. They drew no shortage of stares from passing players.

Henry framed Jay's face in his hands. "Just a few more steps, my boy. We'll have a bit of privacy to talk."

Jay avoided his gaze, glancing at the floor, rapid shifts beneath half-lowered eyelids. He shook his head. "I'm okay. I'm fine. I just, just need a minute. We can go back in. I can do it. I know I can."

His heart, bobbing like a rowboat in a sea of success, ran aground. They'd been so close. He'd thought Jay understood, finally, that using his safeword engendered no shame. That he needn't put on a front for his master to be cared for—that in fact the opposite was desirable.

The harsher lesson, then. More painful for them both. Jay must admit the truth before healing could begin. He wasn't fine. He needed more than a minute. So long as he pretended otherwise, he'd be a danger to himself.

Henry gripped Jay's elbow and steeled himself for the pain.

"A minute? Excellent. Just enough time then, isn't it?" He dragged his submissive forward, into the flow of players moving down the hall. "You'll be ready to play when we arrive."

"I don't—time for what, Master Henry? Ready for what?"

He ignored the questions. Kindness wouldn't help him here. He forced an edge into his voice and hated the need for it.

"How wonderful that you've entirely recovered from your experience. I haven't a room reserved, but we'll find a space, don't you worry. I won't deny my boy what he assures me he's capable of handling."

Jay faltered as they neared the end of the hall. The stairs loomed ahead, filling the space.

"Master Henry? What's—where—"

He dragged the younger man to the banister. "Up the stairs. Go. Now."

Jay shook. More than one player offered a curious glance, and Henry glared in reply.

"You're fine, aren't you, my boy? Put your feet on those steps."

Furrows riddled Jay's face. Hurt and confusion warred in quivering muscles. One foot lifted.

"If you want to play, you'll obey your master in all things." Hardening his voice, he fought the urge to physically block Jay from making contact. "Isn't that the first rule? *The stairs.*"

His heart seemed to stop. His breath certainly did.

Five seconds.

Ten.

At thirteen, Jay lowered his foot.

The floor, not the stairs.

"I'm not ready, Master Henry." Tears drenched his words and clogged his throat, but Jay persevered. "I'm not ready. I'm not fine. And my first, my first rule, it's safety. My safety. My safeword. Tilt-A-Whirl."

Relief burned through him, a cleansing scourge. "Thank you, my boy. My courageous boy."

He kept up a low stream of patter, of praise and comfort, as Jay sobbed. Their prepared room waited far down the hall. Too far. Six steps away, a darkened room. A few minutes to recover, and Jay would be calm enough to take through the hall to the proper room. This conversation wasn't one for an audience, nor were Jay's vulnerability and pain a vintage for strangers to sip.

"Excuse us." Pushing past the gawkers, he pulled his submissive into the nearest room, slapped the red card in the holder, dropped the blinds, and flipped on the lights.

Garish color assaulted his senses.

Jay blinked. His sobs tripped into hiccups. He made a slow turn.

"I'm not—" Jay pressed a hand to his abdomen and sucked in air. "Not hallucinating, right? It's really"—he dissolved into chuckles—"groovy."

No hysterical tinge, thank God. Outside forces made the younger man's moods more changeable than the weather. He'd take providence where it showed itself, even if victory came in the form of a room covered in 1970s VW bus chic. The tie-dyed color scheme, the shag rugs, the beanbag chairs.

The life-size Grateful Dead bear strapped into a sex swing and dangling from the ceiling offered a crowning touch, a vacant-eyed and silent witness wearing an askew canary yellow neck ruffle. Someone's idea of a joke, or a clue to how the club's plushie crowd had been entertaining themselves of late.

He'd strayed into a swirling, mismatched nightmare of chaos, but if it put his submissive at ease, it would do. A source of amusement for one born long after the height of the counterculture era depicted. Youth might make the entire allure of the room as incomprehensible to Jay as the gaudy, excruciating color palette made it to Henry himself.

"Quite. A crayon factory exploded. I believe they left this room in memoriam." He smiled at Jay's giddy release. Hearing that laughter for the rest of his life would make him happy indeed. "I'm so very proud of you, my boy."

Laughter gave way to a beaming face. "I got it right?"

"With perfection," he murmured. "We've a place to build from now, to correct the misconceptions that make you hurt so much here." He laid his hand over Jay's heart.

Jay scrambled to cover the hand with his own.

"And we will set everything straight here." He cupped Jay's head in his free hand, ruffling the short, dark hair. "Discover all that makes you *you*, so you may consider in safety what you want as a submissive, how you want your relationships structured to meet your needs."

Jay tipped his head. "My relationships?" He stepped back. "I thought—"

Henry let his hands drop. He wouldn't chain this roaming boy if he needed to move.

"What I want is you." Challenge rang in Jay's deepening tenor. "Don't you want me, too?"

"This cannot be about me alone." He wouldn't allow his submissive to so warp himself, to develop only to please a single master and not himself. "I know it seems that way to you now, but—"

"No." Jay cut him off with a slash of his hand. "I'm not imagining it and I'm not some stupid kid with a crush."

He thrust a finger forward before Henry could reassure him he'd never meant to dismiss the emotions.

"Maybe I haven't been in love for real before, but I know what a crush feels like, and this isn't it." Throwing up his hands, he kicked at the gaudy purple rug. "Are you—are you gonna tell me I have to go fuck around and make bad decisions just so I'll know you're the one I want? 'Cause I already did that, and it sucked."

He stomped the floor. "I want to be yours, Henry."

Fearless. Unquestioning. He'd never seen his submissive so certain.

"So that's my opening negotiation. I want to be yours, and I don't want you to tell me I need to 'expand my field of interest' or whatever. I know what I want."

Eyes blazing, chest heaving, the boy stood his ground.

No.

Jay.

Jay stood his ground.

My Jay.

Defiant and challenging, demanding what he needed. Jay wasn't dependent on him because he needed to be. He simply wanted to be.

"I see that you do," Henry murmured. He skated his knuckles across one smooth cheek.

Jay leaned into the touch.

"As it happens, so do I." Teasing Jay's lips, he coaxed them open with gentleness. His hands roamed. He tightened his grip on Jay's head and hip. Drove him back with insistent prods until he pinned him to the wall and ground their hips together.

The younger man whimpered.

Henry swallowed the sound with a harsher kiss, nipping and growling.

Jay clutched his shirt, fistfuls of fabric, pulling at him, seeking more.

Henry drew his head back, moving his mouth out of his partner's reach. "Tell me something that frightens you, Jay. A truth you are afraid to share with me."

With a slight nod, Jay swallowed hard. "The nightmares. I'm still having them. When I wake up, I'm sweating, and scared, and—and aroused. Tonight, with the, with the—I didn't want to come watching. How can I feel like my heart's gonna burst with the fear and my cock's gonna shoot at the same time? There's something wrong with me, Master Henry. I'm all wrong."

"*You* are not wrong, dearest." Shame and confusion, as he'd expected. "You've been made to think and feel things, and you haven't been given the time to discover which things are the ones you want and how you feel about them with so much unpleasantness layered overtop."

They could work through this. They would work through this.

"We're going to dig, Jay, until we find the shining boy beneath." He nudged forward, the gentle pressure of foreheads and noses aligned. "You've shown me pieces of him, and he is a wondrous delight."

"We'll do it together? You promise?"

"I promise." He spoke it as a solemn vow. "We will write up a contract."

His first. He'd played with dozens over the years, but their engagements had been defined by these walls. Outside the club, he'd played with submissives bound to Victor's contracts. Never had he offered one of his own devising. Seen the potential and felt the desire for a long-term relationship. This commitment would be a serious one.

"Beginning with no bondage and no whipping of any sort until I judge you ready to try playing again. Control only. You will submit to me, and you'll be my good boy. My Jay."

Em would be insufferable for months, but having Jay would be well worth her smug-but-affectionate teasing. He'd been sketching the truth like mad in the last few weeks, hoping against hope the opportunity, the relationship, might come to fruition. One piece in particular—Jay's back, healed, beautiful and strong, shoulders firm with just the hint of a bowed neck—he would paint for certain. Have Jay sit for it, perhaps, if he could manage to be still.

Photographs. He'd have his darling muse sit for references. Tomorrow? They might spend the day together, in this new contract he envisioned. He kissed the tip of Jay's nose and pulled back to study him.

"More than we have now, Master Henry?" Jay curled his fingers into the fabric of Henry's shirt. "I want more time with you than just our Fridays. I could come here on more nights, give you more control. Please."

"Being here is unhealthy for you, and it likely contributes to your nightmares." He'd watched Jay take an enormous step in the proper direction tonight, but he wouldn't risk a setback.

"We'll find an arrangement that suits us both, but I will not negotiate on this point." Not with Cal's imminent return and the potential for Jay to set his feet on those stairs. "You will not enter this club or any other until I deem it appropriate for you to do so."

He'd wanted complete control for weeks. Jay had granted it on their first night out of ignorance, a vulnerability Henry refused to capitalize upon. Jay knew what he offered now. He understood. He'd had a taste of the trust required and the rewards to be gained. If still he offered it. . . .

The heady desire for that mix of power and responsibility coursed through Henry's blood.

"Not come here at all? You mean like, like hotel rooms? And I can't give you the things everyone here wants?" Shaking his head, Jay yet clutched his chest. "But you'll. . . ."

"I will what, brave boy?" He matched Jay's movement, capturing the skittish gaze and holding it.

"You'll get tired of me," Jay whispered. "If I'm not a good player. If I can't do the things you want."

"You grant me complete control over your sex life, Jay. You allow me to care for you as I think best. Your submission is as lovely as you are, and worth so much more than a few hours here or there spent with other willing subs."

A true relationship demanded honesty. Not only from his submissive, but from himself. Jay would come to know him. Best to start with the truths that would comfort his boy.

"I make their fantasies real for them in the physical world, and I imagine my own. Long-term control over your life so I might care for you properly is no small thing, yet you're willing to offer me that." Running his fingers along the side of Jay's neck provided for his own comfort. The rough edge of emotion deepened his voice. "The question is not how can you compete with the others here, my dear boy. It is how shall they ever again compete with you?"

With wide eyes and blushing skin, Jay wriggled his happy-puppy wriggle and offered a beatific smile. "Thank you, Master Henry."

He paused to savor Jay's reverent joy. The urge to steal a kiss proved too strong. He kept it soft and shallow. They had things yet to discuss.

"And we will not be playing in hotels. Only the best will do for my boy. We will play in my home, Jay."

Jaw dropping open, Jay exhaled on a whimper. "You—me—at your—"

More squirming, and Henry struggled not to laugh at the stupefied wonder filling brown eyes. Jay's erection brushing his hip helped quash amusement, though the arousal constituted a greater temptation.

Jay narrowed his eyes. "I get to sleep in your bed. All weekend."

Oh-ho. A haggler, was he? The confidence reeled him in, a powerful aphrodisiac. How much greater the pleasure in accepting the gift when he knew his lover craved it, too.

"Friday and Saturday. You'll sleep in your own bed on work nights." For now.

"I get to take the sheets with me."

"Agreed. You'll perform housekeeping tasks under my direction while in my home."

"Agreed. You won't abandon me if I'm bad."

Quite the leap. A deep emotional need, then. Did Jay associate the poor completion of chores with abandonment? Always more questions to answer. No, he wouldn't grow tired of loving this man.

"You're not a bad boy, Jay. And I won't abandon you, so long as you agree to one condition."

"Any—" Jay stopped, controlled himself, and started again. "I'm not allowed to agree to conditions before I know what they are."

"No, you are not. It's good of you to remember that, my bright boy." Gripping Jay's head, he held him still and delivered a punishing, rewarding kiss.

Jay whimpered and thrust, grinding his cock with delightful, raw need.

"The condition is this: You will not lie to me. Neither by commission nor omission. If I ask how you feel about something, you will tell me without prevarication. If something upsets you and I do not ask, you will bring it to my attention. If ever you wish to alter or leave this arrangement, you will inform me immediately."

"I won't want to leave." Jay's firm tone and solid stare allowed no sliver of doubt. He believed his words in his bones. "But I agree to your condition, Master Henry. And I have one of my own."

"Do you now?" Wonderful. No matter what ups and downs the future held, his boy could learn to be safe and assertive. The core of strength he'd glimpsed truly existed in brilliant color. "Let's hear it."

"I get to suck your cock." A smirk edged across Jay's face. "I've been waiting eight weeks."

Jay had done the work. He'd made progress. His submission was consensual now, his desire pure and well-formed.

Henry let the leash slip on his own eagerness.

"As have I. As have I." He settled into a low-slung seat and dropped a throw pillow at his feet. "On your knees. You've earned your reward."

Jay stepped forward and knelt, his body the smooth glide of a single brushstroke, the first on a new canvas. Such a magnificent man gazing up at him with adoration and resting trembling hands on his thighs.

"Thank you, Master Henry." Jay parted kiss-swollen lips. "I won't disappoint you."

"No, I know you won't, dear boy. You please me very much, Jay." He ran his fingers over Jay's and lifted them to his belt. "In your own time. This gift is yours."

He let go, leaving the first step to the young man who'd anticipated this moment for so long. Time enough for demands on another night. Tonight, he'd see the truth of what Jay wanted, undiluted by his direct guidance.

Nimble fingers made quick work of his belt and parted his slacks with a speed borne of anxious excitement. Jay's unwavering stare at his erect cock pushing through the flap of his boxers dragged a low growl from his chest. The slide of silk wouldn't compare with his lover's mouth.

Gentle hands dipped inside his boxers, silk parting to allow his cock and balls to emerge.

Jay tucked his slacks beneath both.

The slight pressure of taut fabric under his balls urged him to shift his hips, widening the space between his thighs. The space Jay occupied.

Strong, slender hands cupped the pulse driving Henry's body.

Jay bowed his head and lowered his face. The slow slide of his cheek along the side of Henry's arousal whispered of exultation. He nudged the base with his nose and inhaled. His shoulders pulled back as his ribs expanded, the deep breath followed by a pause.

Henry, too, held his breath, the moment too important for words or even breathing. Time hung suspended like a prayer between them.

Jay shuddered and exhaled on a long, whimpering moan. Extending his tongue, he traced the shaft toward the tip. His gaze flicked upward with anxious hunger.

Henry met Jay's look with an encouraging smile. The teasing warmth of the tongue circling the head of his cock burned through him with the promise of more.

No demands, not tonight, but praise, yes, he might sing his lover's praises. *Sing, O goddess, the love of Henry, master to Jay, that brings countless joys upon their household.*

"Do you know how beautiful you are to me, sweet boy?" He threaded his fingers through the short, dark hair above Jay's ear. "Your head bows with such honor and grace over your master's lap."

Jay moaned and closed his mouth around the object of his worship.

Warmth and waves of suction pulled Henry in, narrowed his focus to the pleasure Jay delivered with enthusiasm and exquisite timing.

"Your tongue dances in delightful rhythm, the fulfillment of a promise long desired."

He snapped an image of each moment, perfection captured in memory. Dark hair waving atop a head bobbing slow and steady. Strong lines, the tendons in an arching neck standing out each time Jay adjusted his angle. Shadowed depths in cheeks hollowing on each pull.

Lovely, each piece an aspect of the whole. His beloved boy. Desire surged. He fought to maintain the gentleness of his grip. No force, no pain, no rushing Jay's obvious enjoyment, his sweet whimpers and squirming body.

Splaying his fingers, Henry slipped his palm down the curve of Jay's neck and out toward his shoulder. Back and forth, stroking, he matched Jay's speed to stop himself from clenching down tight and thrusting into that glorious pull.

"So close, Jay," he murmured. "Your gift leaves me at your mercy. This choice is yours. One we both embrace."

Pressure gripped him, an unexpected push rolling up the underside of his shaft. He groaned.

His brilliant lover repeated the trick, faster. A slip of the tongue, firm and heated, where shaft met head.

Need squeezed his awareness. Urgency built. Tension raced up his shaft and gathered at the tip.

"Now," he growled, control failing as orgasm rushed through him. "My Jay. *Mine*."

Jay pushed forward, draining his master's offering without needing to be told, singing in happy little whines all the while. Slim shoulders vibrated under Henry's hand. More excitement than his dear one might reasonably contain. He tugged his lover from his cock with a gentle pull.

"Up." He kissed him with deep possession, pouring out his strength and contentment to seep into Jay's soul. *You are loved, my boy. So very much.* "Sit with me. I want to see your chest gleaming with your own pleasure."

Yanking the pouch at the front of Jay's shorts spilled his lover's cock into his waiting hand. Five strokes proved enough to ease Jay's release and streak his skin.

"Mmm, we've made a lovely mess of you, haven't we?" He licked Jay's neck, following the cord of muscle to the underside of his ear.

His lover tasted of salt and smelled of sex and earthy musk.

"Perhaps we'll have a quick shower here before I take you home to my bed for unspeakable delights."

Jay wiggled in a half-turn, his expression becoming serious. No, not quite—twitching at the corners of his mouth and the pleased squint of his eyes gave him away.

"I'm not allowed to go home with strangers." A hint of coyness lurked in Jay's smile. "My master says it's not safe."

Was anything more beautiful than the post-orgasm flush of confidence on his lover's face? Jay felt comfortable enough to tease without fear. He nuzzled Jay's cheek, aware of his own utter infatuation and uncaring.

"Perhaps we won't tell him." He traced Jay's ear with his tongue. "You'd keep a secret from your master for me, wouldn't you?"

Shaking his head, Jay squirmed in his arms and pushed at his chest with faux force. "I'd never lie to my master. I only have two rules to follow so far, and I don't wanna break them."

"Two? Is that so?" Nipping Jay's ear, he reminded himself not to progress things too far. His bed waited for them at home. Home. Where he'd be taking his lover. New flutters of desire stirred in his softening cock. "Name them for me, Jay."

"No lying, and safety first."

Concise. His delightful partner had a way of simplifying complexity. "Mmm. So what will we do about this pesky problem? I'd dearly love to take you home with me tonight."

"I maybe—"

Jay gasped, and Henry released his earlobe with reluctance. Distract him with too much foreplay, and he'd lose this time to truly get to know his Jay. The almost-confident joker. The sweet, obedient lover.

"Maybe know somebody I can call to confirm my safety after."

"Do you?" He'd keel over in shock if Jay had confided in a friend about his new lifestyle. They'd made strides, yes, but they hadn't yet leapt canyons.

Jay nodded. "She's great at helping a boy dress right for his master. But I think she might be tied up all night."

He chuckled. Emma, of course. Jay had teased with nary a tremble at the idea of his friend enjoying bondage. Perhaps the night's example had helped more than he'd thought.

Inevitable, he supposed, given he'd all but pushed them together by entrusting Jay's basic table protocol training to her every other week. For all that Emma had been his own friend for a dozen years, Jay couldn't have found a better advocate—nor a more discreet one. She wouldn't hesitate to call Henry out if she believed he'd misstepped.

He kissed his lover with closed lips. "Indeed, I expect she will."

He'd discuss boundaries with her next week if Victor approved, but fostering a mentoring relationship between them might help Jay shed the shame he carried. Submissive as she was to Victor, he'd seen her deliver scathing set-downs to subs and doms who needed a kick in the pants—and been on the receiving end more than once, years ago—and shame had never been in her lexicon. His lover needed good examples. He'd grow into his own skin with time.

"We'll leave a note for her master at the desk and ask one of them to call my phone at noon tomorrow to check on you, shall we?"

Jay vibrated, his eyes alight. "I guess I'll have to stay with you at least until noon, then, Master Henry."

"At least noon," he murmured. "Perhaps we'd best make it later in the day. After dinner."

"Or Sunday, Master Henry." Jay curled closer, his fingers drifting across his master's groin. "I like to worship on Sundays, too."

Or forever, my beautiful boy. With luck, they'd find the right balance to bind them that long.

"Sunday," he agreed. It was a beginning.

Keep reading for a special excerpt of the first book in M.Q. Barber's new Gentleman series

HER SHIRTLESS GENTLEMAN

Her heart is in his hands . . .

After her marriage ends in betrayal, Eleanora Howard finds herself struggling to navigate the dating scene as a thirty-one-year-old divorcee. But feeling undesirable, and living alone in the house she once shared with her ex, is hardly the recipe for finding new love—until she meets Rob. He's just the kind of charming, old-fashioned guy she needs—but he's also eager for intimacy . . .

After serving in the Air Force and getting a well-paid civilian career, Rob Vanderhoff planned to settle down with the right woman and raise a family. But at thirty-six, he's still single and searching—until he meets Eleanora. She's everything he wants. All he has to do is draw her out of her shell. Soon he's taking her on high school-style dates, fanning the flames of her desire—and helping Nora re-discover the sexy, adventurous woman they both know she really is . . .

A Lyrical e-book on sale now!

Chapter 1

Dead last. Again.

The four of them went out after work every Friday, and every Friday Eleanora sat and smiled while guys bought drinks for Sharilyn. Hit the dance floor with Amber. Chatted up Chelsea's breasts.

Even the sidekicks—wingmen, whatever guys called themselves— refused to give her a second glance. She couldn't blame their lack of interest on the ring. She'd taken off the meaningless metal circle before the divorce had been finalized.

But to the endless crowd of broad-smile bar-hoppers, she rated five seconds of stilted conversation between texting or checking sports scores or playing Angry Birds. The highlight of four hours of boredom. Single life almost matched the worst tedium of married life.

That's what she got for saddling herself with David and galloping through her twenties with his ring on her finger. He'd been her first. Her only.

Now she performed rotating roles as babysitter, chaperone, and charity case. She didn't belong at a too-small table packed alongside tight- skinned and perky-breasted girls who flashed their IDs with the affected nonchalance of twenty-two-year-olds.

She downed the final sip of her third beer of the night. She didn't dare hop in her car and head home yet. Given her luck, she'd end up pulled over and facing a drunk-driving charge. David would love any excuse to point out her idiocy. Hiring a lawyer without him finding out would be impossible in this town. She'd never live down the humiliation.

"—and it's deep, too."

Chelsea laughed along with what's-his-name. Dog Collar Dude.

Not attractive, but he had deep pockets. Probably thought he'd be getting in deep with Chelsea tonight, payment in exchange for buying round after round of drinks. God knew he hadn't taken his eyes off her breasts.

Laughter came dangerously close to making Chelsea spill out of her silky, sleeveless v-cut. Eleanora's closet didn't hold a shirt anywhere near so revealing. Boring and staid, as much an accountant in her fashion picks as in her career choices. And in her bedroom habits.

She tilted her brown bottle. All gone. No magical extra swallows remained to knock David's voice from her head.

"Whoa." An unknown quantity stumbled to a halt beside her chair. "Your friend's hot."

Fantastic. The newest Mr. Drunk-and-Horny leaned in close and drenched her nose with the scent of teen body spray. Probably the same disgusting brand he'd used in high school. Probably lived in the same bedroom, too.

"Oh? Which one?" She'd come to this lousy bar with three friends—well, acquaintances—and he didn't have a chance with any of them.

The skinny blond kid blinked as he scanned their table. Jesus. He looked barely old enough to buy the three beers he held, and she'd celebrated thirty-one six months ago.

Sooner or later she'd have to inform her coworkers she wasn't going out with them anymore. They were twenty-four, twenty-five, and poaching college boys was fine for them. For her, the whole scene smacked of desperation. Three months of this bullshit added up to quite enough.

"Uh, all of 'em?" He presented a dopey smile.

"Damn, Ellie. Picking 'em young tonight, aren't you?" Sharilyn swung her martini glass upward, sloshing vodka over the rim. "Good for you."

"Yeah, no, I'm not—"

The kid wobbled into her chair. "I don't feel—"

Vomit splattered her shoulder and rolled down her chest. Ugh. Should've dodged faster. She shoved him back.

Stumbling over his own feet, he landed on his ass, spilled his three beers all over himself, and retched. The acrid stench of puke replaced the flood of body spray in her nose. A toss-up, really.

She laughed over the chorus of oh-my-gods from the rest of the table. At least the night wasn't boring anymore.

"Oh, fuck."

Rob swallowed the last of his beer. Lucas had better hurry up with the refills. "What now?"

They'd hit a handful of bars already. Brian had found trouble with every damned one. With Lucas staying at his place for the summer, he'd been playing mother hen for the last three weeks.

"I think my baby brother's puking his guts out."

"Take him home. Happy beer-buying birthday and all, but he's done for the night." He'd celebrated his own twenty-first on base with a pack of fellow tech geeks. Good guys, including Brian. How had fifteen years gone by so fast? "Pour him into bed."

"Yeah." Brian grimaced. "Soon as I figure out what to say to the woman with puke running down her shirt."

"Try an apology." He shoved his chair back and stood, scanning the tables for Lucas's god-awful sea-green pullover. "Where is he?"

He spotted the vomit-splattered woman about the same time Brian answered, "Your four o'clock."

Shit. Lucas had spewed at a full table, and he couldn't get eyes on him. Man down. Threat?

No punches thrown, so far as he could tell. A circle of horrified and disgusted faces clustered to one side, their owners staring at the floor. One guy held his phone up. On the far side of the table sat a laughing woman with a beautiful smile and a stained shirt. Damn. He hadn't taken a woman home in almost four months, and Lucas had party-fouled the first to catch his eye. "C'mon, let's go rescue Lucas and get out of here."

Looked like tonight wouldn't be the night to break his sexless streak.

"Oh my God, Ellie, seriously, how can you laugh about this?" Light glinted off glitter-speckled fingernails. Amber pushed back from the table. "Yuck. Danny, take me dancing." She dragged her boy of the night away with a theatrical flounce.

"You do kinda reek, Ellie." Sharilyn wrinkled her nose. "Not your fault, but eww."

Waving in front of her face, Chelsea nodded.

Dog Collar Dude flipped through his phone. "Fuck, I missed the kid's first splash. You think he could upchuck again? The visual'd make the video so much better."

Eleanora glanced down with care. The regurgitated beer soaking into her shirt quickly lost its amusement value. The kid had added a puddle beside her chair. He barked out coughs like a hoarse dog.

"No, I don't think he's got anything else in his stomach." She poked his knee with her foot. "Kid? You all right? You got somebody we can call for you?"

No answer, unless she counted more retching. Between the sound and the smell, her stomach started to turn.

A second man with the same pale hair as the first dropped to the floor beside the kid and laid a hand on his back. "Shit, Lucas, I thought you might've passed out."

"Are you all right, miss?"

Sex on a stick. Thick thighs encased in denim inches from her eyes. She launched her head back and her chin skyward. Eyes up. Ohhh, bad idea. The stranger loomed over her with his strong jaw and his short, dark hair and his no-nonsense eyes.

"No, of course you aren't." His aborted hand movement stopped short of her shoulder. "Ugh, he did a number on your shirt. Let me give you a hand."

He slipped around the other side of her seat. Cupping her elbow in one hand and pressing against her back with the other, he coaxed her to her feet. Large hands. Warm hands.

Her body jangled like a change jar spilling on tile.

"Look, he's really sorry, or he will be when he's sober." The stranger glanced down, shaking his head. "He's twenty-one today."

She nodded. The blond guy picked the younger one off the floor. First legal drinking day. Okay. She filed the data under *don't care* and waited for details about Mr. Tall, Dark and Handsome.

"You can't wear that home."

Her chest had snared more attention in the last five minutes than in three months of flaunting herself at bars. She'd found the secret of dating. When introversion and modest assets failed, distress attracted the good guys. Not how she'd hoped to find someone.

The man with the large hands squeezed and let her go. Peeling off his shirt, he revealed a to-die-for body. Solid, toned muscles from top to bottom. Too bad his jeans came almost to his waist. Denim blocked the enticing slope heading into his pants. God, David had never reached such nonchalant bare-chested perfection.

Her rescuer held out his shirt and gestured her toward the back of the bar. "Here, let me give you mine for tonight."

No fucking way. This guy couldn't be for real. She stumbled over her chair.

He steadied her with a quick hand on her clean shoulder.

"Thanks." Oh, hallelujah. She'd started thinking she'd never find her voice. "That's, umm, I appreciate it."

"Least I can do, miss." He guided her in front of him past the line for the ladies' room and stopped at the door.

"Yo, man, you gotta put your shirt on." A beefy guy in a black shirt with the bar's logo over his chest held out an arm. "Carrying it don't count. You can't be shirtless, not in here."

She disagreed with strenuous, silent objections. Her gentleman deserved to go shirtless wherever he liked.

"You wanna run around half naked, you gotta head down the street to the Lazy Eight."

Making that man put his shirt back on would be a crime. Her skin heated at the slow slide of excitement between her legs. Thirty minutes of fantasizing and foreplay with David left her dry as a desert compared to three minutes of standing next to Shirtless Gentleman. The longer she lingered in his orbit, the harder her lungs worked to serve up oxygen.

Lust walloped her with embarrassing swiftness. She lacked the looks and flirty attitude to pull a guy without adding a vomit-soaked shell to the mix. Riding off into the sunset with Shirtless Gentleman glinted so far out of the picture the location didn't exist on her map.

"Yeah, I get that." Shirtless Gentleman raised a hand. "You can toss me out in a minute. Right now, this pretty girl's got someone else's puke on her clothes, and I'm going to make sure she's safe while she's changing." Gripping his shirt, she ducked into the ladies' room past the line of pissed-off, well-beyond-buzzed women. Shirtless Gentleman's presence seemed to deflect any cursing about her cutting the line.

"No, ma'am," he rumbled over the din of music and chatter. "I don't wax and you may not touch."

Ma'am. Polite. Mannered.

She stuffed her shirt in the trash and grabbed a handful of paper towels. Fit. Chivalrous.

The damp paper towels scraped her neck under her hard scrubbing. At least the kid hadn't destroyed her bra. The practical white soft-cup would serve.

Was Shirtless Gentleman military?

Tucking in the shirt didn't give her the fitted look it had given him, but she managed to minimize her resemblance to a child swimming in her father's clothes. Squinting hard almost made the outfit look intentional. A style choice to wear a black wide-neck tee with exposed white bra straps.

Yeah, almost.

She slipped into the hall, her skin electric. His bare chest greeted her from two feet away, his arms crossed and his feet planted in a wide, easy stance. A few hoots and drunken catcalls rose from the women waiting in line.

Shoving aside her embarrassment, she tipped her head back and met his eyes. "Thank you."

His attention stayed centered on her. The unsmiling bulk of a man sported solid pecs and a penetrating stare.

"Again." She fumbled for a classy conversation starter. "Your shirt's really soft."

Your shirt's really soft. What the fuck. Her brains had gone soft. Complete mush. Mashed potatoes held the edge in outthinking her.

His mouth twitched. "Must match your skin."

"Sorry?" She'd heard him wrong. No way had he complimented her skin. Men didn't say those things to her. "I didn't catch that."

He shook his head and dropped his arms. "Shirt looks better on you than it ever did on me, miss. Let me walk you back."

Turning, he swept his hand behind her and landed with a light touch. Five points of pressure, a half circle of fingertips keeping in contact as they returned to the table. More than a few whistles followed them.

"It doesn't bother you? Being"—she waved at the crowded tables— "stared at? Graded? Like you're on display?"

Stupid question. Of course, the attention wouldn't bother him. He had cool, calm confidence perfected. Anyone with his godlike body would want to show off.

"I got over any fear of public grading in basic training." Military. Nailed it.

Not yet, you haven't.

Her face flamed.

"A'course, the opinions of a bunch of yappy drunks aren't worth all that much, positive or not." Shrugging, he tapped her back. "Being on display for the one woman who matters, well now, that's a whole other thing. That'll make a man nervous, sure enough, however cool he plays it."

Great. He had a woman who mattered. Smooth, too, about sliding the revelation into the conversation. No ring, but an empty finger didn't mean much these days.

"I think you've got cool down." Months of going out with the girls from work had taught her how to categorize the bar crowd. The unholy chaos broke into three groups, all ring-free, with the singular difference whether they were ring-free but committed, ring-free and open or cheating, or ring-free and actually unattached. Limiting herself to the third group hadn't done her any favors. "I hope your woman who matters sees through the façade and tells you what a great catch she's made."

He paused his tapping. "Oh, I don't—"

"Woo, I didn't know you were that kind of girl." Sharilyn slapped her hand on the table. "Swapping clothes in a stall?" Her nosy, flamboyant attitude owed nothing to the drinks she'd downed. She came by her perky personality naturally. "What else did he get on you, Ellie?"

Ugh. She smiled through her irritation. Eleanora was bad enough, thanks to her mother's obsession with family history. Every girl wanted to be named for the great-grandmother she'd never met.

Shortening her name to Ellie might as well transform her into a cow. Get along now, Bessie, Daisy, Ellie.

Sharilyn made her sound like a cow giving the milk away for free with a man she'd met ten minutes ago.

"I'm—we weren't—"